THOSE BLACK WINGS

MELINDA R. CORDELL

Rosefiend Publishing.

Copyright © 2017 by Melinda R. Cordell

ISBN: 1545469059
ISBN-13: 978-154546905
ISBN-13 D2D: 978-1-953196-68-2

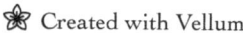 Created with Vellum

"Let me be torn away," then I cried. "Let another help me!"
"No; you shall tear yourself away, none shall help you: you shall
yourself pluck out your right eye; yourself cut off your right hand:
your heart shall be the victim, and you the priest to transfix it."

-- *Jane Eyre*, Charlotte Brontë

ACKNOWLEDGMENTS

I've been writing this book, on and off, for over 15 years. So many people have looked at these pages in one form or another that I simply have been unable to keep track of everybody who has helped me along the way. I am very sorry about that! Many thanks to Shevi Arnold, S.R. Kriger, Kathleen St. Claire, Theodore Curtis, Siobhan Mitchell, Angela Cerrito, Kate Emmons, Tracy Steinhandler Gonzalez, Ella Schwartz, Colleen Subasic, Rose Green, Daniel Holly, Bekezela Broscius, Jane Resh Thomas, Mike Jewett, Michelle Andelman, Janine O'Malley, Polly McCann. Also thanks to Kathrin Gresham for fixing up Wyatt's card in the back.

A high five to Sophie Cordell, the Salty Goddess, who makes the best cover model. What's more, just today she dodged a bullet by heeding the advice of this book. That's my girl!

And, most of all, Brad. I could write 238 pages of mushy stuff about him – actually I already have – and still leave a world of wonderful things unsaid. Thanks for calling me out of the blue on July 14, 1990. You are the best thing that's ever happened to me.

ONE

JUST ANOTHER HEART IN NEED OF RESCUE

WHITESNAKE

Symphonic Band was over, and I was my usual bundle o' nerves. As everybody got up from their seats to put away their stands, instruments, and music, I hurried toward the saxophone section bearing my bass clarinet. Fortunately Rose, the tenor saxophone, was still in her folding chair, tying her shoe. "Rose!" I said. "Can I borrow your saxophone tonight? I need it for Jazz Band rehearsal." I'd never played a tenor saxophone in my life until two weeks ago, when I'd tried out and made first chair in Jazz Band. Now I was playing it a *lot*.

"Sure, Kay," Rose said. "Do you want to take it home tonight and practice it, too?"

"Oh, that would be great, but I just don't have time," I groaned. "Too many accompaniments! Too many solos! Then I'm playing hymns at church next Sunday and gotta practice for that ... I'm sorry I can't talk longer," I said as Rose opened her mouth, "but I have to catch Jenny before the bell rings, sorry!" I hurried on, adding a "Thank you!" over my shoulder.

Muttering, "Catch Jenny, catch Jenny, catch Jenny," to myself, I searched the crowd of students, then quickly climbed over the top of the folding chairs to the next row up, tucking the bass clarinet against my body to protect it from the band students walking past as they chatted.

"Jenny!" I called. The trombonist turned just before she went into the instrument room, trombone in hand, her forefinger holding the slide in place. "Jenny, I'm so sorry, can we switch times for your solo this afternoon? I just found out that my ensemble is practicing at the same time your solo practice is."

She sighed. "Maybe after your ensemble?"

I kind of grimaced. There goes my suppertime! "Sure, if that works for you."

Well, it didn't work for me but I didn't want to let Jenny down any more than I had been. Gaah. I'm not a bad pianist, but my main problem was being too overbooked to practice all the things I'd agreed to do "just to help out." District contest was next week. I was doing a bass clarinet solo, a clarinet choir playing Mozart's *Eine kleine Nachtmusik*, a voice solo (during Mock Contest last month, my voice teacher told the judge that I couldn't sing … nice), AND I was accompanying three solos. Add that to Jazz Band, Sunday hymns, and then the usual chaos with homework and weekend work, and that = over-the-cliff insane.

I carried my bass into the instrument room, a small room filled with yellow wooden shelves. Students rushed in with instrument cases, slid them on the shelves, and rushed out, like bees tucking honey into their honeycomb. In front of the shelf where my bass case lay, I broke down my bass clarinet and put it up, occasionally moving aside for the students putting their clarinet cases under that shelf. Okay, so tonight I had ensemble practice, then I'd accompany Jenny's solo – maybe I could practice her solo for a few minutes after school let out, *before* ensemble – then I'd get my supper out of a vending machine, oh joy, and go to Jazz Band rehearsal. Then I'd get actual food at the drive-thru, then stop by church to practice everything. Then finally home, where I had to do homework in Statistics – why on earth was I even in that stupid class? I wished that math would catch fire and slide into the ocean.

I was *so* looking forward to District Contest next week. As soon as that thing was over I was going to lie down and sleep for three days. No, two days – I had to play hymns on Sunday.

One month until graduation. One month until --

Jo's shriek jolted me out of my brain's nattering. "Aaaa! Don't *do* that!"

The instrument room was right next to the tuba room, and between the wall and the shelves was a narrow gap with a board halfway up the wall. Wyatt, one of the tubas, had put his chin on the board and was gazing into the instrument room from his side, like a decapitated head. A serving of John the Baptist, I thought. Then I had this random vision of sashaying up to him like Salome doing the dance of the seven veils.

Gaah, no no no! Because Salome keeps throwing off veils until she's naked!

I swear my brain is out to get me.

Jo slammed her trumpet case into her cubby and stormed out, muttering about evil headless tuba players.

"Yeah, that bodiless look is seriously creepy," I ventured to Wyatt, tucking my mouthpiece into the case and picking up the gooseneck.

Unlike John the Baptist, Wyatt's head gave me a slow grin, the corners of his dark-brown eyes crinkling. "I know. That's why I do it. BTW, I like your hoodie."

I looked down at my cerulean-blue hoodie, which said *Take me for what I am, who I was meant to be*. "Thanks. It's a line from *Rent*. A musical. I mean, I don't listen to a whole lot of Broadway music, but the show's based on *La Boheme*, and my gosh, you talk about a cool opera, and so I downloaded some of the songs and ... Gaah! I'm sorry! Nobody wants to hear about that crap." I covered my face.

"I did not know *Rent* was based on *La Boheme*," Wyatt said. "That's good to know."

I peeked through my fingers. "Really?"

"Oh, yeah," said Wyatt's disembodied head. "Every day, every match. You never know what you'll need when you pick up the buzzer." His Brain Bowl team was going to Nationals later that month, for the third year in a row.

I shrugged. "I'm glad you like it. Because everyone else is like, 'Kay, stop talking about it, nobody listens to that kind of music,'" I said in a pinched voice, hands on hips. "Or they roll their eyes and start talking to someone else."

"Just 'cause they don't listen to your music doesn't mean they have the right to cut you down about it," Wyatt said.

The breath just caught in my throat when he said that. I don't know why. I blindly put a hand out to the shelf as if I were about to topple over. "Nobody's cutting me down about it." I shot a look at him, like a plea for help.

"I go to the same school you do. I know how people are." He gave me an affectionate look. "To me, a girl with that kind of knowledge is mighty appealing. Even kind of hot."

All the other stuff I totally agreed with. But me? *Hot?* "Aaaa! No!" I brandished the neck of my bass at him to defend my honor.

Wyatt ducked and looked a little hurt.

"I'm sorry, but that's embarrassing. I'm a hermit you know. No: a Kermit. No, I do mean hermit." Then, thoroughly abashed, I giggled my head off.

"Ooookay." Wyatt vanished from the gap.

"I'm sorry," I called after him, putting down the neck of my bass. "Come back! I'm unarmed." Arrgh! Why couldn't I just talk normally?

Wyatt came in through the door of the instrument room, and I perked up again. His camo T-shirt, covered with leaves and shadows, said "Mossy Oak," and he wore sun-faded jeans over scuffed hiking boots. Wyatt was the kind of guy who'd put a friendly arm around your shoulders, saying "Come on, rainy face, turn that frown upside down." A few days ago he'd even given me a hug, out of the blue. I hoped he hadn't noticed my shrinking like a snail wincing away from your finger.

Wyatt leaned against the shelves next to me. "I shouldn't have said that, knowing you. There's a cottontail that lives in my yard that reminds me of you, so quiet and gentle, but easy to startle."

I was surprised into a laugh. "That's sweet." Wyatt laughed too, which I liked. He really had marvelous brown eyes.

His face softened, grew gentle. Was I staring? Confused, I pulled my eyes away.

Wyatt took a sudden breath that made me look back. "Kathy. Would you like to go with me to the prom?"

Instant three-alarm blush. I laughed, pressing my hands to my chest. Had I been asked out? Me?

Wyatt's intent, dark-eyed gaze didn't change. Apparently he required an answer with actual words in it. I fanned myself with my hand, heading to a four-alarm blush. "I'm sorry. I just, I don't know, not the type to go out with guys."

A broken smile appeared on Wyatt's face, like he was trying to be a good sport. "You don't go out with any guys? Or guys like me?"

"I'm sorry! Any guys! Or gals," I stammered. "It's nothing against you. It's like, I don't go out and do, you know, stuff."

"Don't worry. I understand." He laughed, kind of flat.

"Oh, no, it's not your fault. I just sit in my bedroom--" My blush suddenly spiked at a five-alarm. "—I mean, I mean my room, and listen to music. That's my entire social life. It's like I …. What I mean is, you're nice."

"It's okay. Don't rub any more salt into that wound." Wyatt clutched his heart and staggered out of the instrument room.

"Oh, no! I'm sorry!" I cried after him, but it was too late. He was already gone.

I wish Wyatt knew how unqualified I was for romance. My only experience with love was when I got infatuated with Ryan Lawrence during a freshman band trip. I could not figure out why I was compelled to constantly turn around, in a bus full of freshmen, and *stare* at the poor guy all the time. He moved away six months later. I didn't blame him.

Really, they need to have manuals for high-school seniors who have never been on a date, never kissed a guy, to keep them from acting like social dingbats. Though I would be embarrassed to buy a book entitled, *I've Never Gone Out With Actual Guys!*

I clicked the latches of my bass case shut and went to the door of the instrument room. Wyatt had joined his Brain Bowl friends in the band room. "Welcome to Fiasco High School, home of the Debacles!" one shouted, and he laughed with them and said something that I bet was pretty awesome.

So I guess Wyatt was already over my rejection. I hadn't meant to hurt him.

An odd, suffocating feeling settled in my chest as I went back to my chair.

The morning sky was dark; thunder rumbled, making an odd echo through the wall, a sound I hadn't heard all winter. The humid March wind whistled in to cool the heat of so many bodies crowded in the band room.

Outside, rain sprinkled the new spears of grass that pushed through last year's dead blades. Maples lashed under steel-gray clouds. A bolt of lightning spiderwebbed out of a central point, shattering the sky in a sizzling blue trail. Oo! people said, pointing. Did you see that?

The lunch bell rang. Students buzzed around the bandroom, gathering books, putting away nail polish and iPhones, and adjusting jeans over dusty cowboy boots. Wyatt shrugged on his worn brown bomber jacket, chatting with his friends, eyes dark and intense.

I hugged my backpack. For some reason I was hungry for I knew not what.

♫

When I was a freshman, Mr. Ambrose had taken a video for the band's Facebook page. He'd shown it in class. The camera panned across the clarinet section, and there I was, chewing on my lip, my hair oily, wearing my old cheetah hoodie with the frayed cuffs.

When I showed up on the screen, some of the upperclassmen started giggling in the back. "She looks like her dog just died," one of them said.

When people look at a walking train wreck, they don't say, "Oh, sad person, let me be nice to you." They say, "Fresh meat for bullies!" So In P.E. a flock of popular girls screamed at me during volleyball games and blew the whistle in my ear while the P.E. teacher sat in the stands scrolling through her phone. Later that year, some girl wrestled me into a headlock in the library. Someone told her that I'd been spreading rumors about her. Like I even talked! The next day, everybody stared at me, pointed, or cut their eyes at me in the hall. Complete strangers grilled me as if I was on the Ellen Show, and Ellen was saying, "What was your deal?" and I was saying, "I didn't put anyone in a headlock! I'm nice! Doesn't niceness count for anything?" but the studio audience booed anyway.

These were the type of things that would make you sit up in bed in the middle of the night, listening to talk radio just to hear voices that are not yours, trying to get the other words, the hateful ones, out of your head. Those are the kinds of things that make you feel like a caged cat pressing her face against one corner, then another, trying to escape.

So, yeah, people can be evil and wreck you. And, yeah, this is how the world teaches you that you're better off on your own.

Now I was a senior and had found my feet. I kept my hair washed, and I wore cotton tops and comfy jeans and white tennis shoes. I looked nice, no need to be a supermodel, but nice. I played bass clarinet, a wonderful instrument that deserves more respect, and smiled at people. I had buddies in band and in classes, but for some reason I couldn't make the leap from buddies to friends who hung out together after school and shared secrets. Sometimes I still felt like a window, the way people looked through me.

I liked being alone, liked being a little apart from the hectic mob rule that is high school, keeping myself for my very own. Well, let me amend that. I liked being alone, but at the same time I was still in my boat on the Sea of Lonely with no island to get my bearings off of. I was trying to find land, steering by the brightest stars, and had no idea on how to change my course – and not really sure if I wanted to change it.

♬

After band, I ate my lunch in under ten minutes. I debated about running back to the bandroom to practice piano for the rest of my lunchtime, but instead I headed to the library before class resumed. I was so tired and all I wanted was a little fun time break. I rounded the corner of the stacks, grabbing a book of Victorian poetry, but stopped. There, at my favorite table, was Wyatt hunched over a dog-eared almanac, shirtsleeves rolled up, black eyebrows low as if challenging the book to a duel. His worn bomber jacket hung over the back of his chair – a worn jacket that hung loose like an old friend, scratches criss-crossing the soft leather like petroglyphs on the wall of some storm-beaten canyon. You could see the years on that jacket but it still held up fine.

Before I could leave for another table, Wyatt awakened from his reading, looked me over, assessed how I was inching backward. "Hey, Kay. Did you want to sit here?" In an amused voice, like he knew he was foiling my escape plans.

"I don't want to bother you. Really."

"Aw, you're not bothering me." He dragged out a chair. "Come on! Have a seat."

Our chairs were too close; I scooted a few inches to the left and pulled my arm against my side. He radiated warmth and the fragrance of his manly aftershave. "Um, I'm not interrupting anything, am I?" I demurely slid down the sleeves of my hoodie because the library was freezing.

"Nah! I'm supposed to be doing this paper for DECA, but I might or might not be throwing it over so I can study for Brain Bowl." Wyatt gestured to the page he was reading – lists of composers and the symphonies they were famous for.

My face lit as if I'd lifted the bushel basket from off my candle. "There's Schubert! He's my favorite."

"Okay, you asked for it. Lightning round." Wyatt held the book like a hand of cards. "Who wrote the opera Gotterdamer--"

"*Götterdämmerung*. Twilight of the Gods. Richard Wagner." Reekard Vahgner, for those of you playing at home.

"The Four Seasons."

"Vivaldi."

"The Unfinished Symphony."

"Schubert."

"How can it be a symphony if it's unfinished?"

I rolled my eyes. "You write two movements, then you get sick from, er, something, and die."

"Wasn't it V.D.?" he asked.

"Um, syphilis," I said before thinking, and then I died of embarrassment.

Wyatt was kind enough to take no notice. He flipped through the book, smoothing the page's edge with his thumb, making a sound like a brush on a snare drum. His thumbnail was flat, not curved like mine. And his whole hand, with his blunt fingers, his olive skin, the little creases where his fingers bent, the black hairs and the pillowy veins that traveled across the back of his hand ....

Wyatt raised the book again. "Chemistry. List the noble gasses."

"Um ... neon, argon ... xenon? ..."

"Three out of five ain't bad. Math calculations."

"Don't go there. Do not go there. I will throw myself out of yonder window if you do."

"Understood. Literature. Who wrote *Wuthering Heights*?"

"Emily Bronte. And then she died! Um, not of anything … spectacular."

Wyatt grinned and tapped the spine of the almanac against the table. "You know, Kay, I wish you'd been in Brain Bowl."

"Really? Me?" Though I was flattered. I'd thought about trying out for the team, which was really good, but I'd chickened out. What else was new.

"Yes, you," he said, amused. "You can concentrate, and you're always hanging out in the library, so you're not afraid of a little knowledge. You've always got a book or a bass clarinet. Anyone who plays bass has got to have a sense of balance." There was a little wink in his voice.

I liked his nod at the basses. I'd made first chair in State Band on bass clarinet – actually, this is not as hard as it sounds – and in band, Wyatt and I often doubled on the same part. "Thanks. I kind of wish I'd joined, but I would have probably dragged your team down. I have this incredible capacity for working against myself."

Wyatt gave me a long, cool stare until I got all abashed and looked at my book. He said, "It's interesting watching you dodge praise like it's a bad thing. I'm telling you the truth."

"Oh, well …."

"Yes. I am. I've seen you work at stuff. You used to keep a small book in your hat during marching season and you'd read it during football games, even when everybody was yelling and screaming."

"You remember that?" I only did that because football games were boring. "You remember when you let me blast notes on your sousaphone, and then I got so dizzy during the pregame show I had to go kneel?"

"You did? I'm sorry."

"It's okay."

"See, your perception is your reality," Wyatt said. "If you see yourself as confused or terrible at things, you're going to believe it, and that's how you're going to live your life. If you believe you're going to succeed, then that's how it's going to play out."

"It is for you," I said shyly.

"Hell yes. We've been close to winning Nationals for the last three years. This year it's going to happen. But Kay, for better or worse, you make your own fortune. You understand?"

"But what happens if other people get in your way?" I asked.

"Then run over them! Get in your Mack truck and drive that thing up the road." Wyatt glanced at his watch. "Damn. I have five minutes to finish this test. I'd better get to work."

"Too bad. I was having fun."

Wyatt chuckled, a bass rumble.

I glanced up, right into his dark brown eyes. An electric current sparked through me. Confused, I pushed up the sleeves of my hoodie. The library was warm as a strange tide rose in my chest, turbulent, wonderful, frightening.

Wyatt set the almanac aside and went to frowning at his test, his dark face intense, unguarded. Reluctantly, I turned back to my poetry, but now I was super-aware of his presence. Heat radiated from his arm next to mine.

My hands clutched each other. Could he see my loneliness? Could he see how defenseless I was?

Yeah, maybe he'll pick you up and carry you away, some sarcastic thought said.

At once my imagination kicked into overdrive: Wyatt carried me out of burning houses, through war zones, rescued me from the mall during Christmas season. Took me to the dance, where we waltzed like royalty. My toes curled.

The bell jangled: my lunch break was over. Reluctantly, I stood. Wyatt gave my arm a gentle squeeze. It was as if he'd wrapped his warm fingers around my heart, the way you'd cradle a frightened bird.

Confused, panicked, I blurted, "I'm sorry I turned you down for the dance."

"Kay, you're a funny girl," he chuckled, and released my arm. "This ain't my first rodeo. I'll get over it."

I suddenly longed for a hug from him, and AIEE I can't think about that! With one last confused smile in return I fled down the hall to Chorus, dodging students, my heart pounding. I wanted to throw my arms open and sing in a ringing operatic soprano with the full force of my being, sing as the wind rushed through my hair and through my aching heart ....

My thoughts spun around Wyatt: the gentle strength in his hand when he squeezed my arm; the intoxicating smell of cologne charged with his warm hair and his slight vinegar scent; the confiding look in his intent brown eyes.

But as I walked back into the band room for choir, I thought of how I'd shrunk from Wyatt's touch when he'd hugged me. Shaking my head, I got my choir music out of my folder. Yet, now all I could think about was comfort. My heart was in its usual state, on its knees and elbow on the ground, one arm pressed against its chest, groaning in its grief.

All I longed for was for someone to hold out his hand and pull my heart back to its feet; all I longed for was someone who would wrap his arms around me and let me melt like, I don't know, a little melty person. A vast loneliness entered my soul, wide as the gray afternoon outside, and here I was, this sad little kid who just wanted a hug from somebody, somewhere, who she could trust.

But why did such a sweet and delicious thing, something I wanted so much – why was the very thought of it scaring the crap out of me?

TWO
PAPER DOLL
THE MILLS BROTHERS

O n Sunday, after church, I'd only been able to stay five minutes after services to practice my accompaniment for Jenny's trombone solo, because Mom said she needed to go home and get the pot roast out of the oven. I should have driven myself to church that morning, obviously. And then when I did get home, she didn't want me to practice downstairs because I was in the way. So now I was upstairs, crouched over the music score at my desk, listening to Schubert's *Unfinished Symphony* on my iPod, only because Wyatt had mentioned it on Friday. The cellos whispered their theme and I wished he could hear it with me. Then the violins and strings sneaked in, stealthy as catburglars, with their ascending minor theme, stretching the tension as the oboe sang ....

The air horn blasted from the bottom of the stairs with a *bhonk* that mashed my eardrums. I shrieked, my score flew into the air, and I yanked out my earbuds. "Geez, Mom, what!"

"Kay, get down here and help with dinner," Mom said from the bottom of the stairs.

The smell of pot roast, bread, and mashed potatoes drifted up from the kitchen. I attempted to slow my hammering heart as I paused my iPod and picked the music score off the floor, shaky from the gallon of adrenaline that zinged through my system.

In the past, Mom had summoned me with a cowbell, which I always heard over my music. Then one day she rang the cowbell as I listened to the end of Tchaikovsky's *1812 Overture*. Was it my fault that the man ended the symphony in a roar of bells and cannon? Mom declared herself fed up by my uncommunicative ways and got the air horn. Me, I would have preferred to have taken my ivory tower up about 500 feet for some peace and quiet.

So I came downstairs with my little thundercloud into the hot kitchen. I still wore my favorite white dress from church. I considered my dress genteel and sensible, while Mom considered it out of date and Victorian. Mom had the oven door open and was sliding the pot roast out, the glass shrieking across the metal grill. Croissants from a can, freshly baked with their delicate layers of crust, sat in a basket next to the stove, steaming. Grandma Marisa, looking very nice in her slim gray tunic with mother of pearl buttons, had rolled up her sleeves and was doing dishes in hot, bubbly water.

"Brighten up, buttercup," Mom set the pot roast on the stovetop. "Go set the table."

I glowered at the silverware drawer and then grumped into the living room. "No slouching, think happy thoughts," Mom called after me. I slouched. Oh Wyatt. I imagined him gently taking the silverware from my hand. "Let me help you," he'd rumble. My heart melted like butter at the very thought.

Dad and his other brothers were at Uncle Roger's, helping to build a new addition, so he'd be gone for a while. Sunday dinner would consist of Grandma Marisa, Mom, Brandon-who-should-be-working-on-that-addition-with-Dad, and me.

Brandon came thumping down the stairs, his eyes bleary from playing Grand Theft Auto in its most recent incarnation. He wore his old Gutshot! T-shirt and ratty jeans, and his long black hair was poofed up in the back as if he'd spent way too much time on the

couch playing video games. Brandon brought the basket of croissants into the dining room and then collapsed in a chair as if the
effort had done him in. He was a freshman in high school and hated
everything and that's my brother in a nutshell.

"No slouching, think happy thoughts," I told him.

He ignored me. "Get me some tea, Kay."

"Get it yourself, Mister Moody."

Mom came out of the kitchen bearing the pot roast. On rare
moments, all unthinking, she'd hold herself high and walk like a
lioness as if Leontyne was her first name, not her hidden middle
name. When I was little, she'd swish around the house barefoot, her
feet gnarled and muscular from her dance classes long ago, and
sometimes instead of simply turning she would gracefully twirl.
When I was a kid, she wore her hair in a short mane that was this
wicked cool shade of chestnut-red. When she'd stride along I would
run at her side to watch her hair ray out around her face, and she'd
smile and say, amused, "All right, kiddo, I see you." She was like the
Queen of the Night in Mozart's opera, when the mountains slid
aside to reveal her standing in her dome of stars. That all changed
after she started law school.

Mom laid the pot roast before Brandon. "Knock it off, fella.
You'll have plenty of chance for bossing later on, when you're 6' 4"
and own your own company."

"Did you make any tea?" Brandon asked, ignoring Mom's
statement.

Mom brushed back a single wisp of her hair. She kept her hair
all regimented in a tight chignon. "Kay, get the tea," she sighed.

I brought the tea in for my poor, gutshot brother, and Grandma
Marisa dried her hands on a dishtowel and followed. We sat at the
table and started passing food. Grandma Marisa sat across the table
from me. I liked going to Grandma's house and reading *The Feminine
Mystique*, which she kept on her coffee table. In the morning, she'd
do tai chi, and then she'd drink chai tea.

Grandma and Mom talked about a domestic case that had been

decided on Friday. Brandon rolled his eyes like he thought no one would notice. I began sculpting a little castle out of my mashed potatoes as I ate my croissant. Was Wyatt was eating lunch now, too? What would he think of my family? Oh, how I wanted to see him again, just to talk to him, to ease this pain in my heart.

Stop stop stop please stop.

Grandma said, "You're kind of quiet, Kay."

I scooped out tiny crenellations atop the battlements, eating each microscopic bite. "I'm always kind of quiet, Grandma."

A nettle of annoyance from Mom.

Grandma gave Mom a significant look, though she hadn't said anything. Mom shrugged. Grandma leaned forward and looked at me from under her hair, brown streaked with white. "I was thinking about something for you." She reached into her purse, then slid a brochure across the table to me.

To my surprise, the brochure was for the Lyric Opera. I picked it up and eyed it. If they hadn't been watching I would have been drooling over all that delicious music stuff inside. "That's nice." I tried to sound nonchalant.

"Wow," said Brandon through a mouthful of potatoes. "Maybe they want you to sing for the opera."

I shot him a look. "Maybe *you* should. What's this about?" I asked Grandma.

"I was wondering if you wanted to go to the opera on the 18th," she said.

"Seriously?" I tore open the brochure, and on the 18th they were performing *Aïda* by Verdi. Holy calzone! I'd never listened to that one, but I knew enough about it to know that the stage would be full of big feathered fans and reclining queens on couches and glistening jewels and Egyptian dress and people getting stabbed or buried alive, and all the while everybody would be singing like you've never heard. I'd never seen an opera before, much less gone to Kansas City to see any musical performance, so this was huge.

Mom sighed. But then she said, in a kind of cheery voice, "I bet it will be fun."

Which is like hearing a hermit say, "I like talking to people."

I put the brochure down. "What's the catch?"

"No catch. I won some tickets and thought you might like to go."

"It's a school night," I said, looking at the calendar. I often stayed up late trying to finish my Statistics homework. My advisor, who was a math teacher, kept putting me in high-level math classes, even though I kept telling her that I hated math with the heat of a million suns. That never stopped her.

"It's just one night. Do you want to go?"

"Seriously, yeah!"

"Calm down, Kay," Mom said.

I set my jaw.

"I'll pick you up after school that night," Grandma added. "We can go out to dinner at a nice restaurant and then I'll take you to the opera."

Wow. So they were finally taking my love of music seriously. Nobody had ever taken me to Kansas City at night before. I was scared to drive there because there were a lot of bad people down there and my car would probably die and then something terrible would happen.

Mom shrugged. "No. There's only so much of my time to go around. I wish I was in high school. Things were so much easier then."

I gave Mom this disbelieving look. I guess she'd forgotten my lousy freshman year.

"Back when I didn't have to do the laundry and wash dishes for four people while trying to hold down a part-time job and full-time classes," she added.

"You had plenty of other things on your plate in high school, honey," Grandma said.

"Yes. I did. But you did, too," Mom added more gently.

"Well, those days are long gone." Grandma went back to her dinner.

Mom summed me up with her eyes. "You have an easy life. I'm always meeting people who have nobody to help them but us, people on the verge of losing everything. At least you have the latitude and time to see the opera, to listen to music, to do the things you enjoy."

With a tine of my fork, I carved a recessed, locked gate into my castle.

"Kay, stop playing with your food and just eat."

I devoured battlements and crenellations like a sulky Godzilla. Her word was law. It was like talking to a statute.

Just then a car door slammed outside. Brandon, who was sitting next to the window, reported, "Grandpa Arden's here."

"What?" Mom said sarcastically. "Isn't it a little early for him to be up?" I leaned over Brandon to look, and there was Grandpa walking toward the house, head down as if fighting a storm wind.

I perked up. I'd been writing a blues song for Grandpa – at church, where I did the bulk of my practicing these days – and was really wanting to go over it with him. I hardly ever saw him, because he was usually touring or playing gigs with his blues band.

Grandma worked on her mashed potatoes as Grandpa's footsteps thumped up to the front porch. "Ignore him. He wants to stir things up. Don't give him the satisfaction." She and Grandpa had been divorced for several years, I don't know how many. They got along all right, because he'd still visit at her house. He'd bring her blues CD's (which she gave to me) and expensive dinners from Kansas City steakhouses and BBQs.

Grandpa Arden staggered in as if the door had opened too quickly for him. "Well! Don' look surprised to see me," he said jovially. His black, gray, and white hair was in its usual bobtail, pulled so tight that his scalp slid back a couple of inches. He shed his black leather jacket, pipe clenched between his teeth. A few flakes of tobacco drifted out.

"Dad, we have children in here. Don't smoke in the house," Mom said, her professional persona coming out.

"Sorry I'm late," Grandpa said, though it was apparent from the way Mom shook her head that he hadn't been invited. "Y'know how it is … had to play at my gig last night … we played 'til two. I din't get to bed 'til five." He took the pipe out of his mouth and exaggerated a yawn, smoke curling out. "Had a hell of a time wakin up for your little shindig. Nobody told me we were gettin together. Voice mail must not have picked up."

I imagined Wyatt and me sitting at a table together in some smoky venue, rocking out to a blues band playing live on stage. Did Wyatt even like the blues? "Where did you play last night, Grandpa?"

"Arden, put out the pipe," Grandma said, raising her voice as if he were deaf.

He winced, but tapped out his pipe into his palm, crushed them, and put them in his pocket. "Knuckleheads," he said. "It was packed. Big fight outside th establishment there at the end. Ya would've liked it."

I kind of grimaced. Actually it sounded kind of scary.

Grandpa came to the table, bracing his arms against two chairs to look around. "Wadda ya all getting together for today? Wha's th special occasion?"

"Sunday dinner." Mom shook salt over her food with great delicacy.

"Well, I thought ya might've invited me."

"We haven't seen you for two months. We assumed you weren't interested. Sorry."

Grandma Marisa, ever the peacemaker, added, "We wouldn't want to wake you if you were sleeping in."

Grandpa grunted. He placed his hand on the back of a chair, surveying the half-finished pot roast, the full glasses of iced tea, the untouched apple pie. "Hm, good thing I'm not hungry. I know when I'm not welcome."

I laid down my knife and fork, though I was still hungry. I'd stop eating for Grandpa's sake, and I'd start eating again so I wouldn't hurt Mom's feelings.

"Sit down and eat, then," said Mom wearily. "Sit by Kay, there's an open seat there."

Grandpa sat down. Mom dropped a plate in front of him, but he ignored it. I smelled peppermint and something else from Grandpa. He liked to drink. A lot. I wrinkled my nose, then pretended that had been an itch and scratched it.

He watched Grandma, who sat across the table from him. Grandma cut small, careful bites from her roast. Brandon kept slurping down his food.

"What're ya doin, Marisa? Are ya doin all right?"

"I'm doing fine."

It was quiet except for Brandon's chewing. I took a tiny bite of potatoes when Grandpa wasn't looking my way.

"Ya want me to send ya some money? I could send you some money. Got paid yesterday," Grandpa said.

"Keep it. I'm fine."

Grandpa pressed his thumb on the rim of his empty plate so it popped up in the air. He lowered the plate back to the table, then popped it up again. "I played five gigs this week," he said in a low voice, watching the plate as it sprang up then sank down. "I played with Jake and the Heartbreakers for two nights, then I did some background music for some KKFI spots, and I worked some evenings at the bar, playin. Then me and the band played at Knucklehead's last night. It went pretty good." I listened, fascinated. I'd never seen him play – I was too young to enter the establishments where he performed, they all served alcohol. When I turned 21, the first thing I was going to do was go to Knucklehead's and see all the acts I'd been missing.

"Brandon, pass the croissants," Mom said. With a great sigh, as if his heart were broken, he passed them.

Grandpa still looked at his plate. "We're gonna be playin at the American Jazz Museum next month, on the 18th. 'Ts gonna be a big gig. I can get you tickets." He stole a little glance at Grandma.

"The American Jazz Museum! Holy cow!" I sat up. "Oh my gosh, Grandpa, that's the big time!"

Grandpa brightened. "You bet, dolly. We'll be sharin th stage with some big names. The band's tight and it's gonna be a hot set, you bet."

Mon leaned back, her eyes shifting to Grandma. Huh?

"Arden," Grandma said to Grandpa, "We've already made plans for that night."

"What?" I cried.

"Remember? The opera? That's on the 18th and you already said you're going with me," Grandma said apologetically.

I pleaded, "But, but … no! But …." I was so confused – so dumbfounded – I couldn't pull my brain together enough to reply. "Can't we just cancel—"

Grandma Marisa was already talking to Grandpa. "So we can't go, we really can't. I'm so sorry. I didn't know."

I sat there with my mouth hanging open. "Grandma, why can't we just –"

"Well … that's okay," Grandpa flinched, looked at his plate. "That's okay. You call the shots, hon."

"Kay could go next time you play there," Mom said soothingly.

Grandpa scoffed at that. "Once in a lifetime."

"But … I want to go to Grandpa's gig, too." But nobody was looking at me, except for Brandon, who just shook his head and went back to his lunch.

Grandpa spoke up. "Fine. I see how ya are."

"Arden, I'm sorry, but it's already been decided …."

"Ya playin any songs for me today, dolly?" he asked me.

I drew breath to tell everybody what I thought of their little scheme, but I inhaled a tiny bit of spit into my windpipe and started coughing.

"She might not be in a mood to play anything," Grandma said over my hacking. "She already played for church this morning."

"Yeah, church," Grandpa said, waving God off as if he were a mosquito. "I'm talkin about the good stuff. I'm talkin about the music that makes people get up and dance."

I coughed up the last bit of spit. "I have one or two songs. I have to practice at church all the time because sometimes it's hard to practice at home."

Mom sighed.

"Y'need to learn more'n one, two songs, Kathy. Li'l Kathy One-Note. One song's all she has. Ya gotta live your dreams, girly."

"Hey, you know full well I have more than one song," I said.

"Dreams, pah," Mom said bitterly. "They're nothing. When you wake up, they're gone."

Grandma Marisa broke in. "Oh, you two, let's talk about something else."

"Nah, let's not talk at all." Grandma looked taken aback. I felt hurt on her behalf.

In a gentler tone Grandpa drawled, "It never does no good to talk." He got up and came around behind her chair. "I've been quiet for how many years? I've been good, ain't I? Woman, you know I've changed. So," he mumbled, leaning closer to her, voice lowering as if trying to talk in private. "When'm I goin home with you?"

An awful, shocked silence. Grandma's mouth tightened and she lowered her fork, looking haggard.

"So! Would you like to hear my song?" I piped into the silence, my voice way too loud. I winced.

Grandpa spared a sidelong glance to the rest of us; my words seemed to make him realize where he was. I felt weird, like I'd displayed a bit of power I was not supposed to have. I started messing with the mashed potatoes.

Grandpa pulled his hands off the table and stood. "Well, let's hear it."

Mom's lip wrinkled as if Grandpa were handing her an octopus.

"No. She doesn't need to be playing. It's … noisy enough in here as it is."

"Ha. Noisy. C'mon, doll." He unwrapped a peppermint and popped it in his mouth.

"You might let her finish eating first," Mom chided.

But I was already on the piano bench, opening the piano. They couldn't tell me what to do here, at the keyboard. The scent of antique wood and ivory floated to me. The keys were worn at the edges like the pages of a favorite book.

Grandpa sat on the bench. His peppermint candy clicked against his teeth. He ran a finger over the sill, reaching into my personal space. "No dust. Good. So what's your new song?"

Grandpa's clothes smelled mildewy, like they'd been in the washer too long. "Well, actually my new song's actually a Schubert sonata," I joked, playing a few notes of the melody in the upper register, a trilling little dancy song.

"Aw, I don't wanna hear that paper music." All classical music was paper music, because symphony musicians "didn't have the balls to improvise," as he'd so delicately put it.

"Come on, Grandpa, you know I'm a paper gal."

Grandpa's eyes softened. He started playing an old song on the lower register, a song he used to play for me when I was little, which made me smile. "'I'm gonna buy a paper doll that I can call my own, a doll that other fellows cannot steal, and then the flirty, flirty guys with their flirty, flirty eyes will have to flirt with dollies that are real ….'"

Grandma sighed, and Grandpa stopped. "Girl, I thought I set a better example for ya. Ya need some fire in yer belly, girl, instead of playing paper. Blues are the thing ya need, played from down in your soul."

"I have a new blues song I've been working on."

My smile disarmed Grandpa enough to sit back. "Whaddaya call it?"

"Well … I don't know." It was pretty much a boogie-woogie riff that kept my left hand reaching for octave after octave, as if it were a stride piano piece, and a tune that was, now that I thought about it with Grandpa right there, pretty generic. "It's not really finished, and I don't want to sing it until it's finished. All the words I come up with suck."

"Well, go ahead 'n' play your song. Maybe I can help you. 'kay?"

I grinned and started chasing down the notes on the keyboard. My beginning was way too overconfident and I muffed a bunch of notes right off. Usually I could get into the groove and belt my song out. But with everybody right there watching and listening – and as tired as I was from all the District contest insanity – I couldn't get into it.

"My God, dolly, you're playin that song like a fluff piece."

I grimanced. "Yeah ...." I stopped playing. "I don't have all the experience you do, though."

"Here, here, don' do that. Play it again, from the top, let's work on this." I started, and almost at once he said, "Whoa, whoa, whoa, whoa, dolly. Try this." Grandpa moved my left hand off the keys and played what I'd been playing, only with authority, like his music meant what it said. At once my right hand, playing the melody, gained all kinds of confidence. This sounded great already and I hadn't even changed anything! Then Grandpa said, "Now watch this," and busted the left hand down an octave, the bass so low that the stuff on top of the piano vibrated. When my melody changed, he came back up and played some cool block chords, just dissonant enough to make my blues song turn into jazz.

"This is great!" The whole mood of my melody had changed – now it seemed like something you'd play on a rainy day when your man done walked out on you. I tried to remember the chords Grandpa was playing but he'd change chords I just about had one figured out. "Slow down, I want to write this down."

"You don' need to write this down, kitty. They teach you Dorian mode? No? What're they teachin you in that school of yers? My

God." Grandpa switched into a lush over-romantic piano bar version of "Eleanor Rigby" with so much schmaltz that I just about died laughing. "You can't play good if you don' take advantage of all these styles out there."

Grandma Marisa stood at his shoulder. "Arden, I thought she played very well."

"Look, the girl's afraid to touch the keys." Grandpa played a bit of my song with a light touch. "What's she scared of? She can't make music if she's scared."

"She doesn't have to play loud, she's in the house." Mom put a hand on my shoulder, but I shrank away. Her hand hesitated, then withdrew.

"Well, she can't take the piano outside." Grandpa laughed so hard he grabbed his pipe so it wouldn't fall out. I grinned. He leaned toward me. "Look, dolly, ya gotta be heard over all the fun-loving people listening to ya. Play the music so you can be heard. Listen to this, babe. Let me give you an idea or two." With an elbow he nudged me until I scooted off the bench, and then he began to play my song hot and fast, his left hand rocking out that bass line effortlessly though that same line always left my wrist and fingers aching. He bellowed out an old Count Basie lyric to my music. "'I may be wrong but I won't be wrong always. Well I may be wrong but I won't be wrong always. You're gonna fall for me one of these old rainy days.'"

I imagined playing this song the way Grandpa was, with Wyatt sitting next to me on the piano bench, lost in admiration.

Grandpa winked at me as if we were conspirators and I winked back. He bent over the keyboard as if he were a jockey urging his horse on to a win, and I studied what he did, trying to cram as much into my head as possible so I could try it out later. I wanted to tell him to slow down, but I know he loved to show off for me at the piano.

"Arden, that's enough!" Mom stood by the lower register, hands on hips.

Grandpa's face darkened like a thundercloud swept across it. "Don't talk to me like I'm a baby," he muttered in a sharp voice.

I felt a thrill of terror.

Grandpa pushed his foot on the sustain pedal to lift the damper off the strings. His fingers hopping around the keyboard like angry spiders. The loud block chords melted into each other, built to a discordant roar.

Then his hands opened.

With the flat of his palm he shoved the keys, shoved in the piano's face, half-rising from the bench so he could shove harder. The piano rocked under his attack. Grandpa's mouth came open.

He'd never done this before. I stepped back from the bench, wanting to run.

Mom grabbed my shoulders and I flinched. "Go upstairs," she said, projecting her voice over the piano's roar. Grandpa, glancing at her, used his entire forearm to play the bass line and drowned her out. "Go upstairs! Now!"

At the table, Brandon, hunched over his second helping of everything like a stray dog, shouted in a booming voice normally reserved for the basketball court, *"Grandpa, shut up!"*

Startled, Grandpa lifted his hands. Inside the piano, the damper fell with a thump to muffle the ringing strings. The sudden silence hurt my ears.

Grandpa sat back on the bench, staring at the keys. Mom and Grandma stared at Brandon. My heart thudded. *What had just happened??*

The few loose strands of Mom's hair vibrated around her face. Her voice tight, she said, "I think you have to leave."

"Yeah, people are trying to eat," Brandon added, snarfing down his potatoes.

Grandpa didn't even look. Just sat there.

But even though he didn't say anything, Mom stretched her neck as if her collar had tightened. She grabbed the remains of the pot roast and headed into the kitchen, dress flaring behind her.

My work here was done, I guess.

As Grandma talked to Grandpa, as Brandon ate and ignored everybody, I cut a piece of apple pie, my heart pounding. I wished that I could reach back to Wyatt —

My knife paused.

I thought of Wyatt seeing this. For the first time a queasy feeling crept through my gut.

Grandpa had never attacked a piano before. Sure, the grownups always seemed tense around him, but he usually kept to himself. If he wasn't talking to me about playing piano, he would be eating off a TV tray at a corner of the couch, watching war movies. I always felt sorry for him, alone like that.

For the first time I realized that something about this was not Normal.

Forget it, I thought, taking my apple pie to my room. You're just weirded out by whatever just happened.

I shed my family as I climbed the dark stairs right back to my ivory tower.

THREE
YOU'RE DAMN RIGHT I'VE GOT THE BLUES
BUDDY GUY

I hoped that all the practicing I did Sunday afternoon would push Wyatt out of my head. But on Monday morning when I walked into the bandroom for Symphonic Band, my eyes snapped right to Wyatt though he was way in the back by the windows. He leaned across his dented tuba, chatting with the trombone player who sat in front of him. He rocked back with laughter, then looked at them from under his brows as he replied.

The power went out of my legs to see him. I leaned against the stereo cabinet in a swoony delight.

Oh, no.

Oh, *yes*!

Oh cripes, I thought, and went to get the bass.

I was glad of the bass clarinet that day. We were rehearsing Holst's *First Suite*, and I played the same part Wyatt did, our deep, warm basses singing together. When Mr. Ambrose, the band director, laid his baton on his stand to talk about how Holst layered melodies all through his compositions, I rested my hand over the neck of the bass, chin on wrist, and looked at the tubas from the corner of my eye. I didn't want to look at him too much and embarrass him. Yet I felt glad that he could see me, if he wished.

Wyatt was backlit by the sun, his arm looped around his tuba's shoulder. I shut my eyes. Was it so wrong to long for a little comfort? Sometimes I felt so lonely that I felt like something was broken inside.

I practiced the fingering on the bass, listening to the percussive pops of the keys, smelling the cork grease and warm wood of the instrument, the faint metallic scent of the nickel keys that my fingers warmed. I had to break those chains of romance. I could not dwell on him forever – I wanted to get back to my romanceless life and be free of these yearnings.

Yeah, but between classes, I looked for him everywhere, and I'd walk different ways to class, trying to meet him in the hallway. When Wyatt loped past, my heart would press itself against the bars of my rib cage, stretching a skinny, famished arm to him. Sometimes our eyes would meet, and what a sweet feeling would go straight through the core of my body. Sometimes I was afraid to even look at him. Oh, how I longed for Wyatt to give me one clasp of his hand – even a hug, warm and solid! Some small touch, anything, to give me some relief!

Well, this is going to be as close as we get, I thought as we started playing the first movement again. Two rich, dark voices singing together, tuba and bass clarinet, anchoring the orchestra. Isn't a union of voices enough?

After band, at lunch, I was sitting alone when Wyatt and his Brain Bowl friends walked down the hall past the cafeteria doors. A girl I didn't know wore Wyatt's bomber jacket, the tips of her fingers showing from inside its sleeves.

I picked at the apple salad and snorted. I wasn't one of those girls who threw her heart at every passing guy to see if it sticks. I didn't need a man to rescue me from my so-called life. I wasn't a wimp!

Yet the rest of the day, I wished I were that girl, pulling Wyatt's jacket snugly around me, breathing the smell of his cologne. A thrill went through my heart.

The next day, I wore a skirt with a nice blue and white blouse. I tied my black hair into a ponytail with a white ribbon, then covered my face with cold cream and scrubbed it off. My pores tingled. I lowered my head and regarded myself from under my eyelashes. Nice brown eyes with flecks of green, eyes like the inside of a forest. I gave myself a vampish pout. Then I giggled insanely and rushed off.

When I went to my boring government class, I was surprised — but so happy — to see Wyatt there, his hands tucked into the pockets of his bomber jacket, talking to the Brain Bowl coach. The timbre of his bass voice as he discussed the general unworthiness of some competing team made me scrunch myself together in great joy, a mini-hug. I loved seeing him so worked up, like he was going to take his indignation into the streets, flipping cars over as he marched to battle. I put my feet on the chair in front of me and plucked at the skirt to cover my bare ankles. I touched my ponytail for courage.

"Hello," I murmured as Wyatt began to leave.

"Hey, Kay." Wyatt rested his hands on my desk and gave me a quick once-over with his eyes. "You look nice."

Grab him! Wrestle him to the ground!

I felt the blush and ducked my head. "What brings you here?"

"Oh, talking to Coach. Nationals are coming up." Wyatt's manner, though jovial, took on enough intensity to send a low-voltage current through my heart.

"I hope you do well," I said softly.

"Oh, we will. We're practicing two times a day. We placed in Nationals the last six years. This year, we're going to win. All those expensive prep schools and private schools, all those big-city schools that are richer than God, we'll hand them their asses on a platter." Coach was going by and Wyatt grinned. Coach smiled, too, as he left. "Hammer down!" Wyatt added, his hand in a fist, his class ring glinting green at me. "I'd better get to class. See ya."

I slid down in my chair, tipping my head back. Rachmaninoff's "Rhapsody on a Theme of Paganini," with its lush orchestra and supernatural pianist, bloomed like a rose around me.

After class I floated down the hall like a dancer. In band I smiled at Wyatt, and he returned it from behind his tuba.

The rest of the day, though, I didn't see Wyatt again. The delight was an engine revving too fast. When my delight ran out of power, the intense longing flooded back. By the time I got to the last class of the day, the unceasing wanting, needing, had exhausted me. I hated him (even as part of me protested that no, I didn't hate him) for causing these emotions to run unchecked. If only I could climb away from them!

When I got home that night, I was a wreck. I glowered at supper, argued with Mom, went off to church where I flailed around with my music for the rest of the night. My accompaniments refused to come together, my bass solo was meh, the Mozart was decent, and finally I just lay down on the floor in front of the altar, with the evening sun burning through the western stained-glass windows, and cried for no reason whatsoever.

My wretched state of affairs continued all week, even on Thursday when a busload of band students (including me) went to District Contest to play our solo and ensemble music.

Fortunately (or unfortunately) for me, Wyatt was also on the bus going to Districts. Recalling the sad case of Ryan Lawrence from my freshman year, which I am sure pretty much everybody on the bus today remembered, I did my dangdest not to stare at Wyatt through the whole trip. Wyatt sat in the back with a group of his teammates from Brain Bowl, practicing questions and letting the band students quiz them. Somebody said, "Not only is he a science stud, but he can also field-dress a deer."

When we got there, we got our schedules for the day. I was off and running with two accompaniments within 15 minutes of each other. Those went reasonably well. Then I hung out in the gym in the area my classmates had claimed. Played my solo, didn't bomb. Then I played Jenny's accompaniment.

I should have taken Grandpa's advice about playing out. I had my accompaniment in hand, mostly, except for a few parts that I flubbed. But I played softly so that she could be heard over the piano. Even though she played *trombone*. When it was over, her eyes turned red-rimmed and she walked quickly out. Later I heard that she'd gotten a 2, and as far as I was concerned, it was my fault.

I came into the bandroom Friday morning before school. Music students were hanging around in the percussion section as usual, passing time before homeroom began. Some of the band students were gathered around the music stand where Mr. Ambrose put the judges' critiques from District contest. I found my critique. My bass clarinet solo had received a 1, of course, which was an 'A'. The judge had written that I'd made good use of expression and intonation, but I needed to play out more. Of course.

Mr. Ambrose came by and patted Kent, a percussionist, on the back. "Good showing yesterday. You got a 1 on everything."

"So did I," I said, looking at the ensemble sheet. I worshipped Mr. Ambrose because he used to play in a symphony orchestra, but for some reason he'd been snubbing me lately.

"So did she," Kent echoed, glancing from me to Mr. Ambrose.

Mr. Ambrose gave me the side eye, but began to look through the rest of the critiques. "I think your other one is in here, Kent …."

Just then, Wyatt breezed into the bandroom past Mr. Ambrose's office, his bomber jacket swaying lazily over his shoulder. I froze. Oh, Wyatt, my own dear Wyatt! I wanted to pounce on him! I wanted to hide in a little hole in the floor!

With a rustle, Mr. Ambrose set the critiques down and stopped in the middle of the doorway front of me, his glossy black ponytail in my face, fists on his hips. "Wyatt. Come here, now." His vibrant baritone projected so well that the chimes rang.

Wyatt, who had reached the percussion level on the bandroom

risers, turned. My heart jumped to see those dark eyes. His eyebrows rose. "Regarding?"

All the students in the bandroom looked our way.

I tried to scoot past Mr. Ambrose but couldn't escape without touching him. I tried to retreat, but the vocal teacher's pets had crowded behind to watch.

Mr. Ambrose said, "You got a 4 on your tuba solo. That's the lowest score there is!"

Wyatt looked startled for the merest moment, then recovered. "Is this an appropriate topic for a general audience?"

"I'll say it is. Now, explain that 4."

The darkness around Wyatt's eyes scared me. "Now, you were pretty adamant that I take your solo. 'Oh come on come on,' you said, even though I let you know in no uncertain terms that my top priority was getting ready for Nationals. Not District, Nationals. But you kept coming after me and coming after me, so I took your solo to get you off my case."

"You got a 4."

Wyatt blocked his words with an open hand. "I took your solo, I played your solo, and now I am done with your solo. Let's accept it and move on."

"I am not interested in wasting my time." Mr. Ambrose swung his hand, pointed like a gun, down at the floor in front of him. "You're here to play music and excel, not to pull crap on me and the program. Your lack of focus would not be tolerated in the Atlanta Symphony."

Wyatt's face had gone pale and rigid, yet he kept the anger out of his voice. "My focus is on Brain Bowl. I won't win Nationals by practicing a tuba solo."

With a grunt, Mr. Ambrose seized the stand with the judge's sheets and flung it. The stand scraped and rattled across the floor and fell with a ringing crash, sheets scattering left and right. "You are not playing in Concert Band the rest of the year!" Mr. Ambrose boomed.

The students in the bandroom had eyes the size of dinner plates.

Wyatt turned a disgusted, condescending look on him, and gave a small snort of a laugh as he shook his head. As if he'd *triumphed.* "Oh, no you don't. I will finish out the year."

"Not in my band you won't --"

"I will finish out the year in Concert Band. I will have no change in my grade," Wyatt emphasized over Mr. Ambrose's voice. "Or you can meet with me, my dad, and the superintendent, where you can justify your views without throwing a tantrum."

The air pressure in the bandroom dropped due to all the students who gasped – me included. Could you really talk like that to a teacher? But Wyatt wasn't through. "If you'd approached me in a civil manner and discussed the matter one-on-one, I would have returned the favor. But I've put up with your high-handed attitude toward your non-favored students for four years, and what respect I used to have for you is gone."

The heat of Mr. Ambrose's anger radiated from his body. He jabbed his finger toward the bandroom door so hard that I flinched. "Go to the office. Now."

"Okay. And when – if – you recover your temper, you can come down and we can discuss this like grown-ups. Now, you have a quality day." Wyatt walked past Mr. Ambrose without looking at him and out the door.

The bandroom was dead silent for the space of several breaths. Then Mr. Ambrose spun, his face grotesque, shoved past me into the office, and whipped the metal door shut. I yanked myself away, but the flat of the door bounced off my shoulder blade. I staggered. He grabbed the door a second time and slammed it so hard that dust fell from the ceiling. Its explosion drilled into my ears.

"Are you all right?" somebody asked, but I walked out of the bandroom like nothing had happened, ignoring my shoulder. I eased the bandroom door shut until the latch clicked. I took three steps. Then the whatever-it-was coiled up like a spring in my chest suddenly exploded, and I sprinted. I could have poured on the miles and never stopped, flying to someplace I didn't know, but when I burst around the corner, I stopped short. Wyatt was at the end of the hall, striding away, slamming the wall with his fist. With every blow I heard a percussive burst of fury from between his teeth.

I hovered, wrapping my arms around my waist, counting each blow -- four, five, six.

Stop stop stop please stop.

"This is stupid," Wyatt suddenly muttered. He took his phone out of his pocket and dialed. "Hey, Pa. Do you have time to help with a situation here?" He turned the corner and was gone.

Wyatt talked back to Mr. Ambrose -- he defied him!

Well, that's his funeral. He shouldn't have talked back.

Shut up, I thought, though I knew the voice was right. Wyatt was going to be suspended forever. I know I would have been, if I'd talked back. Mr. Ambrose was just overworked and stressed out of his mind. Everyone knew he was doing his best.

But how hateful Wyatt had had looked. I cringed. Yet I wanted to feel my skin draw tight in the heat of the fire, flames licking my hair. To be angry took real strength, strength I'd never had.

Later that very morning, I was floored to see Wyatt back in band. The students were abuzz. Wyatt had sicced the hounds of hell on Mr. Ambrose. Teachers were not supposed to yell or use grades as a means for public humiliation.

Wyatt glared from behind the tuba at Mr. Ambrose, eyes cutting like a laser.

My bass clarinet squeaked. I tore my gaze back to the music, adjusting my volume to compensate for Wyatt's overblowing.

It's the end of the awful toil of romance! I thought. See how he acted? He's dangerous.

So, resolute, I walked away from that which I called love. The end! And every time I remembered Wyatt's anger, love ducked out of sight like a frightened rabbit. After a while, it didn't come back. I could think about my music without being prostrated by unfulfilled longing and misery. How wonderful to be free!

The next day, Saturday, dawned with a sweet haze over the spring-green hills. I awoke, ready to carry out all the plans I'd made yesterday. But to my dismay, my longing for Wyatt had returned, a low-grade fever I couldn't shake. I pulled my pillow over my head and groaned.

I took a morning walk, I played with my yellow Lab, Cricket, I lounged next to my window, listening to Bach's *Goldberg Variations*. I loved the call and response in each thread of Bach's music, so mathematically precise, as orderly as the ticking of a clock. I sighed. Not like my stupid seesawing emotions, where my mind kept saying *Wyatt, Wyatt, Wyatt,* and my heart kept wanting, wanting, wanting.

In a moment I was outside, walking up the hill toward the high pasture and forest.

In the hilltop pasture, where the grass was still short, the world opened to the sky. Nodaway, my little village, was nestled between the hill I stood on and the opposite hill, where the old cemetery was fading away under a sea of grass. I smelled the sharp smoke of a wood stove. The Missouri River meandered through the heart of the floodplain. Beyond the great river, several miles away, were the blue Kansas hills – a place I'd never been, distant as heaven.

In the magical light mist I walked across the top of the hill and imagined Wyatt walking at my side. I must have been thinking of him so strong because it almost seemed that he was with me. I didn't look at him – I didn't dare – but quietly exulted in the sweetness of his presence.

For a long time Wyatt and I walked together across the soft new grass in silence. Fine droplets touched my face. Finally I asked, "Do you think I'm strange? For feeling this way?"

Wyatt said, Not at all.

I began talking more freely with him, looking out at the deep, silent river as birds called from the dark forest behind the pasture. I leaned on a redbud tree, pink blossoms scattered along its zigzag black branches. It was sweet to say all this to him. My words came out haltingly, with long moments of silence, but he always waited for me to speak.

I looked at the bluffs and floodplain, and I imagined that he did, too. The new green on the trees of their forests was so light, so fine, like soft mist. The air smelled of rich earth and decaying leaves and blossoms.

A house finch couple fluttered into the redbud. They chirped and ducked to each other, and when the male scooted up the twig, knocking off a flower, the little dun female followed.

The male turned and stretched his head over the female, who cowed down, looking up at him, her beak open as if breathtaken. He leaned over and took her bill in his. For all the world it looked like a kiss. He kissed her again and again. The wind lifted my hair and played with it. The birds turned from each other to whet their bills on the twig.

Wyatt's flaws fascinated me. Maybe I could help him, open myself up to him, dare to trust him.

"I'm not afraid," I told the wind.

Oh yes you are! the wind replied.

I went to my computer and did a Facebook search, and oh Lord there he was, Wyatt M. Bradshaw. His profile pic was of him all in camo in a deer stand in a tree, holding a thermos cup of coffee with a mock-serious frown on his face.

View pictures of Wyatt (23). In a relationship. (I sighed.) Interests: Winning Nationals at Brain Bowl! Hunting, fishing, studying bats. Saving money to buy land and take an early retirement. Favorite book: *Walden* by H.D. Thoreau.

Here were comments from his friends. *did you hear about caleb punching the deer? lol if not ill have to tell you the story youll laugh!! lol well miss ya!*

In his status update, updated today, he'd written, *I'm working at*

Paducah's from 5-9 to spread the love! Come one, come all, bow season is upon us now.

I glanced at the clock. It was 5:30.

Though all I wanted to do was to drink in all the lovely Wyatt-related information, I grabbed my notebook instead. "I'm going to do it!" My voice ended at a squeak, and I clutched my notebook to my chest like a soap-opera queen.

I set the notebook down and wrote. I wouldn't talk about love. Only mundane things, like how lousy it felt to be labeled shy even though I wasn't, and how nervous I was, writing this letter, and how I couldn't talk to him on the phone because the phone made me sound like a dork.

When I finished the letter, I folded it into a tidy square the way I used to do when I was in elementary school and sent actual notes to actual people. My hands shook.

"I'm going to town. I'm out of paper," I told Mom, who had barricaded herself at the dining room table behind an entire legal library. "I'm going to Paducah's." I grabbed the door frame so I wouldn't fall over.

"Pick up more coffee," she said from behind the barricade. "Oh, God, I wish you were old enough to buy cigarettes."

When I walked into Paducah's, I was fine until the first flash of eye-searing hunter's orange hit me. I got all jangly and had to duck into automotive to practice some deep breathing, my heart pounding in a delicious dizzy rapture. Then I stepped into Wyatt's world.

A whole forest of fishing poles pointed at heaven. Camo and bright hunter's orange. Guns in a cabinet behind the register. Binoculars. Deer bait. Hot Scrape – brings in deer aroused! I imagined a hunter spilling a bottle of Hot Scrape all over his blind and a bunch of bucks racing up and – well, that would end badly.

Wyatt was in the bowhunting aisle among spare barbs and targets, singing "A Country Boy Can Survive" under his breath as he straightened the camo duct tape.

"Wyatt!" I said. "Hello."

He turned, saw me – and smiled!

My legs went all shaky with relief.

He said, "Hey, what are you doing here?"

I would have answered, but my brain gleefully leapt out of my head to snuggle up under Wyatt's arm. "Don't mind me, just go on with whatever you were doing," said my brain.

What was I doing, anyway? Oh, yes, I had to give Wyatt a plausible reason for visiting him, not i.e. that I wanted to gaze adoringly upon his hotness and in this way ease my aching heart. "Um, um, um, I was … why, this was the very thing I was looking for!" I exclaimed, scooping up a couple of rolls that Wyatt had just set down. I clutched the duct tape to my chest. His hands had touched these! "I was, um, going to wrap stuff up in it. And make it vanish."

"Make what vanish, the tape?"

"No, the stuff! Because this is camo tape! Obviously." My Ditz-O-Meter was flashing, but without my brain I could do nothing. I slid the three rolls of tape up my arm like industrial-sized bracelets. "My brother will be first on the list. Mister Moody. I shall wrap him in duct tape and roll him down a hill."

"I stuck my brother to the wall once with duct tape," Wyatt said. "We wanted to scare Mom when she came into the garage. It worked. Now everybody calls my brother Superfly."

Ah! I knew Superfly; he was a freshman. I imagined the kid hanging on the garage wall, both brothers laughing as Wyatt slapped one end of the tape to the wall and unrolled it with a tearing noise. "Did you tape your brother's arms to the wall, too? What if he had to scratch his nose?"

"I only taped his shoulders. His arms were free so he could wave them around. I used so much duct tape that we had to cut him out of his clothes to get him down. It was pretty cool. Do you have enough duct tape, by the way? Do you need more?"

I imagined duct-taping Brandon to the couch when he fell asleep playing video games. "I'd better not do it," I said, handing the rolls back. By now I'd managed to reel in my brain and I could act a little bit normal. "Actually, I just thought I'd look at tents and stuff. I want to go camping someday, but I don't know anything about it." I'd come up with the tent idea on the fly, but now that I thought about it, I liked the idea.

But I worried about what Wyatt might say about my camping alone. Last year I went out of the house after bedtime and walked to the top of the hill because the night was beautiful, with the full moon casting enchantment on the sleeping world. The night breeze and the lustrous moon and the little lights gleaming here and there on the floodplain were so beautiful. When I came back home, Mom freaked out, talking like evil people were going to attack me every time I took a moonlight stroll. I couldn't bear it if Wyatt agreed with her.

But Wyatt said, "Camping, huh? What a great way to spend the night. You get a nice fire going, cook some biscuits and stew, roast some marshmallows for dessert. Then you sit and watch the fire, and it throws up a little red confetti every time it pops, and flames slide around inside the wood. You can listen to the owls calling to each other across the miles. I shine my flashlight into the trees and see if I can catch some bats in the beam."

I caught myself before I could clasp my hands. Stay cool, Kay, stay cool. Yet what a thrill, what an honor, to peek into Wyatt's life so deeply, and how I wanted to join him in it. "That sounds wonderful."

Wyatt's eyes warmed, and he motioned me toward the camping supplies. "I'll show you the coolest tents. Let's go."

I was positively giddy. My thoughts were like the bats I'd seen at twilight, fluttering in the spaces between the trees, like leaves that had developed the power of flight.

For a half-hour, Wyatt showed me tents big enough to house Texas, hand warmers, portable showers, a teeny-tiny party grill, propane heaters, sleeping bags that kept you warm at 0 degrees, an enclosed metal box on a stick to toast bread in. Who knew that there were so many things to keep you safe and comfortable in the wild world?

And here were some little single-sized tents. "Oh, shoot, these are too high," I said, looking at the prices. I had only ten dollars on me – since I hadn't actually come in to look at tents.

He looked over my shoulder. "That's okay. Maybe you can borrow a tent from your uncle. It may interest you to know that these will go on sale this fall."

Just then another customer wandered up with a duck call in his hand and an inquiring look in his eyes.

Wyatt asked me, "Can you handle it from here?"

"Sure." We looked at each other for a long moment, a look so natural, more natural than what I had expected. Before I could change my mind, I slipped him my note. A small bolt of fear curled my toes.

Wyatt seemed surprised, but in a good way. He clasped my hand to palm the note. "Have fun on your trip." He winked.

When I got into my car with my notebook paper and Mom's coffee, I leaned back against my seat for a long, delicious moment, eyes shut. Then I turned on the ignition and blasted my favorite song as I roared away, sweet spring wind in my hair, heading back home to travel Wyatt's web sites.

What a day!

FOUR
ON MY OWN
LES MISÉRABLES

S o I'm leaning on the counter in the hunting and fishing section with Wyatt, and my comment has surprised him into a laugh – my favorite thing in the world – when suddenly a stranger's harsh voice breaks in:

"Freeze! Don't move!"

I look up. I can't register fast enough the gunman with his gun leveled at Wyatt's face. The gunman has a black ski mask pulled over his face, a camo jacket shivering on his frame. His head twitches.

I'm trying to wrap my brain around this, when, "Don't move!" the gunman screams again, spitting. He jerks the gun from Wyatt, to me – I freeze – then back again at Wyatt.

The air's been pumped out of the room. My chest burns. Wyatt can't move, staring down the barrel of that thing.

"Come out from behind that counter!" the gunman commands.

Wyatt hesitates, eyes big. The gunman swallows, and raises the gun slightly. My heart is hammering so hard it hurts.

I swipe a stand of miniature flashlights off the counter and with all my strength, I slam them into the gunman's face. Colorful flashlights ricochet everywhere as he staggers back.

"Run!" I scream to Wyatt.

The gun jerks toward me – I yank back – a huge explosion like a bomb has gone off. Somebody slams a 2x4 into my ribs.

I'm lying on the floor gasping for breath. But I'm so mad at this jerk for pulling that gun on Wyatt that I grab a miniature flashlight off the floor and pitch it into the man's face. Then another and another. All the while, my side feels like it's being stabbed.

While the gunman's dodging flashlights, Wyatt leaps on top of the counter, grabs a crossbow case, and sandbags the man with it. The gunman slumps to the floor, unconscious.

In the quiet, Wyatt pins the man's shoulder under one knee. "Are you all right?" he asks me, his black eyes filled with concern.

"Yes," I say, but whoo I am dizzy. I fall back. It occurs to me that something is terribly wrong with my side. It burns. A pain I can't quite feel yet is making me weak and scared. "I'm … fine …."

"No, you're not," Wyatt gasps. He dumps a full-sized deer decoy on the man to pin him, then rushes to me and lifts me in his arms. I gasp. "You're bleeding."

Maybe I am, and now the pain from my side is just about blinding me, but I don't even care, because Wyatt's serious brown eyes are so close to mine, so concerned.

"Stay with me," he whispers, that deep voice of his quivering with emotion, looking into my eyes. "Please. Stay with me."

"I will," I whisper back.

-- Naturally, that's where my daydream ends.

Real life says, If that *really* happened, you and Wyatt would be hosed nine ways to Sunday.

Yeah, but that's why daydreams are so much better than real life.

Ever since I found where Wyatt worked, it was amazing how many things I needed at Paducah's. Wyatt, who was developing a lovely, deep-brown tan from all the time he spent outdoors, would be straightening up stuff, ringing up customers, or selling deer scent so you could make yourself smell like a deer. Talk about subterfuge!

If Wyatt wasn't busy, I'd stop and see him. If he was gone, I'd put down the item I'd come in for and mope back out. Each time I saw him, my heart would pick up and the blood heated my ears. But once we started talking, I'd feel right at home.

"Look at these raccoons I saw," he'd say, and scroll through the pics on his phone to show me three raccoon cubs hanging off his bird feeder and trying to get at the sunflower seeds. Or a group of deer he saw at sunrise. We'd talk about music, and books, and people at school, and band, and Brain Bowl.

I visited Wyatt three times in May before school was out. In Band I overheard that he went to Prom with a girl from another school. I was sorry I'd turned him down, but at the same time, what would I do at a dance with Wyatt?

But a stray image came to me of the dark gym, the booming music. I stood at the edge of the dance floor with Wyatt, our hands clasped, Wyatt bending close to hear me over the music. His hands would warm mine.

I should have just gone.

Yeah, shoulda coulda woulda.

Graduation day was sunny and hot. When I walked across the platform in my gold cap and gown for my diploma – the bleachers and the hillside filled with spectators – I was so nervous that my mind shut down, leaving just enough for me to walk across the stage, shake the superintendent's hand, and stop to get my picture taken. I headed back to my seat, my heart pounding.

How about that, I thought, looking at the diploma book. I'm a graduate. The wind caught my gown; it billowed like a pair of wings opening, making my heart lift.

Wyatt and I sat near each other the way we had since junior

high – his last name was Bradshaw; mine was Bachmann – and soon he came back down the aisle past me to his seat after having gotten his diploma, looking seriously handsome. I kept my hands to myself and didn't pounce, only grinned. He grinned back and I melted. Once he was back in his seat, the melancholy settled over my heart.

Last night I'd dreamt about a girl with almost uncontrollable grief, sobbing piteously. I was aware of her, but went about my work, ignoring her. I knew she wanted to be comforted, that she desperately wanted to be loved. I wasn't sure what to do. Then she sprang to me and I embraced her, and she clung to me and cried like a baby.

Let that go, I thought with a sigh. I would leave this place and begin a new life at the State University in St. Francis, which was an hour to the north and had smaller classes and a campus where I wouldn't be lost. Wyatt was going to the college in Hardscrabble, the city south of here. We'd be so far apart anyway that a relation-ship wouldn't be worth trying for.

We graduated in the middle of May. No more school-related craziness! I played piano, worked on my blues song, listened to symphonies, and worked part-time at the greenhouse. In my spare time, when I wasn't reading articles online like "Essential Items for Your Dorm!" or "Your Freshman Year in College: What to Expect."

At the end of May, Wyatt changed his status. *We're going to NATIONALS to KICK ASS in BRAIN BOWL. HAMMER DOWN.*

I hope you do kick their rears! I said, joining a bunch of other local folks wishing him the best. To my everlasting joy, Wyatt liked my comment.

For two days Wyatt's page was quiet, which nearly drove me to distraction. Then he updated his status.

I have just been dumped via text message by the world's biggest loser. All hot babes apply here. First come, first serve.

OMG OMG OMG WHAT.

One of his camping buddies, Caleb, commented: *Jasmine dumped you?*

Wyatt: *Jasmine said she wants to see other people. I said, if you want to see other people then open your eyes. She said, No, I want to go out with someone new. Great timing, too. The next match is in 15 minutes.*

Megyn: *I'll go out with you!*

Wyatt: *You'd better stay with Caleb if you know what's good for you.*

Megyn: *Well, okay, but only because you said.*

Caleb: *Wyatt, you're an oak.*

Wyatt listed himself as "single" next to a picture of a little broken heart.

My own heart started hammering so hard that it hurt. I actually leaned my head against the computer screen as if it were Wyatt's chest.

About an hour later, Wyatt updated: *We just leveled the opposing team, 510-280. My current relationship status may or may not have had something to do with this decisive victory.*

Oh, my heart. I could go to Paducah's after Wyatt returned. I'd lay my hands down on the glass counter between us and say ....

"So! you're single now."

Seriously? There ain't no way.

"Would you like to go out with me?"

Aaaaa no. I wasn't that brazen.

"Brazen? I'll show you brazen." I'd grab Wyatt's shirt and pull him to me and plant my lips on his.

A wave of heat seared my heart and rebounded through my body.

Oh, no, this is just wrong, I thought, but immediately kissed him again just to feel that rush of mindless pleasure.

But the strangest thing happened. Out of that feeling came a sharp pain, like a piece of obsidian was embedded in my heart, a sub-zero fleck of hurt that bit deep. My mindless rush dissolved.

I dropped my daydream like it was a fiery coal.

I'd never wanted to kiss any of my crushes before. What was

the point? It wasn't like I was ever going to marry. When I grew up, I'd live in the country with a cat and a rose garden, playing music any time I pleased and working for a symphony. I would be alone because getting married was too much trouble.

But but but but but ….

I holed up in my room, watching YouTube videos of previous matches. Wyatt's team was awesome; all of them were quick on the trigger and absolutely nailed the answers, bang bang bang. But I had eyes only for Wyatt's stern frown, his fist on the table tightening and loosening, his relaxed tenseness. Sometimes, when the team was ahead at the half, they'd would sit back with a sigh of relief and glance at each other and comment quietly. When the game started again, they became tense and still, prepared to spring. When the game was over, Wyatt would set his fists on the table and lean his head back, exhaling.

Watching these videos, thinking, he could be mine. He could really, actually, be mine. I just have to have the guts to ask him!

The next day:

Wyatt's team is heading to the final showdown for the National title. Swissville vs. Oak Heights, 2 p.m. Hammer down.

And finally, about 3:30 the next afternoon, Wyatt reappeared.

405-400, Swissville. WE DID IT. WE ARE THE NEW NATIONAL CHAMPIONS.

I collapsed on the computer desk. "Oh, yes," I said into the varnish.

The day after he returned home, Wyatt's Facebook said, *I'm going to work. Winning is awesome, but a man still needs spending money.*

So I showered, scrubbed my face until it glowed, did my hair, put on my favorite jeans and my favorite cotton shirt, put on deodorant because I was sweating holes through my shirt, put a tiny bit of makeup on, sprayed rose body spray all over me, put on yet *another* deodorant, put on a soft shade of lipstick, hardly noticeable, and popped my lips at myself in the mirror. I looked good, but my guts felt like they'd been scooped out and replaced by a nest of writhing snakes.

I walked into Paducah's, but not with the confident stride I had imagined, because my legs had gone wobbly. At the checkout, a harried-looking mom snapped to a fretful kid, "You don't want that, put it back! And don't touch it again!"

I was on the verge of rounding the corner to the hunting department, but at that moment, Wyatt said "NO" in such a stern tone that I recoiled into the notions department.

A girl huffed, "I was telling the truth. This relationship isn't going anywhere."

"So that's why you couldn't wait until I got home to dump me?" Wyatt said, his voice so angry that my ears rang.

"Give me my ring back."

"And you just had to dump me, by text message, during the most important game of my life? Because your need to dump me was so important that you couldn't wait *three days* for me to get home and dump me face to face?"

"Give me my ring so I can go." Spoken through gritted teeth.

"Why should I?" Wyatt said. "I thought your ring was a gift."

"Don't be an asshole. Give it back."

"You need to come and get this after work. You're just here to screw up my day."

"No, now! Or I swear to God I'll start screaming."

Wyatt snorted and I heard a brushing of cloth. "You want your ring?" he said, his voice hard and trembling at the edges. "You want this? How 'bout you – " He grunted.

Something made a ringing, pinging sound behind me. I turned. A golden ring bounced and spun on the shiny floor, skipping toward the crack underneath the shelves. I lunged and grabbed it before it rolled out of sight. A women's class ring with a dainty green stone that flashed rainbows, the kind that my folks couldn't afford. It felt warm. Wyatt must have had it in his pocket. My hand tightened around it.

Jasmine rushed down the aisle toward me. "Did you see it? Is my ring here?"

My hand, holding the ring, was still at my belly, closed into a fist. My lips parted, but nothing came out.

Now she stopped. "God! What's your deal?"

"Why'd you leave him?" I asked in this soft voice. "Is he bad?"

She scoffed. "You wish. I can do better than him."

Okay, so she was a jerk.

I let my hand open. The ring struck the hard tile and bounced, and when it spun into the air it made an enchanting sound, bell-like and golden, more beautiful than anything I'd ever heard.

Jasmine chased her ring until it had slowed enough for her to catch. She scooped it up and called me a bad name before she stormed off.

Now I had to sneak out of here so Wyatt wouldn't realize that I'd been eavesdropping. I turned to go.

And nearly crashed into Wyatt, who was leaning against the shelf behind me, his stern brown eyes trained on my face.

"Gllgh!" I said, nearly falling over from a heart attack.

He didn't move. Arms crossed, frowning. "It's all right. Can I get you a fishing license or something?"

Somehow, despite my heart having jumped out of my chest, I managed to understand that he was not serious. "No, that's fine, I haven't fished for ages. Gaah, you scared me."

"With good reason." Still frowning. "You came at a bad time."

"I'm sorry! I didn't mean to!"

We were both silent. Some of the heat was leaving Wyatt; he uncrossed his arms. "I'm sorry too. This hasn't been the best day for me. In case you hadn't noticed."

I put my hand on the shelf so I wouldn't fall over sideways like a goof – even though, I reminded myself, I'd been a goof the whole time I'd been here. "Believe me, if I could have stopped by at a better time, I would have."

"Five minutes ago I would have objected to your listening in.

Now I'm cool. Thanks for finding the ring."

I shrugged, still shamefaced.

"So now you've seen a guy get dumped." Wyatt began straightening the tents. "Any questions?"

"No. Ouch."

Wyatt thumped some tents with his fists so they'd fit better on the shelves.

"Well, it's not like she was being really nice to you. Not to criticize your choice of girlfriends. Or, er ..." I couldn't figure out how to backpedal my way out of that.

Wyatt didn't notice. "I'm better than that. It's embarrassing to get so mad in front of someone. I don't like to lose control of myself."

Like with Mr. Ambrose? But I trusted Wyatt – knew he wasn't like that, deep down. "Me neither," I said. "Except it's not so much me getting angry. It's more like I have to keep myself in line. Like if anything threatens to get out of control, I have to nail it down, you know?"

I stopped because I'd been babbling and wasn't sure if I meant what I said.

Wyatt didn't seem to be bothered by my silly outburst. He leaned on his arm, gazing at me, this quiet affection in his face. Something moved deep in my heart, so deep I almost couldn't feel it, the grand kind of joy I felt when listening to some great symphony.

How I wanted to say what was in my heart. How I wanted to take Wyatt's hands in mine and speak those three words I didn't dare say, not even to myself.

But that bit of black obsidian buried in my heart winked, and pain – fear – made me choke. I coughed. The obsidian bit deep. No comfort, not even Wyatt's, could possibly ease that black fear.

Wyatt rubbed my back. "Do you need a glass of water?"

Embarrassed, I shook my head, looking at the tiny model tents.

Wyatt opened a tiny panel on one of the little tents so you could see inside of it, but his eyes had gone tired. "And then … well, it's kind of obvious, but I want you to know that I'm free." And he looked from the tent to me.

Fear struck like lightning from my gut to my soles.

"Oh," I said, gazing at a kid-sized tent on the lower shelf. I reached down and picked it up, trying to pretend that nothing was the matter.

KATHERINE, WHAT IS WRONG WITH YOU? GO POUNCE ON THAT HANDSOME MAN. GET A SPINE! ENLIST!

And what if I did pounce on that handsome man? And then we did start going out? Could you imagine how awkward it would be if we were together all the time? Especially if it turned out that he didn't … love me.

"Don't look so stricken," Wyatt said, and I think he sounded just a tiny bit amazed. "I just wondered if you'd changed your mind about me after turning me down for the dance."

My brain was filled with things I wanted to say, squirming and flopping like trapped fish. But when I opened my mouth, all I could manage was a little squeak. I clutched that kid's tent like it was the last scrap of my sanity.

Wyatt's tentative smile faded. "You okay?"

I can't talk! My brain froze up! Ctrl+Alt+Delete!

"I can't."

Wyatt's brow furrowed as he leaned forward. "What?"

"Can't do it," I mumbled. An electric shock traveled through me. "It's nice of you to ask. But I have some, some issues. Some really stupid ones, I guess. I just …."

My incoherent words sank into the deadliest silence I'd ever known.

Wyatt straightened against the shelf with a small thump. "So … you're saying you're not interested. In me."

"I'm interested," I blurted. "But I can't handle your kind of love."

Deathly silence. Boy, either I can't talk or else I make the dumb statement of the century.

Wyatt's eyes began to turn red-rimmed.

I gasped. "I'm sorry ... I'm sorry."

"That's okay. It's what I deserve for ... but wait. It's not."

Though my brain seethed with explanations, with pleadings, the sudden force in his words stopped them up.

"You know what? For the last two weeks, I kept thinking that it couldn't get worse, and then it does. None of this is your fault. I can't ask you to be something you can't. But ... Christ." Wyatt's face suddenly crumpled.

Kay, you idiot! You broke his heart! "I'm sorry, I'm so sorry. I wish I could help you. I would be a very terrible ... date or whatever." I put my hand out toward him – even now, too afraid to touch him – because everything I said *only made it worse*.

"You don't know yourself very well," he said quietly, and took my outstretched hand in his, a warm touch, solid. I clasped his hand back like he was drowning, willing myself to speak, to come to his rescue. I opened my mouth, but could only stand there helpless.

"Maybe we could have been a good couple." The tremble in his words broke my heart. "It's too bad that ... that you don't think I'm worth taking a chance on. Okay, I'm done. See ya."

He dropped my hand and walked out of the aisle, out of my life.

I waited a moment, clutching that kiddy tent, then slunk out of there, this little doll of a girl who didn't know crap. I bought the tent – I guess because I needed to commemorate the time I broke Wyatt's heart? – then drove out to the river, where I threw myself in.

Not really, but I should have.

Across the river were the Kansas hills that I'd seen all my life but had never set foot on, and I sat by the river and bawled. I was such an idiot, such an idiot, not to mention totally nutso for being so mean to him, and I was never never never never never going to get it right.

FIVE
LEARNIN THE BLUES
ELLA FITZGERALD & LOUIS ARMSTRONG

I followed my family out of the burning hot August sun and into the dark stone hallway of the dorm, which seemed dark as underground for a minute. The hall was crammed full of parents and students and boxes of housewares. I clutched a laundry basket crammed full of towels and sheets, my iPod dock tucked deep among their folds.

My heart was high, like an overfull chalice. So many people around, and though they made me a little claustrophobic, they joked and hollered and said "Oops! Excuse me!" so cheerily that I couldn't help but smile. The hallway was hot, but I carried my laundry basket as if bearing a splendid gift. My own home at St. Francis State! A new life! I tried to keep up with my folks while looking around like a wide-eyed country girl in New York, trying to take it all in.

Mom led us through the teeming masses with a box of my bathroom supplies and the contents of my underwear drawer. Oh God, please, do not let her trip and fall. "Over here, Kay," she said, stopping at a door that said 118A.

"Mom, wait! I want to – Let me do the--"

"Do what?" she asked, unlocking the door, and I wished that I had thought to take the key before she did, since this was, after all, my kingdom. The door swung in. Dad was carrying my little fridge, so I stepped back to let him by (accidentally crashing into an older lady, sorry!). I knew he had to be getting tired. Then my younger brother Brandon cut in front of me, because that's what Brandon does, carrying a carton of my books with a fan on top.

"Kay, somebody, plug in the fan. It's like a sauna in here," I heard Dad say.

"I got it," Mom said.

I stepped into my new room, my new life – and staggered back, stunned at what I saw. Some Goth nitwit – the previous occupant – had painted everything black! The ceiling was black. The floor was black. The walls were black. The window shades were black. Who the heck gets window shades in black?

"Gaah! What underground dweller lived here?" I put down my stuff and ran right to the windows and pulled up those black monstrosities. Light bloomed in the room. Outside was a courtyard with a couple of sugar maples, their leaves tossing in the hot wind, and a lot of blue sky.

"Nice view, anyway," said Dad, a man of few words, and we grinned at each other before he slid the fridge into its little cubby.

Brandon threw an arm across his eyes and went into his melting act. "Oh my God, you have ruined a perfect gamer's lair!" He thumped the counter by the window. "You have to close those things. Then you put a frickin gaming console right here and a big armchair in the middle of the floor, then you stay up all night playing *Cretins of Chelsea Island* or *Man Down*. Or *Sparkle Pony Mayhem*," he added when Mom frowned at him.

"Vampire." I dug my iPod dock out of the towels I'd carefully wrapped it in and put it right in the middle of the counter. "*This* gets the place of honor."

Brandon rolled his eyes and lolled his tongue like the very thought of classical music had fried his brain.

"At least I won't be interrupted by Mom ringing a cowbell at me."

"I do that," Mom said, "because every time I call you, you develop selective hearing." Mom took out the can of sea-green paint we'd bought a few days ago and put it on the desk. "Now, see, aren't you glad I dragged you kicking and screaming to the hardware store?"

I puffed at some hair sticking to the sweat on my face. "Yes, mother." Randy Travis started singing *I toooold you soooo* on my brainradio.

"Kay, don't talk to me like that."

I'm sorry, I know I was being rude, but I just wanted them all to be gone! I had a new life all ready to go and I just wanted to start it already!

Five hours later, after we'd unloaded Mom and Dad's car and my car while Mom painted my room (I begged to do it myself but Mom took over the job), after we went to a pizza place crammed to the gills with overexcited college freshmen and tired parents, after Mom insisted we give the walls a second coat of paint – five hours later, we were finally saying good-bye.

Dad squeezed me tight, his work-roughened hands snagging on the back of my shirt. "You'll do good."

Mom said, "I'm so proud of you. My little girl, all grown up."

She didn't usually talk like this and it made me sad, but the first words out of my mouth were, "I'm not your little girl."

"What are you getting so defensive about? I didn't say you're a little girl now."

I huffed. "Just ... don't."

"Why do you always have to be like that? I don't know why I bother." And the moment was ruined.

Brandon gave me an overenthusiastic fistbump (ow), and my family filed out, Dad waving, Mom sighing, Brandon making a goofy face (I made one back), leaving me in my room.

Alone.

At last.

I took a deep breath, looking around my empty new room. Outside, heard through my open windows, the crowds hummed and murmured, but in here was quiet and safe. My heart fluttered with excitement. At last. Now I could start over and be the person I'd always wanted to be.

But first, though I was eager to get started, I sat on my bare mattress and tapped the Facebook app on my phone. "Oh, seriously, are you doing this again?" I asked aloud.

I brought up Wyatt's page. Maybe he was just getting started at his college, maybe he'd updated ....

No updates. He hadn't been on here since June, when he'd commented on a news story about the Missouri deer population growing out of control. He was still "in a relationship."

I couldn't look directly at Wyatt's profile pic – those dark brown eyes smiling into the camera as he sat in a deer stand, taking a selfie.

I opened my email app.

Hey Wyatt –

I'm in my new dorm at St. Francis U. I don't have a roommate yet – they told me she was stood up at the altar and then she dropped out of college! Isn't that crazy? But I feel lucky, because can you imagine how awkward it would be, living with a married woman? What a weird story, though. smh.

I'm supposed to get another roommate later, though I don't know when.

Are you moving into your dorm in Hardscrabble? Or are you driving back and forth from home? I wish I could see you but we're so far apart – well not that far – but I don't have a whole lot of money for gas.

I'm still sorry about

I tried several times to write more, then sighed and closed down my email, letting the letter go to my Drafts folder. The fourth letter in

Drafts now. I'd sent Wyatt two emails with huge apologies, one in June, one in July. No reply.

Yesterday I had gone to Paducah's, where he'd worked, for the first time since June, supposedly to buy college supplies. Mainly, I had to admit to myself, it was to see him. I'd rushed through the store, excitement building up to such a pitch that I was dizzy as I approached the sporting goods department. There was Wyatt's counter! But there was a shock that knocked me cold and dead – he was not there. The excitement that had been building up in me crashed down hard, leaving me all trembly-weak and laughing nervously as I chatted with the wrong person (she asked, "Are you all right?" – I couldn't just tell her "No! I just want to lay down on the floor and die in the middle of sporting goods!" That would have been a little weird.) I walked out of the store without my college supplies because I didn't want to stay in the store any longer if Wyatt wasn't there.

But I was also just a little mad at Wyatt for refusing to answer my emails. Even if he just wanted to say, "Go to hell," I'd rather hear that, than wait on this damned silence that drove me crazy!

I sighed and tossed my phone onto my bare mattress. New life, remember? No more dwelling on the past.

I set up my iPod dock and speakers on my desk and played "Riviera Paradise" by Stevie Ray Vaughn and Double Trouble as I hung up my clothes and filled drawers with my stuff. The excitement came back. My new life. I couldn't wait to explore my new home.

My walls were a pale sea-green. They really did look so much better than the awful black walls, I thought. I just wished I'd gotten to paint them myself.

I checked to be sure I had my key, shut my door (it locked automatically), and headed out to explore the campus while the paint dried.

My residence hall was connected to stairs and halls and more halls lined with rooms. As I walked, I peeked into the rooms, so many doors wide open, and everybody was decorating and putting sheets on their beds or setting up gaming systems. People looked up and waved and said, "Hi!" and I'd stop and chat for a while. Some of them wore St. Francis U. shirts, the unofficial ones with St. Francis wearing shades and giving the peace sign.

I found a few people from my old high school, but I was more interested in meeting new people who didn't have some preconceived notion of me. I ended up going to supper with several girls from around St. Louis after I helped them install their sound system and showed them a nice music streaming site that I liked to listen to.

When I came back after supper, the paint was dry. I put my sea-green sheets and Grandma Bachmann's green and blue quilt on the bed and hung up sheer lace curtains. I hung a yellow umbrella upside-down from a little hook in the ceiling, and put a big spray of red silk peonies on a shelf. I covered the walls with sheet music covers, enjoying how the colors of those old lithographs popped against the green. I was bothered to see that, here and there, specks of black hid in the little dings and dents in the concrete walls. Oh well, my room still looked great.

The first couple of weeks were a whirlwind of activity. I ate at the university food court, though sometimes the food was ... indescribable. But every table had other freshmen, like me, who wanted to talk and be funny, so I could sit just about anyplace and be welcomed. This definitely wasn't like my old high school, where joining a friendly-looking group got you the Laser Glare of Death.

One thing, though: Here at college, my name was Katherine. Not Kay. I was leaving my childhood nickname with the people who'd known me forever. If I was going to have a whole new identity, I was going to make it a good one.

I sat at lunch with different people every day – Bob, LouAnn, Sally, Julia. I started hanging out with the foreign students because I wanted to learn more about life far away from home. I chatted with a guy named Carter at the bookstore. He bought me some expensive chocolate that was so sweet and smooth and rich that I just about passed out. It must be nice to have the money to buy stuff like that!

I started making friends. Yvonne walked me through the college computer system. I got pizza for Jodi and lent her my white dress for her sorority pledge thingy. I went on a Rubbermaid run with Gretchen and Chris. Ko from Hong Kong gave me a dragonfly made out of silk yarn. She said it was a key chain, so I kept the key to the pipe organ on it – I was taking organ lessons this semester (Mom complained when she found out). Sally played Cui Jian's music for me and I ended up buying a bunch of it online and blasting it in my room.

I was too cheap to get a whiteboard for my door, so people would stick notes on my door with tape and Post-Its:

"Hello to a sweet person."

"Thanks for the pizza after class yesterday. It was sooooo good!"

"WE ARE GOING TO PADUCAH'S TO BUY SCOTCH TAPE. JOIN US. WE ARE THE COLLECTIVE."

"Get a message board!"

So, because I was cheap, I taped together two pieces of paper and labeled it, "Temporary Message Board," and people wrote on that instead.

The next week, classes started. As I walked to classes, I looked everyone in the eye and said "hi," and they'd generally say "hi" back. I strode around campus, confident, sure of my place in the world.

I was just about bouncing off the walls at our first Wind Symphony class. The bass clarinet next to me patted my arm to settle me down. "Girl, you're making me jittery. You'll be fine." I settled, though I was still vibrating with excitement when they passed out the music.

"Omigosh, Holst's Second Suite!" I crowed when the oboe player, an upperclassman, dropped it on my stand. "I love this piece." I opened the music so Yolanda could see the third movement. "This time signature is whacked out but it's so awesome."

"Have you played this before?"

That took off some of my excitement. "I *would* have at Four-State Honor Band, but my band director left without me because I showed up five minutes late."

"He did what?" I nodded. "Oh my God, I would have put him on my permanent shit list if he'd done that to me."

It was nice, hearing somebody say that. "I think I'm going to like it here," I sang to her, and she giggled.

When we played it, I actually nailed the whacked-out time signature part. The director, Dr. Byrd, gave me a nod – she noticed my playing! Me, a freshman bass clarinetist, who'd been snubbed by my own band director though I'd made State Band; me, who the choral director at high school said "couldn't sing!" I was so happy that after Wind Symphony I went to a practice room and pounded out the blues on one of the pianos, the way Grandpa had taught me.

But as I walked back to my dorm, I looked through all those faces on the sidewalk, all those people my age, wishing with all my heart that I could see Wyatt walking toward me – that maybe he'd come up here just to see me. Even the simple thought of his dark brown eyes studying me, his serious expression, made my heart lurch. Then I took a deep breath, sighed it out, and continued on alone, lost in sad daydreams –

Until I reached my dorm and saw, scrawled in big black letters across my Temporary Message Board, "Do you like sucking dicks?"

SIX
MAD WORLD
GARY JULES

My whole body went cold and hot at the same time and I couldn't move, stunned. Then I ripped down my Temporary Message Board, rushed into my room, and shoved it into the trash.

Who had written that? Wasn't I getting along with everybody? Did I somehow do something wrong and somehow make somebody hate me?

And whoever wrote that didn't know me at all! I was a social dingbat who had never been on a date, never kissed a guy. They were talking about third base to a gal who had never even been on the field!

I sank trembling on the edge of my bed, staring at my trash can as if it was going to burst into flames.

Okay, I thought, maybe it's just a one-shot thing. Some jerk walking down the hall wrote an awful note. Won't see him again. Just let it go.

But when I came back from supper with Yvonne, a flugelhorn from Wind Symphony, laughing and singing parody songs from YouTube, I stopped singing. Somebody had moved the sign with my name on it ("Katherine's Room! 118A!") to the door of the trash room.

"What's that doing over there?" Yvonne asked, following my gaze.

I just went over and moved it back. My across-the-hall neighbor came out of her room to watch. "Do you know anything about this?" I asked, since her door had been open.

"No, I don't," she said with a surprised look.

Yvonne said, "That's kind of a dick move."

I couldn't answer. Yvonne saw this and rubbed my shoulder. "It's okay," she said. "People are idiots. Don't let them get to you. I gotta get to English. Later!"

I smiled – until I got inside and found that somebody had slipped a picture under my door that had been cut out of a porn magazine.

I wanted to throw up.

The obsidian fleck in my heart began to bite, the same one that had bit into my heart all through my high school years. At first I shook it off. But now, when I sat with someone over lunch, or when I leaned on someone's doorway to chat, I felt that sub-zero blackness lurking. When its hard glint winked, my laughter went hollow and my smile felt forced. Each time, I would leave, afraid that somebody would notice something wrong and blame themselves for my discomfort.

As the week went by, that black feeling spread through my chest, clogging my insides with loneliness and grief.

It got so bad that my fingers, instead of hovering over that email message to Wyatt, finally finished it and hit send. "Please, please, please," I whispered.

But an hour later my heart stopped when a message from Wyatt actually appeared in my inbox.

I stared at it for a long moment before I opened it.

• • •

Kay —

I'm sorry I didn't write sooner. My girlfriend tends to lose it when she finds something of yours in my email or on any of my sites. I shouldn't be writing this at all, so don't reply.

I've been busy with school, sounds like you have been too. Don't be sorry about July. It was a bad day for all of us.

Cheers, Wyatt.

And that was all.

I brushed my fingers over his words. I could hear his deep, rumbling voice so clearly, as if talking only to me. My throat grew tighter and tighter. And just like that, I was crying again.

I remembered how he'd liked my blue hoodie that said *Take me for what I am, who I was meant to be.* How he liked to put his head on the partition between the instrument room and the tuba room, looking like a serving of John the Baptist. One time Jo, putting up her trumpet, looked up and screamed at Wyatt's bodiless head grinning at her. After she stormed out, our eyes met, his dark brown eyes, that serious look, and I didn't want to pull my eyes away for anything.

But he wrote, *Don't reply.*

That hurt worst of all.

On Wednesday, when I came back from class, they had slipped a condom under my door. I picked it up with just the tips of my fingers, skin crawling, and flung it into the trash. Then I lay down and just could not move. What was I supposed to do?

But it was almost one o'clock, and I forced myself to get up and go to Freshman Seminar. I tried to take notes, but I felt like half of my soul had been sliced away, leaving my spirit to bleed uncontrollably. I lost track of what the professor was saying. I clutched my notebook against my belly, head bowed.

Class ended. I walked with the river of students, alone. Maybe I should wade into Colden Pond, which wasn't very deep, and let the muskrats attack me. Ha.

I'd reached the entrance to my dorm when Carter loped toward me on long legs. His sharp face lit up to see me. He wore a navy blue polo shirt, khaki Dockers, and shiny black dress shoes. Carter kept his blonde hair in a neat, short ponytail. He was always super-nice to me (case in point: chocolate).

Though I wanted to turn away, I said, "Hi." The strain showed on my face.

He stooped to look at me, his sharp-edged face sobering. I smelled his musky cologne. For some reason that made the hurt in my heart sharper.

"Are you all right?"

I stared at my notebook. "I'm fine."

"You don't look all right. Do you want to talk about it?"

I shrugged, then pressed my lips together, something inside my chest fluttering. "I don't know." Vexed at the shake in my voice.

"Here." He tugged my notebook out of my hands and wrote his cell number on the cover in a strong, blocky handwriting.

"Please. Call me if you need anything." Carter handed it back, flame-blue eyes searching my face.

"Thanks," I said in a dull voice.

I lay down on my bed, my hands cold though it was late summer. A phone number. You're not supposed to talk to strangers. But he was a stranger who, for the first time, saw that I was suffering and chose not to ignore it.

I gave him five minutes to get back to his dorm, then called.

"Hello?" Carter said.

At the sound of his voice I burst into tears.

We found a study room at the library to meet in. I sank into a chair, feeling as if I'd suddenly ended up at a job interview. He slid into the seat next to mine, his hands resting on the table in front of me. I stared at his long fingers. I wondered if he played basketball.

"What's the matter?" he asked.

I shrugged. Maybe this wasn't such a good idea. "It's nothing. There's not even any reason for me to feel this way." But even as I spoke, a lump swelled in my throat so I could hardly speak around it, and the next thing I knew, I was sobbing. I put my head down on the table under his stare.

"Shh. It's okay." Carter stroked my arm as if it were a kitten. "Tell you what. I'll tell you about myself, and you tell me about yourself. Okay?"

I lifted my head and scrubbed my eyes, disgusted with myself.

"Okay." He straightened his ponytail. I wondered why he wore his blonde hair long like that. "I'm from Omaha, where I live with my mom. I don't see dad much; he has this political career." Said with a slight sneer. "Mom's a florist. Me ... I don't have any career plans yet. In high school, I played golf. I'm pretty good. My team went to State." I had to smile. Golf was definitely not my game. "But that's enough about me. What about you? Are you Native American?"

I squirmed. "No." I just had dark brown hair and brown eyes – that didn't make me Native by any stretch of the imagination.

"You look like an Indian princess, that's all."

I definitely doubted that. That "Indian princess" story sounded like some vapid white foolishness that made Native people these mythological beings, while in real life, whites broke treaty after treaty and ignored all the grief they put the Native people through because of centuries of lies. That seemed much more believable to me.

But he was so nice that I let all that slide, and I shrugged. "I'm from Nodaway, which is a teensy river town that keeps getting flooded. I went to Swissville High School and came here to school because of music stuff. I play clarinet in Marching Band and bass clarinet in Wind Symphony. I used to play hymns in church. I'm not bad, but I'm not really good, either. I have an annoying younger brother named Brandon."

"I had a sister. Hannah. She died when I was 10." He squeezed his hands together.

"Oh! I'm sorry!"

"Don't worry about it. So do you like college?"

"Well … yeah."

Carter smiled. "So those were tears of joy, earlier."

I laughed. "Well … no."

"You want to talk about it?"

"Yes. No. I don't know." Oh, I was so exasperating. "I mean, I don't know, I'm just feeling so depressed and I really don't know why …." And here go the waterworks again.

This was about the time to get disgusted with this whiny female. Instead, Carter leaned forward. "It's okay to feel this way. It's okay. I felt the same way myself, a couple of months ago."

I looked up, so surprised that for a moment I forgot to hide my stupid tears. "Really?"

He nodded, slow and serious. "I was broken up over a girl I loved. I had a really hard time, but I got through. I know you'll get through too."

"Thank you." The poor guy.

"Are you scared to be on your own?" he continued.

"I don't know. Maybe a little. I shouldn't be. But at the same time, everything's so different."

"Yeah," Carter said. "I'm not crazy about being on my own, either. I – I already spent time on my own, and I hated every minute of it. Out here, though, you're surrounded by all these people … but it just makes it seem worse. It's like the more people there are, the more alone you are."

"I know!" I said. "And I don't feel like I can talk to anyone, really talk, you know? I can't tell them about the important things. What's going on inside."

"But you're telling me. Right now."

I paused. My God, I had no idea that I could feel so safe, talking to someone. But Carter listened as if my silly rantings actually were worthy of consideration and not just a bunch of racket coming out of a goofy girl's mouth.

Then to my astonishment he said, "Would it be all right if I held you?"

I hesitated. But I had to trust somebody. Running away screaming had to be an option of the past.

Awkwardly, I scooted toward him. From his chair he reached one arm over my shoulders and pulled me against his side, his other arm going around my front. My arms were crossed against my chest like a mummy's. "This is so weird," I said, but didn't move. My nose pressed against his shirt, which held that lovely musk fragrance.

One part of me went, Watch out! It's a MAN and he's touching you! But another part was relieved to have shared my burden. I had no idea it could feel so sweet.

I waved to Carter as we left. The smell of his cologne clung to me. That made me smile.

As I rounded the corner far up the hall, I saw, way down at the other end, a girl come out of my across-the-hall neighbor's, walking straight toward my door, carrying something in her hands – and smiling.

"Hey!" I shouted. She looked up, smiling and bland, as she shoved something in her pocket. "You're the one who was doing that! Who was harassing me!" I was being loud, yes, because I wanted everybody in the freaking dorm to hear.

"I wasn't doing anything," she said, all bland and laughing. Laughing! How could she laugh about this?

"Oh, yeah, right. Sticking all that ... stuff under my door, writing all that nasty stuff. What is the matter with you? Do you not have a hobby? Nothing to do? Can't get a boyfriend?"

I don't know why that popped out, but now the bland was gone from her face. She expressed herself in words of one syllable, none of which I will repeat except for the words "off" and "you."

"Nice *friends* you have here," I told my across-the-hall neighbor. "Real quality."

People were beginning to look out their doors. The bland girl turned around and left. She wasn't smiling any more.

"Stay away from my door," I said, absolutely shaking with adrenaline.

SEVEN
A LONG WALK
JILL SCOTT

That evening as I crossed the Commons to supper, still exulting – and amazed – over my victory, Carter ran through the crowd of students to me, laughing, his short ponytail bouncing at his back.

"Here you go." He placed a bouquet of sweetheart roses into my hands, delicate red blooms wrapped in green tissue paper.

Roses! I gasped and laughed and didn't know what to do with them. I'd never gotten roses before, except once from my mom for my birthday. "Seriously, what are these for? I really don't need …."

"Because I want to say thank you for our talk today." Carter pulled his hands away when I tried to hand them back. "No, no, they're yours."

I kind of laughed. "I'm not one who gets into romances," I said, holding the bundle with as much trepidation as I'd hold a newborn baby.

"Oh, no, no. I'm not giving these to you for … *that*." Carter went a little red, which was cute. "No! Not at all. I just wanted to make you happy. I wanted to make you forget all the trouble you've had. I hope that's okay." With one long hand he adjusted the tissue paper on the roses, settling them in my hands. He smiled at me with those flame-blue eyes.

I went four-alarm red and looked away, still grinning, but *whoa*.

We walked back to my dorm, where I put the roses in a vase, leaving my door wide open just in case Carter tried anything funny. (And maybe to show off a little to the across-the-hall neighbor — though her door stayed shut.)

Carter was too busy looking around my room, his face all lit up like a kid in a candy store. "I really like your place. You have a neat sense of style. Nice umbrella."

I had my yellow umbrella hanging upside-down from the ceiling for color as well as storage. It picked up the red from my bouquet of red silk peonies and the colorful old sheet music covers I'd stuck to the sea-green wall with ticky-tack.

"Thanks," I said, pleased as punch that someone liked my room.

Carter picked up my iPod. "What kind of music do you listen to?"

"A little bit country, a little bit rock and roll. A lot of classical."

He was scrolling through it. I kind of wish he'd asked before picking it up, but at the same time, I'd always wanted somebody to ask me what I was playing so I could rhapsodize all about my favorite songs.

"Ooh, I like this one. Mind if I play it?" When I nodded, Carter plugged it in and turned on the speakers. "With or Without You" by U2 started up. A classic song, I liked that. "So how do you like your roses?" he asked, coming over to where I was finishing arranging them. "Those look nice. You're a good arranger."

"Thanks. I worked in a greenhouse this summer. But don't you think these are a little too soon?" I asked, a little wary.

"You don't like them?"

"They're pretty. But I hardly know you."

Carter smoothed out the green tissue paper that I'd discarded on my desk. "This may sound crazy, but ... but I feel like I've known you all my life," he said, so quiet he was almost talking to himself. "I don't want to scare you off. I've never felt so strongly about a woman before I met you."

Double whoa.

"But hey, it's okay. Let's not get too deep, Carter," he told himself, laughing.

"You think?" I joked.

"Yeah. Sorry," he said, a little shamefaced. "You wanna come to supper with me? If you want to eat on campus, that's fine, but there's this little Chinese restaurant I've been wanting to try out. And campus food is kind of corroding my insides." He put a hand on his stomach and made a face.

"I don't have money for Chinese food."

"It's okay. I'll pay your way. You don't have to pay me back. My dad gave me a credit card." Carter pulled his wallet out of his back pocket. "Dad's kind of a dick, so I try to max it out. I haven't had much chance to since I've been on campus. Maybe you can help me."

"Are you sure?"

"Hell yeah! After what he put my mom through, he deserves it." Carter slid the wallet into his pocket and said, "Come on, let's go."

As we headed across campus to his car, I saw a couple of band students carrying big bags from the parking lot, Yvonne (flugelhorn and trumpet) and Elizabeth (tuba!) and Elizabeth's boyfriend (flute). "Hi Kay!" Yvonne called. "We have cool Rubbermaid products, look!"

"You're living on the edge," I called back.

"Do you want company?" Carter asked me. "They can come along if they want."

A great idea! So they did – for which I was grateful, since I wasn't up to going on a DATE or anything.

I sat next to Carter at our table, and he passed me some of his mushrooms when I said they looked really good. Our group sang goofy songs we swiped the food we liked off each others' plates. We (the band students) talked about today's marching band practice, when the trumpets and clarinets collided and the music practicum student who'd drawn up with the maneuver fell over and died on the sidelines. Carter wasn't in marching band, so he listened and laughed and ate.

When we came back to campus, Yvonne and Co. went on their way – their mission was to organize their dorm rooms – and Carter said, "You want to go for a walk?"

Not really, but he had just taken me out for supper, so I said, "Sure. But only a short one. I really need to get home and get some stuff taken care of." While in the car, I'd checked my phone, as I always did, for an email message from Wyatt. Still nothing. All I had was a message informing me about a concert series in Mass-achusetts, which of course was like 2,000 miles away so maybe a little difficult to attend.

The heat of the day was fading into coolness, though the late August sun still had not set. A flock of sorority girls skittered past on the sidewalk, bearing bags of paper cups, plates, and plastic forks. Far away, some guy on the tennis court yelled, "Hai! Hai!" Tennis as a form of martial arts, I guess. Locusts whined their summer songs in the treetops. I thought of Wyatt on his own campus, or maybe at home. I wondered if he was looking up into the summer sky and even thinking of me at all. Wishing I could somehow take back those words I'd said to him so he'd still … he'd still care for me. I twisted a leaf between my fingers.

But Carter was at my side, walking quietly, so I roused myself. "Why are you trying to max out your dad's credit card?"

"Because he's a dick."

"I think that has already been established," I said.

"No, seriously, he is," Carter replied with a little heat, and I backed off. But he blew out his cheeks and ran a hand through his blonde hair. "Sorry. You want to know how much of a dick he is? After my sister died and my parents divorced, he insisted that he have custody of me because Mom was having such a hard time. You know what my dad did? Left me alone in his house for about a year."

"Alone?" I gasped.

"Not alone alone, but he was hardly ever there. So busy with his legislative career that he couldn't come home for supper, or hang out with me on the weekends. I'd come home from school – he wasn't there, but at least the maid was, finishing up the housework. She'd make me a sandwich and I'd talk to *her* about my day. Then she'd go home and I'd play video games for most of the night. Sometimes he'd be home for breakfast. Usually not. And I was never supposed to talk about Hannah. Never."

"Wow. Hannah's your sister who …."

"Drowned." Carter shoved his hands in his pockets as he walked on. "One day I was really upset and Dad was actually home for once. You know what he said? 'Stop bringing her up. It's over. You gotta live in the present. You gotta grow up and move on from this shit.'"

"He said that?"

"He didn't say 'shit.' But all the other stuff he said. It was like a slap in the face. My own sister. His *little girl*."

Wow. Harsh. "I'm sorry, your dad is not a dick." Carter, looked up, shocked, but I added gently, "Your dad belongs in a category that's way, far, beyond that."

Carter laughed. "You're good. But I know you don't want to hear about me. Why don't you tell me about yourself? I'm more interested in you."

"In me? Nah."

"Yes. All my life, I've wanted to meet someone like you. Someone who listens to the stuff I say – I mean really listens, not just pretends they're listening while they're scrolling through their Facebook page. You know? Someone who's interesting."

"I'm not interesting."

Carter smiled at me, shaking his head, but the smile died away into something much deeper, a longing that thrilled me even as it made me squirm. "Yes, you are. Those stories you told about your life today in the library were amazing. Your struggles to be understood – I totally understand them because I feel the same way, all the time."

"You do?"

He nodded. "Katherine, I know this is crazy, but I feel like we really have something special – something other couples don't have." He took my hand gently in both of his. We'd stopped in the middle of the sidewalk, facing each other. "I feel like we have that connection between us. We can be amazing friends, but I think we could be so much more."

This was all maybe just a little nuts, but when Carter said those things, a thrill went through me. The evening was quiet, the sun down and Venus was barely visible in the dark blue eastern sky. The leaves whispered above us. Was it possible? Could such a connection exist?

But Wyatt, I thought.

But Wyatt had a woman who had him on lockdown. But Wyatt told me not to reply to his emails. I couldn't stop my life for someone who was clearly not available to me.

"I don't know," I said, timid. But Carter looked a little hurt. "I don't mind talking to you, though. It's so nice to have someone actually listen to me."

"I know." His hands tightened on mine, warming it, and I smiled. "Talk to me some more. Tell me more about yourself. I really want to know."

"Get a room!" some guy yelled as he pushed past on the sidewalk.

Red rose in Carter's face even as mine heated up. But we both laughed.

"If two people holding hands is going to make him say that, what's he going to do if he sees someone making out?" Carter asked.

We told each other our stories, walking around campus until

late. I talked about my Nazi chemistry professor, the goofy things that happened in my classes. I told him about Grandpa Arden, a bluesman down in Kansas City, playing at all the clubs. Carter told me about his past — how his father ignored him after his sister drowned. He told me about his high-school golf coach, who was like a real father to him, and he told me about the long talks he and his coach had when they were on the road.

At bedtime, when Carter dropped me back off at my dorm, I was almost giddy, and waved to him as he left.

Over the next week, I opened up to Carter more and more. We wrote notes back and forth, texted each other all the time (sometimes I'd be surprised by my phone buzzing in class and, embarrassed, quickly turn it off while the professor gave me a sour look), and sent so many emails. Nobody had ever paid me the kind of attention that Carter was giving me. Here was a handsome guy just about doing cartwheels to comfort me, a guy who was listening to every dumb thing I said and telling me that no, this stuff wasn't dumb at all but actually really smart. And he treated other people well. Carter chatted with the cashier lady at the food court. He picked up everything on the table when we'd finished so the girl bussing the tables wouldn't have to. I always thought of rich people as being snobs, but Carter was the most down-to-earth person I knew. Well, one of the most.

Now, I didn't go to sleep thinking about Carter. Even now, Wyatt inflicted a tangle of feelings upon me that I couldn't clamber out of, feelings so intense that they scared me. Not so much with Carter. But maybe if I tried my best to go along with it I'd eventually fall in love.

On a walk around the campus a week after our meeting in the library, I said casually, "You know, maybe we could go out."

Carter's face lit like the sun. He grabbed me in his arms and gave me a big squeeze, and whirled me around. I clung to his neck and squealed.

We didn't kiss. Not yet. We figured we'd take it slow.

Friday night, on my way home to see my family, I stopped by Paducah's again. No Wyatt. I slinked away, ashamed of how sad I felt.

Sunday night, when I came back, Carter took me out for a date at a swanky restaurant. I felt like a church mouse among elegant society.

"I want you to have the best," Carter told me over wine. (We were cheating.)

I swirled my glass, dizzy from the alcohol. I wondered idly what wine would go with Grandma Bachmann's fried catfish and throwed rolls. "Sometimes the best doesn't cost anything. Sometimes the best is free." I looked over my glass at him. "This whole world is beautiful; it's like a gift. Fog off the river, the smell of apples, a great oak that's been growing for hundreds of years, and the birds that hide in its branches ...." Whoo-hoo! I liked this kind of talk. I took another swig.

Carter covered my hand with his. "The love of a good friend."

My giddy mood vanished. Wyatt had squeezed my arm in the library the day I'd fallen in love with him. How tightly he held my hand on the awful day I broke his heart. Regret spread through my heart like a dark stain.

Come on, Kay, I thought. You've lost your chance with Wyatt. It's time to move on.

Carter and I walked side-by-side back to his dorm. White pines crowded around us, pitch-black against the starlit heavens. The breeze shushed through their long, soft needles. Carter, all lanky, slouched at my side, his hands in the pockets of his lambskin jacket.

"I wasn't depressed, though everyone told me I was – after the fact, obviously." With a short laugh, Carter raised his eyes to the starry sky. "I was in love – more in love than I had ever been. But that love, it turned out, was unrequited.

"Rebecca was a wonderful girl – I'm not telling you this to make you jealous," he added.

"It's okay. I'm not jealous." I figured that if Carter liked her, I probably would have liked her, too.

Carter sighed. "Well, there's not much to be jealous of. Last April – over lunch at school – she gave me back my stuff and said, 'I don't want to see you anymore.'

"I went to my golf class and we went out on the course. Mr. Jenkins was talking, but I wasn't even listening – I couldn't hear. I kept staring at the lake. I kept thinking I could walk in there – I could put rocks in my pockets – hold a big rock in my arms —"

I gasped. "What?"

The hurt in Carter's face was so deep. "I could use the rocks to keep myself underwater until … until I was done. The lake was so black and while I stood there, I found myself holding my breath —"

He took a deep breath and exhaled.

"I broke down. I went to Mr. Jenkins and said, 'I need help.' They put me in the hospital under observation for a week. I hated it. All I wanted was to see her. I wanted to see her so bad." He rubbed his eyes.

This huge dizziness came over me. "Oh, boy, help, I gotta sit down." I sat on the sidewalk, but the wooziness got so bad that I had lay down. Good thing that nobody else was nearby. Snow curliqued before my eyes, like angels in their liquid dances between the stars. I concentrated on them, trying to clear my head of that image of him sinking into the lake, inhaling that black water.

Carter gave this amazed little laugh as he knelt at my side. "Katherine? Are you okay?" Through the static I heard a strange new excitement in his voice.

"Yeah …." After a moment I pushed myself back up, not quite sure what had just happened. "Sorry about that. Help me up?"

"Are you sure you're all right?" Carter's intense blue eyes searched mine. His hands rested on my sides, holding me up. I wobbled. They tightened to support me, and a little rapturous thrill went through my heart.

"Do you really want to hear about my dark side?" he asked, his intense blue eyes so serious. He put his arms around me, pulling me close. "Nobody else has."

I wrapped my arms around him under the shadows of the pines. "I'll listen to anything you say."

After a squeeze, he let me go. "Mostly it's about my dad," he said, pulling some pine needles off a twig. "Sometimes people say, 'I bet you take after your dad,' because we look alike. But that's a lie. He made me stay at his house every weekend even though he wasn't there. It was like I was a prisoner there, a real prisoner. Mom finally changed the custody agreement to *make* Dad spend time with me. He hated it." He exhaled and shook the pine needles from his hand.

I thought about my own dad, who, though he was pretty quiet, loved us very much.

"All that time alone did something to me. I still get depressed so bad that it hurts. I want so much for someone to share my thoughts, my dreams, my hopes, and those people are so hard to find." Carter's eyes turned to me. "I need someone to help me fight my demons. You can help me, because I love you, and I know that you love me too."

The words hit me like a thrill. *He loved me.* I'd never had somebody outside of my family say that to me.

I clasped his hand the way Wyatt used to clasp mine. "I'll help you. I promise." Because when I make a promise, it's for keeps.

Carter took in his arms. I clung to his neck. I smelled the peppermint on his breath as he gazed at me, intense, a little fearful. I wanted to draw back, but stayed still.

He kissed me. His lips were soft and wet and as soon as they touched mine, I winced away.

"You ever been kissed before?" he asked shyly.

"No."

"Let's try again."

He kissed me again. This time I didn't spring away like a startled antelope, but I wasn't sure if I was doing it right. All the same, that kiss also felt very very good, and when we were done, I kind of wanted to try again. And then Carter didn't seem to know how to follow up and neither did I, and we laughed and he gently set me down.

"I guess we could use some practice," he said, and we shared another little kiss, and it was very sweet.

I loved the nobility of my sacrifice. I would be an angel, wrapping my wings around him, though I wore the ashes of my old love on my forehead, invisible and pure. I would raise him up, I would make him a new man, I would save his life.

Except the next morning I woke up depressed. In the cafeteria, I shunned people and glowered at my cereal. I kept going over last night, hoping to revive that sunshine-and-roses feeling, but my heart was busy sinking through the ocean like a stone. Why had I nearly fainted? Out of pity? Why that excited laugh from Carter?

After breakfast, I came out to go to class. The sunlight slanted through the sycamores like light through a cathedral, and through its dapples walked Carter. He brightened and changed his path to meet me. As I walked toward him, I opened my arms to honor his pain.

Except I suddenly realized that my show was fake. I was lying with my whole body. I fought to ignore it, to keep smiling, to keep my arms open. He was going to see that I honored him, that I would sacrifice myself for him, whether I liked it or not.

EIGHT
LETTERS I'VE WRITTEN, NEVER MEANING TO SEND
THE MOODY BLUES

S omehow, before I headed back to school on Sunday night, I found myself standing in the sporting section of Paducah's again. Wyatt was not there – which, as usual, broke my heart into a million pieces. Lonely, missing him, I took the liberty of leaning on the countertop again, the way I used to. And Wyatt would lean on the other side of the countertop in his Paducah's vest as we talked about school, and work, and good music we'd been listening to.

I put my head in my hands for a moment. I hated that I was torn this way – to miss Wyatt so much when I was going out with Carter. It wasn't fair to Carter that I felt so strongly about Wyatt to be standing here now, wishing for something I wasn't going to get.

Don't reply, Wyatt had written. But I still wrote him emails. Then I quietly, one by one, relegated them to the Drafts folder. Letters I've written, never meaning to send.

In History class on Monday morning, my mind wandered as the professor rambled on about the Jacksonian Democrats who hated the bloated aristocracy. As I'd walked to class with Carter, we'd held hands and swung them like carefree children. Now that I was alone, I sighed. Every time I turned around, Carter was coming at me like a heat-seeking missile. He'd catch me between classes – as he did just now. Or he kept me at his dorm way past my bedtime, ignoring me when I said, "Man, I've got to get home so I can get some sleep." He'd want another kiss, another cuddle. When I tried to spend a quiet evening at my dorm to catch up on homework, there he was knocking on the door with his newspaper (which we shared), or Chinese take-out, or more flowers, or scented candles, or a card. Even if I'd loved him, romantically loved him, it would have been too much.

With Wyatt, talking was like fencing. Wyatt could always surprise me into a laugh, and sometimes I could do the same with him. Wyatt was smart, and he and I could talk and talk for hours and it never seemed we could run out of things to talk about.

With Carter … not so much.

And yes, even now when I thought of Wyatt, the same wish was still there, constant, like a little sprig of English ivy that grew up the side of my heart. It wouldn't be torn loose. It kept putting out shy new leaves, fresh, perennial, evergreen.

But Carter's face had been so vulnerable when he'd told me how he wanted to die. My heart convulsed. I shouldn't be a source of sorrow for him.

But was that the only reason I stayed – my wanting to protect him? Wasn't there supposed to be more to it?

When history was over, Carter was waiting outside the classroom for me as he always did. "It's so good to see you," he said, smiling, and he put his arms around me.

And boom, just like that, I started to cry. Right when there were half a million students filling the hall to stare at me as they went by.

Carter started back, his flame-blue eyes concerned. "Oh my God. I'm sorry. What happened?"

"I don't know," I stammered, trying to wipe the tears away, like maybe I was just having an allergy attack. I gave up and threw my arms around him again, trying to hide the fact that I was making a scene. "Just hug me back. Please."

Carter took me down to a bench by the pond. "Is it something I did?"

"No. I – I just don't know what the matter is with me. I don't."

"Are you wanting to see somebody else?"

I sat there in shock. That was exactly what I wanted. But yet – "We've been together an awful lot," I said. "I don't want us to get tired of each other."

"I'm not getting tired of you."

"But I am." Whoa! I backpedaled. "I mean, I need some space, Carter. You're getting kind of pushy."

"Why didn't you tell me I was getting pushy? I would have backed off."

"I didn't know how to tell you without making you upset."

"Making me upset?" He laughed, a hollow sound. "My God! What makes you think I'd be upset?"

I sighed. "I don't know about this relationship. Maybe we shouldn't continue it."

And I was aghast!

Way to throw a bomb into the discussion!!

This big hurt rushed into Carter's face. He sat back, mouth agape, like a little kid who got smacked for no reason.

I backpedaled frantically. "I'm sorry – I didn't mean it like that."

Carter's hands went to his hair. "What did I do to deserve that kind of response?"

"I don't even know where it came from."

"So what part of this relationship is a mistake? I thought we were okay. Wasn't I treating you well?"

"It's not a ... You do, but ...." I flailed my hands.

"So you don't love me?" He leaned forward and put both hands over his mouth, blue eyes fixed on mine.

"I thought I did," I whispered. "But...."

Carter rose, completely undone, arms at his sides, a hollow longing in his eyes. "So you're breaking up with me."

I started back, shocked. "I didn't say that ... oh." The realization sank in. "I ... guess I did." But that helplessness on his face stopped me in my tracks. I had no idea that breaking up could be this traumatic, even after a short time together. "I mean, it's okay, isn't it? We'd still talk."

Carter put his head in his hands.

"Please don't do that. I'm so sorry. Am I doing this wrong?" I pulled his hands into mine, making him raise his head. He didn't look at me, though, but turned his face off to the side.

"Why are you saying this relationship was a mistake? I don't get it." Frustration came through in Carter's voice. "I'm sorry, but I don't see what I did wrong."

"I'm not in love with you." Such cruel words, though they were true. "I'm so sorry."

And the hurt in Carter's eyes as he unwound his hands from mine – and the corresponding black fear that splashed across my heart as he shook me free – was something that I would never forget.

The next morning I woke up in a panic, thinking of Carter's hollow eyes. And I. Felt. *Terrible*. I'd betrayed him. How would I fix this mistake??

It's my fault, not his, I thought as I pulled on my jeans and piled books into my bag. I'd always been selfish about keeping my own space. I was so used to my solitary life that I really didn't want to bother letting other people into it.

Except for Wyatt ... oh, stop that!

Geez. I was such a mess of a person.

I ran to the cafeteria, hoping Carter was there – and to my immense relief he was just getting into line.

I rushed up the stairs to him. "I'm, I'm so sorry," I stuttered. "I hurt you, and I feel absolutely terrible."

"It's okay," he said, and such relief was in his voice that my eyes prickled from tears. "God, I'm so glad you're saying this. I missed you." We hugged tight. It felt so good to have his arms around me. Don't forget, I told myself sternly, you need him just as much as he needs you.

"I said everything wrong yesterday," I told him. "I don't want this to end. I just want a few more evenings free so I can recopy my awful History notes and read my newspapers."

"That's okay." He got trays and silverware for both of us. "I was thinking last night that maybe we are moving a little too fast." He looked close at me as we went into the line. "I'd do anything to keep you. Anything. You mean too much to me for me to ever let you go." Those words warmed me through and through.

We ate breakfast together and I felt so comfortable.

"I woke up this morning and I decided I wasn't going to give you up," he said, taking my hand.

"Never gonna give never gonna give, never gonna give you up," I sang, rebounding to an old Rick Astley song.

I got that blank stare again. I broke off my song, unnerved.

Carter went on as if I hadn't just Rick-rolled him. "This relationship means too much to me. I need you."

"But I don't need you," I blurted out. "But …." And right there, once again, I started to cry.

But Carter would not give me up, he would not let me down. That evening we met for a walk and he kept us talking and working on the relationship. I cried a lot. But somehow – I'm not sure how it happened – at the end of the night we were together again, and kissing, and I'd agreed to go with him on a trip to his home in Omaha that weekend to see his home and meet his mom. Just like that.

Wyatt seemed so distant, like a star in the heavens. I was a moth that kept fluttering up towards his light, never reaching it.

NINE
FALLIN'
ALICIA KEYS

C arter and I headed to Omaha on Friday morning, skipping our classes for an early start. We cruised up I-29, river and floodplain to the left, tall loess hills on the right. The occasional houses and farms tried to climb their sides; a cemetery seemed to be sliding down.

Both of us bubbled with excitement. "The Old Market is great," he said. "Great food, great shops. I'll take you for a carriage ride. And you'll meet my mom. I'll take you to my old school first, while they're still open." He grabbed my hand. "I can't wait to show you the stuff from my life." We kissed. Then we kissed again. And again! Boy, those kisses were addictive. It amazed me how much I wanted them. I was disturbed by how much power they had over me.

The first thing he did when we hit Omaha was pull into the florist's shop where his mom worked. "Come on, you'll love her," he said as he opened my door. "Don't be shy! She's excited to see you too."

As soon as we walked in and the scent of cold roses and leaf-shine spray hit me, smells of my old job at the greenhouse. But this was nothing like the little greenhouse where I used to work, with roses, carnations, and baby's breath in a little refrigerated box, potted African violets and peace lilies sitting around the counter, the humid scent of sun-warmed potting soil, tomato leaves, and spring drifting in from the hoop house, and an old gray cat cleaning itself in the middle of the floor.

Here, sprays of butterfly orchids cascaded down. Delicate ferns in miniature hothouses with elfin mosses and tiny flowering plants tucked around their feet. A gigantic, flashy bird of paradise plant with brilliant red and yellow blossoms. Big potted hydrangeas with flowers the color of pink and blue cotton candy. Some really high-end flowers in the glass coolers behind the counter – calla lilies, yellow roses, each petal tipped with hot red.

A lady with short salt-and-pepper hair came around the counter. "So good to see you!" She and Carter gave each other a big hug. "Oof!" she said, laughing. "So is this your sweetheart?"

My face heated up and Carter was blushing too, which was sweet. "I guess you could call me that."

She just came over and gave me a hug, too. "I'm Stella. You must be Katherine. I hope my son hasn't knocked you down in giving you a hug. He's just a giant puppy dog."

"Mom!"

"Well you are," she said, smiling at him. I liked her right off the bat.

"Can you make a bouquet for Katherine? I want to take her around the city in style."

"You don't need a bouquet for that."

"Aw, come on, Mom, just a little one. Don't make me take this to your competitor!" he teased.

She rolled her eyes. "Oh, no, if I lose your sale, this whole business is going to go under."

He gave her a hug with one arm. "I hope not. Come on, Katherine, what flowers do you like?"

I chose a few deep blue delphiniums, a pink gerbera daisy, a few pink roses, and some yellow whatchamacallits, for a small and tasteful bouquet.

"Now give her double," Carter said.

To my consternation, the bouquet was so big that I had to carry it on my arm like Miss America.

But his mom frowned when Carter pulled out the credit card. "Put that thing away."

"But I'm trying to max it out."

"What? I thought I raised you better than that."

"*He* didn't."

"It doesn't matter. Nope! Up. Now." Stella flicked her finger at the offending card. "I don't want to see that thing ever again."

Carter pulled out his wallet, put up the card, and got out some cash.

She rang him up. "I'll see you two tonight after work. No funny business," she added to Carter, raising her eyebrows.

"Mom! I've been living on my own for the last month!"

"We haven't been doing any funny business," I added. "No worries there."

"Good. You'll understand when you're a parent. I'm really looking forward to talking to you more," she added to me. "He's said a lot of nice things about you."

I glanced at Carter and back to his mom. "You raised him right."

"Lord knows I could have used more help! But for all that happened, he turned out fine." She patted Carter's hand. "You two have fun. You make a lovely couple."

We pulled up to his mom's house, a little bungalow on a maple-shaded street. Carter swooped me up and carried me in, even though I protested I didn't need to be carried, but he was high-spirited. He carried me straight to his room and set me down. "Here's my place," he said. "Do you like it?"

I had figured he'd have a high-powered manly-man den, but no. A small room with a big TV, a big bed with a tan bedspread, a rack full of games and CD's, no books. A desk sat next to the window with a little ship in a bottle on top. The rest of the desk was clean except for a pencil mug and an autographed picture of George and Laura Bush. I frowned (I was a Truman Democrat) but didn't say anything. On the wall was a print of an old-time baseball player hitting a home run.

"I thought you didn't like baseball."

"Dad got that for me. He didn't know it either."

"Why do you have it up there?"

Carter shrugged.

It was weird to look around the room and not get much of an idea who lived there.

Carter's hand stole around the back of my head, his fingers threading through my hair, and we kissed. And kissed again. He opened his mouth. I pulled back so fast I thwacked the back of my head on the door frame.

"Oh my God! I'm sorry!" he said, and we were both laughing and apologizing at once. "Did I scare you?"

"Well, I didn't expect it ...."

"You want to try again?"

So we did. I leaned back against the doorframe. His hands slid into my hair on both sides of my head – my hands slid over his back and pulled him closer. I was a little shocked at myself for being so needy but this felt so good.

He broke off the kiss to scoop me up into his arms and carry me to his bed, where he lay down at my side. Fully clothed, we made out. But when he climbed on top of me, I suddenly got scared and broke off.

"No, not this." I put both hands on his chest to stop him.

Carter kissed my face so gently but climbed off. "Are you sure?" he whispered.

Even though my heart was thumping and all of this felt very good, I put my hands on his face. "Yeah, I'm sure. Sorry. The only way you're going to, um, do that is with a wedding ring."

He lay on his side, pulled me to him, and we kissed some more, a long session that made me feel like I was floating. Finally we pulled apart, but only a few inches.

"Don't you ever want to?" he asked, his voice hoarse. He swept some of my hair out of my face.

"I do." The afternoon light was so dim that it seemed closer to twilight than afternoon. "But I can't. Not even with you. Sorry."

Carter was quiet, studying my eyes. It seemed amazing that someone could see something in my eyes that was beautiful – but at the same time, the love in his gaze was so deep that it hurt me. His breath was hot on my cheek. "You're the only one I want to do that with."

I wasn't comfortable with that … but we started kissing some more and I kind of forgot about it.

We finally climbed down and rearranged ourselves and I brushed my hair again. My lips were puffy and a little red, and the blood still pumped hard in my veins.

Carter leaned over my shoulder as I brushed. "So you really don't want to do that? Not even with someone you've invested a lot of time and emotion in?"

"Well, no!" I said, still trying to get all those little strands of hair out of my face. "My luck, the birth control would fail and I'd end up with a baby. There's no way I could give it the life it needs. Also, babies are boring."

"They aren't boring. They're beautiful."

I dropped the brush on his desktop as if offended and pulled my brown hair behind my head. "I don't care if a baby looks like the Queen of Sheba, I don't want one. And I'm not going to do anything that could potentially cause one."

"What if we doubled up on the protection?" Carter said, dead serious.

I could see my four-alarm blush in the mirror as I finished my ponytail. Wow, that felt a lot redder than it looked. "I'm not going to do that with anybody other than the guy I'm going to marry. And that's final."

"What about petting? What about oral sex?"

I clamped my hands over my mouth. "That's so gross, aiee! I'm sorry, I don't mean to laugh."

Carter lifted my hair off my neck, stroking it. "This is amazing, seeing a college student laughing at sex like a middle schooler."

"A thousand pardons."

He noticed my sulk. "That's okay, it just seems weird. You haven't talked with anyone about this?"

"Well, who? Not my family!" Once my mom caught me hiding behind the bed reading a Health Department pamphlet about sex. I handed the pamphlet to her and left. We never spoke of it again.

"It's no problem. I mean …." He went red, and dropped my hair. "I haven't done anything either. Like that."

"Oh good," I said without thinking.

Carter seemed to take heart from that. "So if you want to wait for marriage, that's fine. I can wait."

This would be a bad time to mention that I planned on a long courtship before marriage.

"Come on. Let me show you the guest room. You'll be staying in there."

Now this room had personality. A Strawberry Shortcake comforter underneath a heap of stuffed animals, a pink desk with worn Babymouse paperbacks in a cockeyed stack, an empty goldfish bowl with colorful gravel and a little castle. A hand-painted picture of a girl sitting on top of a tree playing a lute. Wallpaper border with butterflies and ladybugs. A gorgeous butterfly rug in the middle of the floor. A framed shadowbox with shells inside.

"Wait. If I sleep here, who am I kicking out?"

Carter looked at me, then around the room as if surprised. "Oh. Nobody. Come on in."

"But what's with all the stuff? Didn't you … don't you …?"
Didn't you have a sister?

Then I said, "Oh."

Then I said, "Are you sure it's all right to sleep here?"

"This isn't really her room." Carter dropped my bag on her bed. "We sold that house. Mom brought her stuff along when we moved here."

I walked cautiously into the room, my eye caught by a black, rabbit-fur cat, no bigger than my hand, curled up asleep in a basket. It looked as if it might wake up with a pink-mouthed yawn any moment. I stroked it with one finger. "I don't want to upset anyone."

"Stop worrying about it," Carter snapped. He softened. "Come on. I want to take you out to see the city."

But my eye was caught again, this time by a pink photoboard with white ribbons that held a million pictures. I pointed at a little girl in a My Little Pony swimsuit, wet curly hair plastered to her head, who seemed to be yelling "Yeah!" at the photographer.

"Is that her?"

"Her name's Hannah," he said, his voice rough. He touched photo after photo with his long finger. "This was her cat, Blackie. That's Mom with the sideways birthday cake. That's our cousin Nicholas holding the smoke bomb. The girls in the water-gun Mexican standoff were her friends; Hannah's the one with two guns, naturally. And that's me."

I squawked with laughter. She'd displayed a picture of a young and skinny Carter picking his nose as he grinned at the camera. "I would have made that picture vanish years ago!"

Carter shrugged, the shadow of a smile on his face. "I tried to, but she found it again."

We stopped by the kitchen, grabbed some cookies, and off we went toward his school.

But Carter announced, "I'm going to make a short detour here." He drove slowly over a small hill, through an ornate iron gate, and into a huge cemetery. "Though I'd rather skip this."

Hannah's stone was pink granite with the picture of an angel on it.

We got out. I said, "Hi, Hannah."

Carter gave me a funny look. "What are you doing?"

"Talking to her. Don't you talk to your people?"

"Why? They can't hear."

"I think they can." I knelt down to rub the dried grass from the mowing off her stone. "If you were dead, wouldn't you eavesdrop on the world now and then?"

"I haven't been here for several years now."

"I'm sorry."

As I cleaned off her stone and pulled up the grass that had grown up around its edges, he stood there, hands in his pockets, staring toward a great oak that stood alone the next hill over.

After a moment he said, "Well. Time to go."

I paused, surprised – we'd been there all of two minutes – but when Carter walked toward the car, I followed. Then I saw my flowers. "Wait."

I carried the bouquet to Hannah's grave and opened the pink tissue paper, picking out a few delphiniums and yellow thingies for myself. The rest I laid at the foot of her stone, tucking the paper back. "Here you go, Hannah. These are for you. I wish I could have met you."

I headed toward Carter by the car. I was not prepared for the tightness of his hug, nor for how long he held on to me. "Katherine, you teach me so much about love every day."

I hugged him back, loving the feel of his arms around me, hoping that my hug made him as happy. Oh, I just wanted to take him into my heart right there, give him a little refuge, a little peace.

The rest of Omaha was a lovely blur. I wandered the halls of Carter's school and met some of his classmates and his very nice golf teacher. We went to the Old Market, where I bought a million books at Jackson Street Books and Carter got me a bracelet of jade turtles at Souq, the South Asian store. We went for a carriage ride, and had dinner at a nice bistro. We came back home and talked to his mom and looked at pictures.

When I went to bed, moving Hannah's stuffed animals onto the floor – the girl was obviously a zebra fanatic – I looked at the picture of Hannah yelling "Yeah!" at the camera. I wished that she hadn't died.

Carter had talked a little bit about Hannah's death on the way back home. The shouting between his parents. Their divorce. His staying, nearly alone, at his father's house for about a year, playing video games and watching TV. He hardly ever saw his father, who had thrown himself into his legislative career. Finally moving in with his mom. When Carter had moved out, his father did not say one single blessed thing about it. Wow. Classy.

"What about Hannah? What was she like?"

He shook his head. Five miles went by.

"I'd rather not talk about it," he said. His eyes leaked.

I took Carter's hand in mine. By the headlights I saw his slight smile, and he squeezed my hand tight. We didn't speak. We didn't need to.

TEN
TURN THE PAGE
BOB SEGER

The Wind Symphony went on a mini-tour of area elementary schools – though we used the term "area" loosely because the farthest school was about 100 miles away. "Cause that's just how we roll, baby," said Yvonne, my seatmate, settling her sunglasses over her eyes. At each school, we played some music and showed off our horns. Yvonne played the theme from the *Big Bang Theory*. I played the cat's theme from *Peter and the Wolf*. After we totally blew away the little kids with our awesome wall of sound, Dr. Byrd would smile and say, "How many of you want to play in band when you get older?" and all these hands would go up.

We'd let the local band directors conduct. The first one conducted the march way too slowly, so everyone said the piccolo soloist paid him off. "No no no!" she protested as we all settled into our seats in the bus.

"Next time he does that, can we add three flats and play it in minor?" Ky asked.

We started rolling up the road in our big lumbering University bus.

"Augh! Fight! Fight!" The euphonium player was pretending to throttle the guy next to him. "Twenty thousand miles of this: The bus mate from Hell."

"The seat partner that wouldn't sleep," added the percussion gal in front of me.

Yvonne and I talked for a while about band, but after a while we fell silent, the way you do when you're driving along a hundred-mile stretch of road and run out of topics to talk about.

We stopped at Hardee's for lunch. I sat with Bayo, who was second-in-command in the band. I'd noticed that the more instruments you played, the more of a boss you were. Bayo played *everything*. We passed the funny papers back and forth, reading and commenting on various comic strips, which was fun.

But yet, coming out of the restaurant, I was engulfed in the feeling that I didn't belong here, not in this awesome group, not in the human race – I felt how isolated I was, like no one cared. The feeling was so acute and overpowering that I wondered why I didn't self-destruct from it.

"I give my love, and ask nothing in return" – *and get it*, I thought to Wyatt. And now he was so distant – almost like he didn't exist. It was so hard to believe in his existence. But I tried.

We raced down the road to Red Oak for the next concert. Bayo gave me a lemon drop for dessert, which was sweet of him. He lived on the same floor as Carter, so we'd see each other once in a while over there. The lemon drop cheered me for a moment, but as I settled into my seat and Yvonne settled into her novel, I felt the bite of that black obsidian fleck. I wondered if I would ever be free of it. I longed for Carter to hold me tight, just to ease that pain.

A vague discontent crept into my heart, wishing that it could be Wyatt holding me. But he was gone – and I'd made my choice.

The director, Dr. Byrd, played a recording of our Atlantic concert in the front. I sang along (quietly), and when I paused in my song I could hear others around the bus singing their parts quietly, little shadow-songs. We were heading to our next concert, and I'd told Dr. Byrd that I wanted to announce "Jesu, Joy of

Man's Desiring." I wasn't a huge fan of baroque music – if it ain't baroque, don't fix it – but I really liked Bach. She said that would be fine.

The "Jesu" came up on the recording and that saved me. I could hear how the woodwinds sounded like the organ while the trumpets and trombones sang the voice part – I could almost imagine hearing the singers:

Well for me that I have Jesus,
  O how strong I hold to him
  That he might refresh my heart,
  When sick and sad am I.

The bus was quiet, except for a card game going on behind me and the stereo playing the concert music.

At the next school, I announced the Jesu. "Be sure to listen to how the orchestra plays two parts," I told the crowd, my heart pounding at all the young eyes (and the critical eyes of all those music majors in the Symphony) watching me. "The woodwinds will play the part of the organ, while the trumpets and low brass will take the part of the singers."

I heard a low murmur as I went to sit down. Nervous, I looked around, but one of the trombones gave me a thumbs up as I went by. I guess that's okay. Relieved, I sat down and Dr. Byrd took the podium, and gave me a nod as she flicked the baton.

After we left Red Oak, where I announced the Bach, Yvonne looked at me from over her sunglasses. "Hey, good announcing. I hadn't even thought of the Bach like that until you said that, and then when I was playing it, I thought, 'Hey, yeah, she's right, we are playing the choir part!'"

"Thanks," I said, glowing like a happy little light bulb.

"Are you majoring in performance or music education?" she asked.

"Well, um, neither. Mom says there's no work for musicians."

Yvonne made a little pssh noise. "There's plenty of opportunities out there," she said. "If you're smart and good at what you do, you'll get them. My family's the same way. 'You won't make any money as a musician!' Well excuse me, guys, but I've been performing in local bands and making more money than the other sister who goes out and wrecks the car on a regular basis. Oh, sorry," Yvonne added, "Where'd all that bitter come from? That just happened without me thinking about it."

"That's okay. What bands are you playing for?"

"Oh, back in St. Louis we had a ska band and that was a lot of fun. It's not like I made millions off my gigs – more like 20 cents – but I had a blast, and I get a little cut of the album proceeds as well. They treat me well. I make better money playing for weddings, but we get a lot of really freaked-out people coming at us all the time. We raised our rates after one incident that was … interesting. I bet we could raise them again … I'm sorry, I didn't mean to talk for three hours."

"That's no problem. I have a hard time talking at all."

"But you did good on the announcing."

"With conversing, then. I always feel like I'm saying dumb stuff." Which sounded dumb.

"Stop thinking like that. You need to believe me, not that little warped critic up in your head."

I laughed, imagining a little hunchbacked old man shaking his fist at me from some upper recess in my brain. "Can you throw him out for me? He never gives me a moment's rest."

"I wish I could, because I have one of my own," Yvonne said.

"Well, I guess that makes us sisters in solidarity, then," I said, and we fist-bumped.

Then we pulled into the parking lot at the next school, and in the bustle of unloading and the excitement of the other Symphonians I forgot my gloom. We settled down in our chairs and set our music on our stands and warmed up over the hum of young voices crowded on the gym floor. I rattled through some scales over two or three octaves, loving how my fingers snapped down on the notes, loving the percussive pop of the keys.

Across the stage, Yvonne blazed through a fanfare on her horn, her face perfectly serious – grinning would have messed up her embouchure – but her eyes were smiling. I grinned back, then from the wings Dr. Byrd motioned to Bayo, the oboe guy, who stood up and gave us our concert A, and I loved the hush that settled over everything at the sound. Yeah, maybe Yvonne is right, I thought, and tuned up with all the rest of my people.

ELEVEN
I CRISANTEMI
GIACOMO PUCCINI

On a stormy October day when Wind Symphony was done, amid the chaos of everybody breaking down their instruments and putting their horns away and dropping music on the floor, I returned a call from Mom – but when she spoke, I stopped dead in the middle of the bandroom, my bass clarinet in one hand.

"We have to go to the hospital," she said. "It's your Grandpa."

I set the neck of my bass over my shoulder and tucked the instrument against my body to keep everybody from crashing into it. "Oh, no. What happened?"

"Just … just come down here as soon as you can."

An hour later, after an intense drive through a thunderstorm, I speed-walked down the hall in the Hardscrabble hospital, my hair dripping, my arms wet and chilly. Rain blasted against the windows as if the hospital was in the dishwasher. The rain obliterated the wide space of grass and trees that bordered the parking lot. Water slid down the pane in such thick lines that it seemed as if the window was melting. The wind shoved its way through the resistant trees, flinging leaves and twigs to the ground. Each time the trees would try to straighten, the wind would shove against them again. Fallen leaves were mashed into the grass.

When I reached the CCU, Mom stood outside the thick double doors, some of her lion mane wisping out of her chignon. "Kay, what took you so long?" she said in a gravelly voice. "I was going to have you paged! We only get a half-hour to visit Grandpa."

I shrugged. "What happened?"

Mom pushed open a door with her right arm, stepping into second position. "He drank too much last night," she said steadily, and my heart thudded. "The doctors said he vomited so much he gave himself a heart attack." Her eyes shone. When she blinked, a tear fell, struck her cheek.

I felt a strong, unpleasant pang in my heart, the wink of black obsidian, and looked down. "Oh, Mom, I'm so sorry."

Mom squeezed my shoulder. I put my left arm around her. We did a sort of awkward hug. Then we broke it up and I followed her into the CCU.

In the partition next to Grandpa was a tiny white-haired woman, alone. She had slid off of her pillow, eyes shut, mouth gaping. I ducked behind the curtain to Grandpa's side. The hospital smelled of floor wax, medical alcohol, and pee. Grandpa's heartbeat scrolled across the screen of a machine on a pole. Once in a while the screen would flash and say "missed beat." The back of Grandpa's wax-paper hand was black with bruises under the clear tape that held the IV needle in. He stared at the ceiling, the lines in his face drooping.

I squeezed his other hand. His eyes, red-rimmed without his eyeglasses, shifted to me. His freckled skin felt soft and loose, the fingers bony. I studied that hand of his that had played piano all these years, afraid to see what was in his face.

In an uncertain voice I said to his hand, "I love you." I'd never said that to him before.

After a moment he nodded once.

I looked at Grandpa then. A tube carried a black, tar-like poison out of his lungs through his nose. He didn't seem scared, only tired and sad. He looked at me with raw, vulnerable eyes I'd never seen.

Brandon was texting. Mom and Grandma talked to a doctor in a low voice. Grandma Marisa's hand was over her mouth as she nodded.

Nobody looked at Grandpa but me.

His mouth moved. "Katherine," he mumbled.

Off guard, I leaned closer.

"I want you to play because I want you to do something good with your life."

I swallowed around the big lump in my throat. Nobody seemed to notice that he'd spoken. "You're the best," I told him.

His mouth moved as if he wanted to speak again. Instead, he nodded sadly and closed his eyes. I wondered if I should close mine, too.

The lady in the next partition moaned something that sounded like, "Owen. Owen," over and over, as if hardly having enough strength to call aloud. Or maybe calling aloud even though she was unconscious, an idea that frightened me.

Then Mom and Grandma turned back to Grandpa. Grandma said that we'd better let him sleep. She pecked him on the cheek, and Grandpa's lips puckered a little but he seemed to be too tired to do more. Mom pecked him on the cheek, leaving a little flower of moisture, and patted his hand. Brandon kind of gave him an awkward hug. I patted his hand exactly the way Mom did, three pats, and we all filed out.

"Owen. Owen," the old lady slurred as I passed her. Her tongue moved as her mouth formed unheard words.

A second nurse watching a bank of monitors nodded as we left, his forehead creased. The monitors, which showed the heartbeats of the patients, beeped softly. Sitting atop the nurse's station was a red rose that had been in its vase too long. The rose had begun to shatter, revealing the seed at its heart. I picked up a satiny red petal and put it in my pocket.

In the waiting room, Mom and Grandma Marisa leaned their heads together and murmured about Grandpa's funeral arrangements. I ignored their talk, ignored the lady in the corner who was pressing a Kleenex against her face. I turned on my iPod and listened to "I Crisantemi," *The Chrysanthemums*, an elegy for string quartet by Giacomo Puccini. I thought about playing the piano in concert halls, in smoky bars, for a wedding, to accompany a choir. To live a life like Grandpa's, even one where I freelanced music for a living and stayed clean, scared me.

Even though I was surrounded by people in Wind Symphony who succeeded, I felt like they were given luck and I wasn't. That I'd pursue opportunities and would fail and fail until I had to move back home with Mom and Dad.

Much later, when I was deep into a symphony by Shostakovich – all those tombstones – a doctor appeared framed in the doorway, a young woman from India with a stethoscope draped over the back of her neck, her hands in the pockets of her white cover coat, somber black eyes roving the room. I tapped the pause icon. Put the whole world on pause.

"Marisa White?" the doctor asked.

Grandma hesitated. She took the chair's arms, pushed herself to her feet, looked at her.

It was a brilliant October day. The sun warmed the back of my black dress and flashed off the marble grave markers in the little country cemetery. I leaned with one arm against the rough, lichened bark of a crabapple, still vibrating from the shock of the three-gun salute. The blue canopy luffed in the cool breeze that lifted the yellowing crabapple leaves and spun them to the ground.

Under the canopy stood women in black print dresses, men with suit jackets draped over one arm, occasionally blowing their noses with a handkerchief. Grandpa's casket, shiny as a Cadillac, sat above its final resting place, the hole hidden by a platform, the mound of dirt concealed under a huge green square of permaturf. A mounded arrangement of white chrysanthemums lay atop the casket, stiff and unmoving in the breeze. Grandma, Mom, and her brothers sat in the front row of plastic blue chairs before the casket, their faces strained and pale. Dad stood behind Mom, his broad hands resting on the back of her chair. The pastor read the 23rd Psalm. In the pasture in the next field, a sorrel horse walked alone, nose brushing the ground as it browsed for grass. Even at this distance I heard its snort.

Grief over someone who shouldn't have died is a lot like being lovesick. But grief is a dull ache with nothing sweet about it.

I leaned against the crabapple. Though the obsidian fleck winked in my heart, I could not cry. I was aware of my sadness, but it was in a place separate from me, deep below the surface.

Several years ago, when Mom pulled into Mrs. Sandusky's drive to drop me off at piano lessons, Grandpa Arden had driven past, his car drifting out of its lane. Mom said, "Oh, Daddy, why can't you stop drinking?" I pretended not to hear, fiddling with my sheet music.

I thought of all those years at the piano, where the smell of peppermint always made my heart pick up with the hopes of learning something powerful that I could take for myself and use brilliantly. I would miss that smell. It would be Grandpa's, and Grandpa's alone, for the rest of my life.

That Friday, after having checked my email for the hundredth time, I sat down at a piano in a practice room to practice an arrangement of Beethoven's 7th for Sunday services.

Paper music for a paper gal, I thought, and sighed.

"Well, it's not like you can play the blues in church," I told Grandpa sadly, and dived in.

I chose the Beethoven because it always made me think of Wyatt. I sent him a shy little email after Grandpa's funeral, when I'd felt particularly lonely and blue. Still no answer.

I wished that Wyatt could listen to me play this. I loved how grand the music sounded, indomitable, storming out of the piano like Beethoven on a mountaintop, calling down the lightning.

Not that Wyatt would ever get to hear the Beethoven. Carter was my man now.

But that's the thing! I thought as the music rang from my piano. I love Carter, yes, but I ... care for Wyatt, too. With Wyatt, the stakes go up in a huge way.

This is life and death.

And I just lay my entire left forearm across the keys and filled the music with discord. Let the strings ring.

"Overdramatic much?" I asked.

I couldn't keep feeling this way over something I'd lost. I had to crush what I felt for Wyatt – give no quarter. I'd given up my chance. *I had to move on.*

Something moved in the window on the door. Yikes! But then I saw it was Carter, peeping in. He brought a hand up where I could see it and gave me a little wave. He had a habit of showing up unexpectedly – he knew my usual haunts well enough to surprise me with a visit.

I pulled my arm off the keys, embarrassed at being caught like this. "Come in."

He did, pulling off his cap. He clutched a little paper bag. "What song is that? That sounded neat."

"It's Beethoven." I began pressing random chords into the keys, listening to the discords and accidental harmonies strike off each other.

"You're really good. Here. I got something for you."

That cheered me up. "All right!" I reached into the bag and pulled out an oatmeal raisin cookie – my favorite – and a card.

Carter had written, *Anytime I'm sad, you always find a way to make me happy again. I love you.*

I melted. "Aw, thanks. You didn't have to."

"But I like to." He reached over to me and we hugged. "Could you play that song for me?"

"Sure," I said, and he sat on a plastic chair by the door. But when I played the Beethoven for him, the spirit of the music had fled.

Carter actually clapped when I finished playing. "That was great! I can't believe I know somebody who plays the piano that well."

"Thanks." I liked his praise, but I ducked my head. I found a bittersweet cluster of notes I liked and played it softly several times. "Carter, do you ever get crushes on people? Besides Rebecca?"

He shrugged. "Sometimes. It's no big thing. I never think about her anymore. You're the only person I'm interested in."

I deflated. "I – well, I – sometimes I get crushes too."

"You mean like Wyatt?"

I jolted up and yanked my hands off the keys. "What! How do you know about him?"

Carter crushed his hat between his hands, looking shamefaced. "I looked at your journal."

No no no! It wasn't like I had any state secrets in there, but hey, that journal was mine! "How much did you read of that thing?"

"I was just curious. I just read a little bit about how you were visiting your parents and stopped to look for him and he wasn't there, and you were sad. Then I stopped reading because I felt bad that I'd been snooping."

I let my breath out. Okay, that had been a relatively harmless entry. "Well, you should feel bad, you trespasser." I grinned. "No more kisses for you."

But then he looked so sad that I cried, "I'm sorry! I didn't mean it."

Carter didn't recover. "So who is Wyatt?"

"Just a guy I went to school with. Played tuba, which is one of the best instruments out there." I played some chords from "A Mighty Fortress is Our God" a couple of octaves down in the bass side. "A good guy."

"You really like him."

My face warmed. "Yes."

"So ... how much do you like him?"

Something about the way Carter asked this question kind of stopped me. I don't know if it was that pause in the middle, or the serious look on his face. But I softened my answer.

"I've liked him for a while. But these days, I don't know. It's been so long since I've seen him. He never answers my emails. The jerk."

Carter stilled seemed calm, though watchful. I played a few Beethoven chords. "But I'm with you now," I quickly added so he wouldn't feel bad.

I played a few lines from one of the songs Grandpa used to play for Grandma.

I got those St. Louis blues, just as blue as I can be,
Oh, my man's got a heart like a rock cast in the sea,
Or else he wouldn't have gone so far from me.

Carter didn't even notice. "How often do you think about him?"

I slipped my hands off the keys, disappointed that he didn't listen – and now sad because I was thinking about Grandpa again. "Once in a while. Don't you ever think about Rebecca?"

"No." Then Carter shrugged and said, "Maybe sometimes. She's not a big deal. I don't like to live in the past."

I pressed my fingers into the keys so they didn't sound. Must be nice.

"What's Wyatt like?"

A wave of misery swamped me. "I'm sorry, could we just leave this alone?"

"Why?" Such concern in his blue eyes.

I shook my head. "I'm sorry. I shouldn't be a jerk. I don't want to upset you."

"You're not making me upset." Carter put his arms around me. I leaned back on him – his hug felt so good, so needed.

Just then my phone in my coat pocket started singing Grandma Marisa's song, "Climb Ev'ry Mountain." I dug around for it, answering it a millisecond before it went to voice mail.

"Kay, I'm going to your grandpa's place this afternoon to finish cleaning out his apartment. Can you give me a hand? Everybody else is busy right now."

Even though Grandpa lived in Hardscrabble, the city we went to for shopping and food, I'd never seen his place. "Sure. Just give me an hour or two to get to your house. I'll call when I'm getting close. Carter says Hi," I added, because he was waving.

I hung up and gathered my music. "That was Grandma," I told Carter. "I'm going to help her with Grandpa's stuff."

"Do you want me to come with?"

I thought about saying yes, but changed my mind. "Nah. I'll probably just spend the rest of the weekend at home instead of driving back and forth. Maybe I'll get my laundry done this time." I played a few last chords, closed the piano, and grabbed my backpack.

Outside, a misty drizzle came down from a white-gray sky, and a chilly wind blew. The streets were dark with water, but no puddles.

Carter gripped my hand as we headed up the sidewalk toward my dorm. "I don't want to scare you …."

"Hm?"

"I have a bad feeling about this weekend." He fixed his blue eyes on mine, his face gaunt and serious as a starving man's. "One of us might not return."

With a thrill of horror, I thought of Hannah. "Are you saying that one of us might die?"

"I don't want to scare you. You've been so good to me." Carter looked into the brilliant red maples that lined the walk. "I wouldn't be able to stand it if I lost you."

"Oh, Carter, don't. There are so many good people out there who would be happy to love you. I'm not the only gal."

He stopped and held me tight. "I keep having this dream about a black hole, a vacuum big as the sky," he murmured into my hair. "It's pulling away everything I love. I can't make it stop. I can't hold on to anything."

I pressed my cheek against his lambskin jacket. Sometimes it seemed like I could never give him enough love.

"Katherine, don't go home. Stay here with me."

"What?" I looked: The man was serious. "But I just told my grandma I was coming out."

He kind of shrugged and released me. "This Wyatt guy ... what does he mean to you?"

I pushed my hands in my pockets so he wouldn't notice my trembling arms. "Not much. Why?"

"Because ...." Carter cleared his throat, walking up the sidewalk. "You seemed a little bothered when you told me about him just now."

I looped my arm through his so he wouldn't be able to look too closely at me.

"Are you planning on seeing Wyatt this weekend?"

"No, of course not." I sighed. "I've screwed up big time with him. I don't think I'm ever going to see him again." I stopped talking because this lump ballooned in my throat.

A gray day, getting colder, and a wind that tumbles yellow and red leaves down around your head as you walk, and all those brave colors against the dull sky is heartbreaking.

"Do you love him?"

"Urrgh." I put my hand over my face. "*Yes*. But not in the way I love you."

Carter was still studying me. "Is that good?"

"Damned if I know." Wyatt had said that to me, back in the instrument room when he was a disembodied head. It seemed ages ago. "Wyatt's a lost cause, anyway. I mean, if he was interested, he would have gotten back with me by now, right?" I kicked at some wet leaves sticking to the sidewalk.

"That's not good of him, leaving you hanging like that."

"Yeah."

"It's obvious he's not interested in you," Carter added. "What a jerk."

I nodded just to get Carter to leave Wyatt alone, since it was I who was the jerk. "So you don't have to worry about me. Okay?"

Carter gave me a gentle hug. "Okay." His voice sounded better, like I'd reassured him.

TWELVE
HE STOPPED LOVING HER TODAY
GEORGE JONES

O n the way home I drove more carefully than usual, in case
Carter was some kind of psychic. But the only situation I
met was that of an old man with a fedora driving 45 mph, and I
could not pass him for 15 miles due to all the damn hills.

But once I hit town, despite what I'd said to Carter, I made a
beeline to Paducah's, my heart pounding as I got out of the car. Oh
please be there please please be there!

I shot straight through the store to sporting goods. No Wyatt at
the counter. No Wyatt by the duck calls. No Wyatt around the
corner helping a customer.

I rushed through the aisles, finally stopping, weak-kneed, in
front of the tents – the place where I'd shattered his heart into a
million pieces. No Wyatt here, either.

My heart cracked under all the sad as if it had been a walnut.
Why couldn't I get a tiny bit of a break? All I wanted was to see
him! I missed him so much!

And just when I was about to howl, somebody tapped my shoulder. I turned – and he, Wyatt himself, stood at my back, his deep
brown eyes shining.

My face lit up like a thousand-watt lightbulb. I burst out laughing, even though I suddenly teetered on the edge of tears. "Oh my gosh! Where have you been? I've – I've been looking for you everywhere!"

"Sorry I wasn't here. I had to help someone out in Automotives. Hey, now, come on, you seem a little overwrought." Wyatt clasped my hand and swung it back and forth. "So how have you been? Has college life been good to you?"

With a short laugh I looked down at the tents, because all this light was coming out of my face and I couldn't make it stop. I never felt so filled with light around Carter. "Yeah," I said, then, embarrassed, "I have a man now." Wasn't I supposed to say that as if I were happy?

"Good for you." And Wyatt wasn't supposed to sound so pleased.

I looked at the class ring Carter had given me. "I can't stay long – I'm on my way to meet my Grandma. She needs some help this afternoon with Grandpa's house."

"My condolences. I saw your email."

I snapped to attention. "So you *have* been getting my emails? I wasn't sure." I couldn't help the sarcasm.

"Yes, I have." he said. "Listen, I'm sorry I couldn't write you back. My girlfriend saw them and got jealous – I don't know why – and told me not to write you. I told her I needed to write to you and explain what was going on, but she got so mad at me that I gave it up."

"Wow. I'm sorry." Though my actual reaction was, Hold up! Wyatt doesn't know I'm interested in him? HOW DOES HE NOT KNOW.

"No, I'm the one who should be sorry," Wyatt said. "I even thought about sending you a snail-mail letter but I didn't know your address. I'm so glad you stopped by today because I was thinking about how I was going to get a hold of you without my girlfriend having a Grade A meltdown."

Even as I thought, *I'll give **her** a Grade A meltdown,* my heart shouted AAAAA HE WAS THINKING ABOUT ME and ran in circles and threw confetti all over the place.

"So ..." I swung our hands, tentatively. "You're not mad at me?"

"Mad at you? For what?"

Wyatt seemed so genuinely puzzled that I said, "Um! No problem. Forget it."

"No really, what?"

I grimaced. "Oh, when I ... turned you down back in June."

Wyatt grimaced too, and ran a hand through his black hair. "Yeah, I was ... I'd really been a dick that day. You caught me at a bad time – and that wasn't your fault. Aw, don't be sad. Let's talk about something more interesting than that old news."

I wanted to tip my head on his chest and we could wrap our arms around each other. But I didn't dare.

So his jerk of a girlfriend knew that I was in love with him.

But Wyatt didn't.

Well! This was interesting.

Later that afternoon, Grandma Marisa and I pulled up to the curb in front of an old duplex on a maple-lined street in Hardscrabble. On the radio, Brad Paisley sang "Whiskey Lullaby." *He put the bottle to his head and pulled the trigger.* I rested my forehead on the window, studying the duplex where Grandpa had lived. Prickly junipers had overgrown the sidewalk, which was buckled by maple roots and had drifts of fading maple seeds along its edges. Dust darkened the spaces under eaves and windows.

I had been rocketing around in a whirlwind of Wyatt thoughts during the whole drive because HE'D BEEN THINKING ABOUT ME, HE'D ACTUALLY BEEN THINKING ABOUT ME, but now that I saw Grandpa's house, the feeling settled down.

Just as Alison Krauss starting singing the next verse in her angelic voice, Grandma shut off the ignition and the music. "That part doesn't apply here," she murmured. "And there's not a single thing romantic about it."

Wow. I didn't usually hear that kind of conviction in her voice.

Mist speckled the windows of the car. Sparrows chatted as they hopped around the sidewalk, pecking at bugs and grit. Grandma shook her head as if waking from a trance and tapped a cigarette out of the package. "Let's finish this job," she said in her rough voice, and got out of the car to light up. Sparrows scattered with a whirr of wings.

Frowning around her cigarette, Grandma jimmied the key to unlock the door. We entered a dark, echoing apartment with bare wooden floors and yellowed shades closed tight against the afternoon gloom. The place smelled of pipe smoke, sausage, and a sour odor I couldn't place. Grandma snapped the light on. I pulled my coat tightly around me in that cold room.

A small table with one wobbly-looking chair sat against the wall by the kitchen. Over the table was a calendar from a tavern, still at March, with a picture of a raccoon peeping warily out of a hole in a tree. And Grandpa's piano! An old upright piano, black from age, sat in the corner, and on the music sill sat a plastic bowl with a dusting of broken peppermints at its bottom. To say the old black piano was beat-up was an understatement; it looked like somebody had taken a 2x4 to it. Outraged, I ran my hand over its rough side as if to comfort it. Some of the polished veneer had been kicked or gouged off, exposing the plain lumber underneath. I imagined Grandpa sitting on the piano bench, drooped over the keys, and I blinked back sudden tears.

"You and Arden, always hanging around a piano," Grandma said, but her voice sounded sad. She shook her head again and quite suddenly walked into the kitchen.

I opened the case to play Grandpa's piano. I immediately slammed it shut, horrified. Vomit. Dried vomit caked between the ivory keys, though someone had tried to wipe it off.

Grandma came back into the room. Her eyes looked a little puffy. I scrubbed my face and took a couple steps back from the bench.

"The boys picked up most of Arden's stuff yesterday, so you and I will be finishing the job. There's not a whole lot left." Grandma pursed her lips as if the sight of the water-stained walls and gritty wood floor was distasteful to her. "Kay, child, I need you to listen." She took a drag from her cigarette, then let the cigarette arm swing down, exhaling with a sigh as she studied the old piano in the corner.

I stood straight and frowned. Something about Grandma's voice …. "What is it?"

"Well, let's sit down first." Grandma pulled out the wobbly chair by the kitchen table and began looking for another seat. I grabbed the piano bench – it was clean – and pulled it up to the table. The raccoon in the calendar picture eyed us warily.

Grandma slid the empty ashtray to her with one finger, and flicked a tail of ash. "You've been hearing a lot of things about your Grandpa in the last few days. He drank. He was an alcoholic. Arden and I have been divorced now for years. He didn't live with me anymore, but sometimes I'd let him come back and stay for a few days, when he was down on his luck. That was a mistake." Grandma looked at me, her mouth straight, a hint of a frown between her brows. "Kay, I need to tell you this. Your grandpa was not always a good man. Sometimes he hit me."

The walls and floor absorbed Grandma's words. I couldn't get my brain around what she'd said. "He what?"

Grandma's cigarette was burning down, getting close to where her fingers held it. "It went on from the time we got married until I left him. That was … thirty years? But I didn't leave him. Not until the kids grew up and moved out. I held our family together," she said, meeting my eyes. I sat silent, listening hard. "I held it together as long as I could. And once the children were out, only then did I leave him. Then

Arden couldn't say that I was taking the children to hurt him," she said. "Then I wasn't putting the children into danger by leaving. Then I felt I could face the Lord on the Judgment Day and say, 'Lord, I held the covenant together as long as I could. I did my best. I just wish I could have had a man who followed Paul's commandment, 'Husbands, love your wives, and do not be embittered against them.' Staying with Arden was the hardest thing I've ever had to do. But I did it."

I couldn't speak.

I couldn't believe I was hearing this.

It couldn't have been that bad, if it took her that long to leave.

Grandma sighed a cloud of smoke. Dragon, I used to say when she did that, back when my dolly and I helped Grandma weed the begonias under her maple tree. We'd pick dandelion clocks and blow on them, and the seeds would float high and wide, silver umbrellas in the sun.

Grandma ground her spent cigarette in the ashtray, crushing every spark of its little fire. "Some of those people at the funeral were mad when I had the preacher talk about Arden's drinking. After the service, they told me that Arden was a good man. That this was a funeral, that we shouldn't have talked about such hateful things. But it was the truth. His drinking defined his life. His drinking made our lives a misery. His drinking killed him. We can't ignore that."

She slid the ashtray away, eyeing her crushed cigarette. "Then again, who am I to talk about self-destructive behavior?" Grandma reached across the table to pick up the salt and pepper shakers. "Well, let's pack up Arden's stuff. The sooner we can get done, the better."

Relieved at having something to do, I followed Grandma into the kitchen. The kitchen light was burned out, so we worked by the light from the living room and a tiny, dingy window over the sink. In the half-dark we wrapped grimy dishes in newspapers and put them in a box for Goodwill. With both our hands busy, our eyes on their tasks, it was easier to talk: less dangerous. "So this went on the whole time you were married?" I ventured.

Grandma wrapped two glasses in newspaper before she replied. "He was handsome. He worked at the candy factory, so he was always bringing me chocolate. That was a big selling point," she said with a faint smile. "Back then he was good to me. But he wanted to play the club circuit. He toured for a while with some blues group, I don't know their name any more, and then they broke up. After that, times were rough, and he drank more. He'd threaten your mom and the boys.

"The mercy was that Arden would often be traveling. When he was gone for a couple of days, we'd breathe easier. When he came back, we'd wait for the storm to break. You'd never know what would set him off. Never. It's as if he were taking his time, looking for the tiny detail, the one detail that you'd never expect, before he exploded. And yet he blamed us for his blowups. I blamed myself, as a good wife should do.

"I was so afraid for your mom. She was the last one to grow up and move out. I prayed she'd find someone good for her, not like Arden! But your father is a quiet, gentle man." As I wrapped a greasy glass in newspaper, I felt a glow of pride for both of them.

"After your mom left, I decided to leave. I had to find a home and I wanted a new job where I wouldn't have to drive a car so I could stay out of sight. The boys found me an apartment over the square and I found a job at the courthouse, so I left my car at your Grandmother Bachmann's house, because she was all for me leaving. One fine morning, my children helped me move, and that day I dropped out of Arden's sight."

"Wow," I said. How had I missed all that? "Was that the same apartment on the south side of the square that I used to visit?"

"Yes."

I remember her making me a cake with the Easter bunny on it there. I remembered sitting in her lap looking through the TV Guide at the new fall cartoons, and the dim hallway and the toy room with the gooseneck lamp in the corner and the blocks on a cart and the funny couch thingy in the corner where I slept. In fall we'd sit at the front window and watch the marching band practice on the square, and I thought I'd die of excitement.

"It made me furious that I had to scuttle from place to place like a fugitive, when the culprit could walk free and go any place he wanted without fear!" Grandma looked off in the distance, then shook her head and went back to her packing. "Every night, as I crossed the square to my apartment, I was afraid that he'd see me. That he'd come knocking. Because then it would be, why did you leave me, you made me hurt you. Because he never stopped loving me." Grandma looked at me, as if to be sure I understood. "He kept coming back to me, kept asking for another chance. Even though we lived apart, even though I tried to make him understand that we were over, I could never break those ties to him. He always came back. He loved me until the end. But," she added, "he didn't love me enough to stop drinking. He loved the bottle more than he loved me."

"I'm sorry." I rearranged the glasses in my box, trying to make them fit. It wasn't working.

"That's the way some people are." Grandma lifted her box to check its heft, found it acceptable, set more in. "I'm never going to marry again. You don't know what people will do."

My heart was pounding, but when Grandma stood, I gave her an awkward hug. Grandma laughed, a soft metallic sound, and squeezed back. "I worry about you. You can be so trusting, so naive."

"What? I'm not that trusting." Come on, you ought to see some of the defenses I've put up!

Grandma let me go and regarded me. "I don't want you to make the same mistakes I made. Sometimes I would see you two at the piano, and I'd worry."

I looked at her askance. "That I'd turn out like Grandpa?"

"Noooooo. Of course not." She began checking through the

lower cabinets. "Oh, look," she said. Added, "Oh." When she lifted the little turtle off the shelf it fell into several pieces.

I gasped. "My turtle! The little turtle I gave to him! I must have been about nine."

It was a white porcelain turtle with a candle in its shell. I took the pieces from my grandmother. The pieces were no longer white; now they were yellowed, and felt tacky from years of grease in the air. I blew away a piece of fuzz.

When I had seen the turtle in the store, I told Mom I wanted to buy it for Grandpa for Christmas. Mom had snapped, "No, put that back. He'd never use it." At that moment, Brandon had ducked into a rack of clothes and vanished, distracting Mom long enough for me to check the change in my pockets.

I got that little turtle for Grandpa because he'd seemed so lonely. I thought its light would make him happy. I couldn't figure out why Mom was mad.

When Grandpa opened my present at Christmas, he seemed confused. "It's from Kay," Grandma said sharply. He winced.

I had picked the turtle out of the box for him. "Look. It even has a candle."

He wheezed a chuckle, and his nicotine-stained hand took the turtle. "Now, look at that. What a good girl."

The little turtle smiled through a yellow patina, smiled though he was in pieces. Grandpa had kept the fragments all these years. "I'm sorry," I whispered, cradling the fragments in my hands.

"He'd thrown her down the stairs." Dad leaned against the kitchen doorframe at home, his burly arms crossed.

I sat on the kitchen counter, where I'd been scavenging for Oreos. "I asked Mom, but she was busy." I felt like I was apologizing for disturbing Dad's silence. "I thought this would be a good time to ask, since Mom's out grocery shopping …." I shut my trap. I hadn't expected an answer from him at all. Dad was a good guy, but not much one for talking.

Dad opened the fridge and surveyed it. "She's right, we don't have any leftovers. Get out the Hamburger Helper," he told me. I did. Mom kept Hamburger Helper in stock specifically for Dad dinners.

He came over to the counter with the hamburger and I hopped down and poked his spare tire.

"Hey, I'm working on that," he told me as he always did. He unwrapped the ground beef with his rough, cracked hands. Though he always scrubbed, the cracks in the sides of his fingers and around his fingernails were black, where even the gritty pumice soap Dad used couldn't reach.

I opened the box of Hamburger Helper, shy of the question I wanted to ask. "Um. Where did he throw her?"

Dad dumped the hamburger into the Pyrex bowl. "At her apartment." He started chopping it up with a fork.

I waited for more of an answer until I realized I wasn't going to get it by waiting. "So what happened?"

"Well, one night when you and your mom were visiting Marisa, Arden came up. He was going off the way he always did, cussing and complaining about whatever."

"No kidding?" I asked.

"You don't remember that?" Dad asked. "Oh, yeah, he could be really a pain when he wasn't getting his way. One of the foremen at work does that to the boss, complaining and cussing, until he gets what he wants. My God. Anyway, Marisa didn't want to hear it. She started to close the door, but then Arden grabbed it from her and started hitting your grandma with it. With the door." Dad put the hamburger in the microwave and started it. "Your mom hustled you outside. Before your mom could go back, Arden pushed Marisa down the stairs."

The microwave hummed in the silence. Dad looked at the box of Hamburger Helper as if the story was printed on the side.

I remembered a dark hallway, a woman halfway down a staircase slamming into a wall and falling backwards. Or was I making it up? There was no way to know.

"How old was I?" How like a toddler's voice mine was.

"About four. You had nightmares about Humpty-Dumpty for weeks."

I cleared my throat to ask what happened next, but Dad moved to the kitchen doorway to watch TV while the hamburger cooked.

I bided my time with making a quick salad while Dad watched TV. When he came back during a commercial to drain the fat from the hamburger, I said, "So what-all did I witness? I didn't know Grandpa was hurting Grandma. And yet I was there when he pushed her down the stairs. What's up with that?"

Dad dumped the drained hamburger back into the bowl. "I don't know."

"So what else happened? How bad was it?"

Dad shrugged. "One time Marisa was visiting us, and Arden wanted in. Marisa told us not to let him in. I went outside and picked up a 2x4 and told Arden to leave. I was just a kid, really, barely 20, and Arden was an old soldier, been to Vietnam. He just laughed at me. But he left."

Dad turned on the microwave and headed out of the kitchen, where his armchair and Pepsi and *Star Trek* waited. Captain Kirk held the evil people at bay with a phaser. "Stop! Come no closer." Dad sat down and started watching.

Nothing but a space alien attack was going to budge Dad once he'd fixed his eye on the tube, so I trudged up to my room and sat at my desk to glue the turtle back together. Though most of the turtle was there, several chips were missing, so he looked something of a mess by the time I'd finished reassembling him. I set the turtle on a piece of paper to dry. Fault lines ran all over the poor little turtle, the enamel all crazed. I gently placed one finger on an unbroken part of its shell.

Would I have been as eager to play piano with Grandpa if I'd known?

A car pulled up, and the front door open and closed. I went downstairs.

Mom and Dad had switched to "Law and Order." Mom's gnarly, panty-hosed feet rested side-by-side on the coffee table, toes pointing and flexing like she was doing a dance exercise. She moved a magazine off the couch so I could sit, but didn't speak. That meant she was beat. She took out her pearl earrings and stretched magnificently toward the heavens. Chignon was still perfect, pulled tight, only two tiny hairs wisping out.

Dad headed out to take a bathroom break. As soon as he'd left the room, I blurted to Mom, "Why didn't you ever tell us?"

"Tell you what, honey?" Mom said, coming out of her stretch.

I hemmed and hawed. "About Grandpa, um, and Grandma. Why didn't you tell me what was going on?"

"What are you talking about?" Mom asked, incredulous. "I thought you knew."

"I didn't! I knew something weird was going on, but nobody ever talked to me about it. Why didn't anybody ever sit down and explain all this?"

"Don't yell at me," Mom said with her authoritative voice. "There's no reason to be talking about that stuff. Grandpa hit Grandma, but now, obviously, he's done. Simple as that."

If it was simple, why am I so confused? If it was so simple, then why does it scare me to talk about it?

Mom touched the mute button on the remote. "Besides, honey, you don't need to think about those things. There's no point in going over the past."

"It's not pointless. It's all part of …."

Mom interrupted. "All part of what, our glorious family heritage? Is this something you want to pass on to your children?"

"Nieces and nephews," I corrected.

Mom sighed. She got her cigarettes off the coffee table and

tapped the pack against her hand, her voice calmer. "He's gone. It's over and done. You have no call to get angry about it. None. It never happened to you."

It's not over! I'm not angry! It did happen to me, in a way! The three thoughts, hitting my brain at the same time, overloaded the wire between my brain and tongue. I sputtered. I wasn't sure why I wanted to know this, either. All I know was that it was important.

Mom frowned at me. "Kay, what is the matter with you? Stop that."

I was all ablaze. "I am perfectly calm!"

"Don't yell at me."

"I'm not yelling!" I yelled. I ran up the stairs and slammed the door.

Her word was law. It was like talking to a statute.

A while later, Mom came into my room, smelling of smoke as if she had not quite finished smoldering. Out of the blue I started crying. She sat on the edge of the bed. I wished she would hug me, even if hugs made me uncomfortable.

Mom blew out her cheeks, slouching for once. "Listen. For the last month I've been working on this awful domestic case, and that, along with what happened to your grandpa ... it's just bringing a lot of bad back. Honey, you don't need to go looking for misery. There's plenty of it in the world to seek you out. I wonder why you'd want to think about your grandpa at all."

Despite her pensive words, a hot current of anger moved through me. "Those who forget history are doomed to repeat it," I said in a low voice.

"What is that supposed to mean?"

I wasn't sure. I looked at my hands and shrugged.

"There's no call to be hostile."

Unfair! "I wasn't!"

"Muttering cryptic remarks? Then not being able to explain them? I don't know. You used to be such a happy girl, but you hit adolescence, and it all went downhill."

I crossed my arms and clamped down on all the things I wanted to say.

Mom frowned. "Case in point. There you go sulking again."

Can't win, especially against a lawyer-in-training. I rubbed my face and tried to go the candid, truthful route. "What I'm trying to figure out is if this whole thing has made me into this timid little mouse, or if it's just from my temperament when I was little, or what."

"Are you saying that you think you were trained to be shy and afraid of everything that happens? That it's my fault?"

"No! Geez! But if you wake up every morning being scared of setting someone off, wouldn't that sort of leak over into other things as well? And other people?"

"Well, I don't hide in the corner every time something bad happens." Mom's eyes flashed with that lion's look.

"That's not what I meant."

"I never told you to run and hide instead of facing the world. I'm the one who's always trying to drag you, kicking and screaming, out of your hidey-hole to make friends."

"Yeah, and then you'd talk to them the whole time so I couldn't get a word in edgewise," I snapped.

"Would you stop that?" She got to her feet. "You're doing it again, throwing barbs at me. Thanks."

"But it's true," I muttered.

"This is ridiculous. All I want is to have a nice conversation, and then I get this. Sometimes I don't know why I talk to you."

I threw myself backward onto my bed. Likewise, I'm sure.

"But it's not that simple," I added. "I want to do music stuff, but I know that you don't want me to do music stuff because of Grandpa."

"Your grandpa has nothing to do with it."

I gave her a funny look.

"He doesn't," Mom said. "I don't hate music. What about those playlists you made me? I liked those."

I softened a bit. Brandon, Dad and I had pitched in for an iPod for Mom's birthday, and I'd put her CD collection on there, but then I downloaded other songs for her. I'd worked really hard to match songs according to what she already liked. "Thanks. But it just seems like you come down on my music. It's not like I'm wrecking cars or shooting up drugs or anything."

"I never said that," Mom said. "I only want to see you looking for a career that will give you a chance for a good life. Music won't do that."

"But Mom ...."

"You saw Dad's house. Is that how you want to live? In a duplex you can't pay for? Mom had to pay his electric bill several times because they were about to shut him off."

"Mom. It wasn't the music. It was because Grandpa drank. I'm not going to drink."

"He said the same thing, years ago, when I was little. But then what happened? He couldn't get work. Mom had to get a job to support all of us. It would have been so simple for him to get a day job. He could still play at night."

"I'm not going to be like Grandpa," I said, but I felt the heavy ooze of failure seeping out through my every pore. No, I'm not going to be like Grandpa. I will be normal so I don't give myself anything to grieve over. It hurts to fail, whether at love or at life.

I lobbed a question like it was a hand grenade. "So who-all did Grandpa hit? Did he hit any of us grandkids?"

Mom's face went dark. "He'd never hit any of you."

The pain in her face made me stop. But I asked anyway. "So ... who did he hit?"

"Sometimes he'd hit my brothers. And he hit me around, once or twice. Though my brothers usually managed to protect me. Is that what you wanted?"

Yes.

No.

Grandpa said it best: It never does no good to talk.

THIRTEEN
STILL GOT THE BLUES
FOR YOU

GARY MOORE

*W*yatt *had been thinking about me.*

I couldn't stop thinking about him, either. It was embarrassing how much I had been thinking, and how my mind was engaged in a constant, non-stop conversation with him. "I have loved you devotedly for so long, and yet you have shown my heart no mercy," I imagined myself saying. Dumb stuff that would make me cringe if I even had the guts to say it. But in my mind, I said that, and more, so much more.

Despite all the vows I'd made to Carter, I couldn't stay away from Paducah's. I had to go back before I returned to school, because Wyatt said he was going to be there until 9 – and I was going to get an extra visit in there to make up for all the times I'd missed him. So in effect, I was breaking my word to Carter twice.

I was sure this made me a bad person – but at that moment, I didn't care.

I was wearing my long black coat when I ducked into the notions department and peeked into sporting goods. Wyatt was being attacked by hordes of customers. Well, I couldn't save him, so I decided not to compound his distress with my appearance. From the other side of the shelves I could hear little scraps of his warm voice and I wanted to tuck them away for later.

When things settled down, and the customers had been all helped, I stepped out.

Wyatt was paging someone when he saw me standing there gravely. Now this caused my heart to flutter: He saw me and froze. Stopped in mid-sentence, eyes full on me.

After a second he regained his poise, finished paging, and hung up the phone. "Couldn't stay away?" he asked, smiling.

I couldn't stop grinning as I joined him at the counter. "I was bored."

"Not ready to go back to your dorm yet? Not even for your boyfriend?" he asked with a little smile.

Wyatt's smile made my guilt vanish in a happy little puff of smoke. "I ain't been gone that long. Besides, I ...." I clamped my mouth shut before I could say *I missed you.*

I rested my arms over the track lighting in the glass case to warm them. "Where've you been the last couple of months? I keep coming out and looking for you, but you're never around."

Wyatt leaned in on the other side of the counter toward me. "Oh, now that I'm in college, I've been working during the week. The high-school kids usually get the weekend shift. I'm here because I traded with Jean. She had a cross-country tournament today."

I sighed with relief. A schedule conflict had been the cause of my misery: nothing else. "Oh, good. I was sure I'd made you mad."

"Are you still worried about that?"

I shrugged. "Well, yeah. I'm pretty good at saying the absolute wrongest thing without even realizing it."

"It would take a lot more than a simple statement to make me angry. Especially at you." Wyatt focused on something behind me. As I turned he said, "Hold on a minute, we have a customer."

It's a gunman! I thought, but no, it was a mom all in camo with a little girl who needed a deer license. As Wyatt rang her up, she told Wyatt how she hadn't been able to get a single decent deer when she was in her stand but later she managed to hit two does with her car – by accident, of course, not on purpose.

"I've had that kind of season, too. An ironic one." Wyatt handed over the goods and the hunters left.

I traced designs on the scratched-up glass with my finger. "That's a heck of a way to bag a deer."

"Bag a deer, lose a car. Okay, not lose a car, but you'd pay out the wazoo for the deductible. Anyway, no, don't worry about me being mad at you. You're too sweet."

"Aw! You're not sweet-talking me, are you?"

"Maybe, maybe not."

"Flattery will get you nowhere," I said primly.

Wyatt gave me a long cool look, so long that I got confused about whether I should talk. "It's not flattery if it's the truth. So what have you been doing this weekend?"

"Oh. Helping Grandma with Grandpa's stuff."

Wyatt leaned forward on the counter, concerned brown eyes on mine. "That's right, you told me that already. Are you okay?"

I shrugged. "I guess I am. Well, actually, no." Because out of nowhere my throat tightened.

"I'm still lucky enough to have both sets of grandparents, so I can't imagine what you're going through. It must be rough." Wyatt lay his arm on the counter, hand open in front of me. I lay my hand in his, and he clasped it. We stood like that for a moment, heads bowed. We probably looked like we were praying. I was okay with that.

I gave in to that easy comfort between us. "Grandma said that Grandpa … gave her a hard time." Soft-pedaling because I still couldn't get used to the truth.

"Gave her a hard time emotionally? Or physically?"

Boy, he didn't dodge around, did he? "He … hit her. But I expect the emotional stuff was there too." Now that I remembered the time Grandpa attacked the piano, it made sense. Well, okay, only up to a point. But I remembered him chasing down notes at the piano and then was a little overwhelmed.

When I was little, I stood on Grandma's lap to watch the marching band through her apartment window. I remembered that. But I had also seen Grandpa push her down the stairs *and I had managed to forget the whole thing.*

Wyatt's gentle voice woke me from my thoughts. "You probably already know that stuff can continue from one generation to the next." Like he was concerned about me.

I thought of Dad, so quiet, so gentle. "I'm lucky. Mom and Dad are cool, though they have their goofy moments."

"That's good." Wyatt tapped his class ring against the glass. "Sometimes people get trapped in cycles and can't get out. I had a friend who got stuck with this real jerk. I talked with her about leaving sometimes and she said, 'I don't know.' Finally she did get away, and ... she went out with me for a while." His face went so tired all of a sudden. "She was such a great person, so full of life, but when she was with that jerk she was just so beaten down. I guess she missed being beaten down, because after a little while she left me and went with some other jerk who wore heavy boots. The better to kick her with, I suppose."

"Oh, no! I'm sorry."

"I'm not. Okay, don't look so shocked, I *am* sorry. I try to think about it as little as possible, but .... I just don't get why a gal will do that to herself."

I shrugged helplessly, for he stood drooped at the counter. "I don't know. I wish I could help."

Wyatt raised his eyes. "You know, she's going to marry him."

I gasped. "Did you try to talk her out of it?"

"I ran into her just the other day, in fact. I went to the hardware store to get some bolts for Dad's lawnmower, and ran into her just as I went in. She didn't want to talk, but I caught up to her — maybe she let me catch up — and told her that maybe we're not together any more, but if she ever needed any help, to email me. No questions asked, no strings. I told her she'd made her choice, and I respected that, but I wanted her to be okay. She said she would be."

Wyatt thumped the counter a few times, frowning. "But I could see some bruises on her arm." He laid his fingertips on my bicep as if he was going to grab me, but so light I could barely feel them. "In that kind of pattern. And my heart sank, seeing that. Maybe it was an accident. Maybe it wasn't."

Wow. The poor girl. "I'm sorry."

"Me too. And it hurts worse because I really do care about her. I thought we had something special. And it's a helpless feeling when someone you care about a lot is in a situation like that. She had to unfriend me on all my social contacts because her so-called husband said …."

He rubbed his face. My heart tore a little, watching him. I wished I could contact her. Get her free. Heck, if Wyatt wanted to spend his life with her, I would have stood aside and let him. Did it make me weird, to be like this? I hoped not. Sure, I would grieve for what I couldn't have. But on the whole, all I wanted was to see him happy, even if it was with somebody else. I could put up with that.

Wyatt cleared his throat. "But hey, I don't mean to drag your evening through the mud over something you and I can't fix."

"You're fine. I don't mind hearing this. You know, Grandma stayed because was trying to hold the family together."

"She was probably trying her best to get by. Do you blame her?"

"I haven't really thought about it." I traced designs in the scratched-up glass. "No. Yes. I mean, no. I mean, Grandpa really loved her. I guess she used to love him, but he … it couldn't work. Oopsie," I added as a customer hove into view. I moved aside.

A young man asked Wyatt if could get his rifle scope calibrated after his kid ran over it with the ATV, and Wyatt looked it over, tried to look through it, and told him he might have to get a new one, and the hunter said, well shoot, and headed off to look at gun accessories.

"It's busy today," I said, coming back.

"It's deer season. A lot of folks get really excited. Have you ever seen hunters at the taxidermist's, going through a box of antlers? It's like little kids playing with crayons. Hello there." Three customers in a row came up, so I moved aside again – leaned on the far end of the counter, watching Wyatt as he dealt with each in their turn. He had this easy way of chatting with everyone, of putting them at their ease, and being perfectly friendly with them. I was fascinated. I watched Wyatt talking with a customer, his dark brown eyes meeting theirs, then explaining the Missouri Department of Conservation regulations about deer feeding. I wanted to study him, not just because I was so crazy about him, but because he could teach me how to talk, really talk, to others.

The customers left, and Wyatt said, "I don't mean to talk about sad things."

"It's okay. It's nice to talk to someone who understands."

Our eyes suddenly caught and held, and we shared a long gaze. Somehow, it seemed like we had connected – his eyes seemed to hold mine – and then I dropped my eyes with a small laugh, not knowing why.

"What time do you get off work?" I asked quite suddenly.

"Nine." His warm brown eyes now curious.

"This is a stupid question, but … would you like to get together after work? I'd wait for you." I'd wait for you forever, I thought.

"That's sweet of you. I'd take you up on that except I already have plans tonight."

Abashed, I said, "Well, I guess you already have a girlfriend."

"Actually, I'm running around with my friends this evening. My lady isn't coming along. It's a guy thing."

I grinned a little. "Sounds boring."

"Nah. They're the salt of the earth." He clasped my hand in his and then released me.

The rest of the evening I wished Wyatt could see everything through my eyes. I imagined him in the passenger seat of my car, listening to my cool playlist with me as I drove back to school. I imagined him walking across campus with me back to my dorm, our breaths vaporing to cloud. Oh, how I wanted him here so we could keep talking and talking. I wanted him to see all the things that made up my life. I wanted to learn so much about him. I tipped my head back to watch the winter constellations, the first stars of Orion peeking over the eastern treeline, the stars like diamonds scattered across black velvet. My heart cracked open with love.

How I could have been so wrong, all this time, being so afraid of Wyatt?

I didn't bother stopping by Carter's room. I went right to my dorm and opened my laptop.

Hey Wyatt!

It's only been an hour since I talked to you down at Paducah's. A couple months ago I wouldn't have had the guts to write this letter, but I've learned more about communication in the last two months than in all my years in high school.

This worries me, even scares me. Here at college, I have my significant other, which is Carter. We've had our ups and downs. It's usually me that causing the downs, because sometimes I don't want this relationship. But he's a good person, and we talk, and we get things straightened out. Not too long ago -- Monday, was it? -- I nearly ended the relationship. We talked on Tuesday, and I kept saying, "Maybe we should end it," and the next minute I'd say, "But we've come so far." In the end, we spent a few days apart, and yesterday we met again and were glad of it.

It is a ticklish subject. I have no idea as to how this affects you, but as for me, I am torn up, and I don't know what to do.

Mainly, it's how you stand in my life. ("What the heck??" he says. "What is this??") -- I'm taking an awful risk, but I may as well let you know

—

Well, I've been infatuated with you since my junior year, and when I started going to Paducah's to talk to you all the time, the feeling became full-fledged.

There. I said it. (Well, almost.) I never said anything before because I didn't want to throw your world into confusion. You have a lady, and I have my guy, and as you can see, all hell will break loose sooner or later.

I'm sorry I kept turning you down. I was really bad to you. But

--At this point I was stuck for about 5 minutes, sitting with my head in my hands. But wasn't it time I owned up to my mistakes?

I was a jerk and an idiot. I was afraid that I was not ready for you. I am deeply sorry for having caused you any pain, especially at a time when you probably needed my help the most.

You can haul out the old bazooka and hunt me down or you can hit reply, whichever makes you feel better. Anyway, I need to find out what you think, so I can go on from there.

I hope I haven't depressed you.

Take care of yourself! Don't work too hard!

Kay.

"Please don't kill me," I whispered as I hit send. Then I put my head down on the keyboard. Oh great, I have acted upon yet another stupid idea.

What if Wyatt is actually with his girlfriend tonight and they're having a great time, and suddenly this email shows up – and she sees it! I've just wrecked Wyatt's nice evening!

Even worse – what is Wyatt going to think about this?

Just then, a knock on my doorframe. Carter leaned into my room, his fist still against the frame. "Hi."

"Gaah!" I shut my laptop quick, as if I'd been watching porn. "I mean, hello."

"You all right?"

"Yeah! Sure!" Yeah, my behavior isn't suspicious at all. I got up, surprised at how weak my knees were, and we put our arms around each other. I wondered what I'd do if I checked my phone while Carter was here and found a reply from Wyatt. Or, worse, if Carter noticed.

"So you changed your mind about coming back tonight?" Carter said. "I didn't expect to see you... but I am so happy you're here. I felt so alone without you." He squeezed me again.

I squeezed him back, but not as enthusiastically. "Carter, I need to tell you something."

His blue eyes searched mine closely, concerned. "Are you all right?"

I looked down. "I saw Wyatt tonight."

"Oh, so now you're scoping out new boyfriends?" he joked.

"No no no no no no no! I'm so sorry! I should have kept my word to you."

He nodded, his eyes going somber. "Do you love him?"

I looked at my hands. Yes. But I couldn't say it out loud. As true as they were, I had never spoken those words. They were my treasure, buried deep, not to be cheapened by scrutiny or scorn.

Instead I blurted, "I want to be single. I need to end the relationship."

Carter released me. His face went stark and white.

"Please. Don't be angry."

"I'm not angry." Though meeting his eyes was like having a fire hose turned on my face.

I wanted to touch him, but I felt like he'd resent it. His anger made me feel so stupid and false, like I'd been playing a game with his heart.

"So why did you lead me along for all this time?" he sneered.

"I don't know. I didn't mean to. But you deserve a lasting relationship ...."

"You have a nice way of giving me a lasting relationship. Going out, scoping other men. Real nice," he said sarcastically. He'd never spoken to me like that before.

"I didn't hook up with Wyatt. I swear that nothing happened. I just ...."

"You just broke your word to me, that's all. You said 'I'm not going to go see him.' That was probably the first thing you did, too, as soon as you hit Swissville, wasn't it?"

I put a cold hand on my forehead, turning aside. "I just need to end it. Tonight. I'm sorry." Then I started to bawl.

Carter stared at me for a long moment, anger draining out of his expression. Finally he sighed and took me in his arms, calmed me down. "That's what Rebecca said to me. She said I could trust her. Then she dumped me."

Rebecca, the girlfriend he'd wanted to kill himself over. He bowed his head and covered his eyes with one long hand.

Disgusted with myself, I rested my head against his side. "I'm sorry I upset you."

"I don't want to scare you. But sometimes I want to stop living. I know I have to fight it. Then I see you, and I'm like, okay, I can handle it."

I held him tight.

"But I don't know, Kathy. Sometimes I feel like I'm in another cycle, just like with Rebecca, and I don't feel like I'm going to be able to break out of it. This scares me. More than anything, I hate it. But I don't know how to make it stop."

"I'm sorry." His words astonished me – they held an extra ring of conviction.

His voice broke. "And what scares me more is that sometimes ... I don't know ... I'm afraid that I might try again. I keep thinking and thinking about hurting myself. The other day, I went to get the laundry done, but I was thinking about you, and how you couldn't decide … does she love me, yes or no … I got so frustrated that I just punched the wall."

The walls were made of concrete bricks. I gasped. I'd noticed the other day that he'd skinned his knuckles pretty badly, but he just told me that he was horsing around.

I stared at the wall in my room, gathering up my determination.

"You look like you want to say something."

"Forgive me." I sent a punch sailing at the wall, but managed to miss. How on earth did I miss something as big as a wall? "Wait," I said, and tried again – but Carter grabbed my hands. I tried to pull away, but his hands held mine too tightly. We stared intently at each other.

"Take it out on a pillow," I said, my voice steely. "You could even take it out on me. But don't you ever, ever take it out on yourself."

"Maybe I will. And maybe I won't." He threw my hands from him and left the room.

That night, shaken by my serial inconstancy, I sent another e-mail.

Wyatt –

I can't believe what I've done. I've jeopardized so much -- now I'm oblig-ated to two people. So much for loyalty. But what have I done to you? It seemed right to say what was on my mind when I sent you the e-mail, but after I sent it I realized the repercussions. So here I am, trying to cover it up. It won't be much use, I guess. I don't know. I'm horribly confused.

I am sorry.

Wyatt never wrote me back, of course. I could imagine him saying, "Well, there she goes again, telling me what's in her heart and then taking it back. Do I need this kind of hassle?"

How could I go back to Paducah's after this and face him?

Maybe I *was* playing a game with Wyatt, and with Carter, teasing them and then pulling away.

It was winter, with dark skies and constant snow piling deeper and deeper. I couldn't concentrate on my reading, I couldn't play my music.

I kept checking my email, but nothing from Wyatt ever showed up. It seemed like I'd written my emails to empty air, and my confused words were only a figment of my imagination. I couldn't remember what I wrote – except for that one sentence that was the heart of the first email.

I didn't care anymore. I was sick of fretting and worrying about how Carter felt. Carter this, Carter that – what about what I felt? Wasn't that important too?

But he would simply die if I left him – couldn't I see what kind of pain I would put him through?

Something strange was happening to my heart. Carter and I still had good times. He'd take me out to dinner. If one of us had to work on homework, the other would bring over some food. We'd go on walks when the weather was decent. It was like we were this little married couple, except we lived in separate apartments and didn't go all the way.

One time I discovered that my slick-soled shoes would slide over the slushy ground. And suddenly, with a boyish grin, Carter seized my hand and started running, pulling me down the sidewalk, and I was powersliding over the slush, shrieking with laughter and holding tight to his hand. When he stopped, winded, we sort of collapsed on each other, and all the students that went by smiled and gave us the thumbs up.

But when I pushed Wyatt way back in the corner, and transformed Carter into the love of my life, my emotions misfired, sputtered, quit working. I stopped feeling love. I felt despair and gloom just fine, but happiness faded away.

♫

One early December night, Carter took me to another fancy restaurant, wooing me back after yet another split. Ever since November he'd been watching me closely. I'd been good; Lord knows I'd been good. It's easy to be good when you're stuck in a cage.

We stood by the checkout as Carter handed the maitre d' his credit card. I stared at the bowl of peppermints. Though I hated peppermints, I unwrapped one and put it in my mouth.

Grandpa Arden. The smell of peppermint brought him back at once.

My hand reached into the bowl. My fingers dug into the crackling candies and took out a fistful. I put my hand in my pocket.

I rolled the smooth peppermint in my mouth. It clicked against my teeth.

And it was almost like Grandpa was there, saying, Don't be a paper girl. Stay true to yourself. No matter what.

FOURTEEN
HEMORRHAGE (IN MY HANDS)

Carter talked about it, wrote email after email about it as winter darkened toward the longest night of the year.

I keep thinking about killing myself. What a relief it would be to take the pills or cut my veins. Just to stop thinking about you ... anything to ease the pain of needing you. Sometimes I think about doing it in front of you. Then I start to shake. I can't do that to you, Kathy. I love you too much to hurt you so bad. I don't know what to do anymore.

I listened to Johnny Cash's "Hurt." The music worked on me as a drug: loneliness was an elevator descending, basalt speeding past its bars as I sped down. Loneliness was a fallen angel on a barren mesa, opening those black wings like the petals of a rose to expose its unearthly, beautiful face before it ate your soul.

I have tried to deny my feelings for you. Doing that almost destroyed me. Death would be better than to live my life without you.

Without the music, it was hard to breathe. Getting through the day was like walking through molasses. I'd go to class and then wrap my black mood around me like a blanket and sink into it. This is definitely not a way to get good grades.

You say that it would be all right if I found another girlfriend. I don't think it would. It would kill me to see you with another man. I think you would feel the same way.

I spent a lot of time with Carter trying to bring him out of his depression, but even with everything I did – urging him to go for walks, asking him to talk to other people, holding him – it was never enough. I'd manage to cheer him up one evening, and I'd walk home feeling relieved, like maybe he'd turned a corner. Then the next day I'd find that he'd sunk back into his depression.

I was helping him, I was saving his life. Yet I grew weary of the limited conversation, my own thwarted desires, of the captivity that sapped my strength and left my eyes dull and heart sullen. I worked so hard to save his life – but who was doing that for me?

You don't need anybody to save your life, that voice said. You are fine. It's Carter you have to worry about. Because if you think it's bad now, how do you think it's going to feel if he carries through with this?

Oh, Jesus, I did not even want to imagine the guilt, the grief if he went through with it.

I keep dreaming of you at my side, but then I have to push the dream away. I want you to be my lover, my wife. Yes, my wife. But then you lie to me again. You say you love me. Then you don't. But you must love me, because you keep coming back to me.

And yet we had argument after argument, then we'd come back together and be very loving, then tear apart again.

On one such evening in his dorm room, we'd had another long argument. He'd been reading my journal again – I caught him at it – and when I called him out on it, he got mad.

He was reading my journal, even though I'd sent him so many emails and quoted all kinds of stuff from my journal to him – just not the current stuff, which I was ashamed of because it involved Wyatt. But he still had to read my journal to see what I was hiding. Well, I had plenty to hide, according to him. Why wasn't I thinking about him? Was I going to walk out on him when he needed me most?

I ended up crying as usual. He left to go to the bathroom to cool down. I sat on his desk, where I'd been going through his Kleenexes pretty handily, as the door shut behind him.

So I opened his laptop and looked at his email. Okay, Mr. Perfect, if you think it's okay to look at my journal, maybe I should look at your email. No secrets, right? And I opened his Sent Mail folder.

Right at the top of the sent emails was Rebecca Hadley's name – his ex-girlfriend. And 126 messages sent to her.

126 messages?!

I'd emailed Wyatt only 21 times since I'd known him, and about 10 of those were unsent drafts!

I scrolled to the bottom of the list to look at the earliest emails. Well, okay, those emails he'd sent to her while they were still in high school. *I miss you … it's so good when we're together and I wish we could spend more time together.* And, *Do you want to meet in the library after school to study for history? Or I should say, "study."* And, *Did you hear about Mrs. VanBuskirk squaring off against Tank? So awesome!* Rebecca had replied to those emails. Then the dates broke off for a while – that must have been when she broke up with Carter – but then he'd started emailing her again after we started college.

He'd emailing Rebecca the whole time we'd been dating.

He'd even emailed her yesterday.

Kathy wants to break up with me. I don't know why. I'm hurting, Rebecca. I wish you would listen to me. Why don't you ever write me back? All I wanted was to be your friend. But you didn't want to bother, did you?

Didn't look like she'd replied to any of those.

I clicked on the last email that Rebecca had written him, from last March.

· · ·

I'm sorry. I've already talked to Mom and Dad, and you can't come to my house any more. They also said that if you call me again and threaten suicide, that they will call the cops immediately. Please stop.

I can't do anything more for you. I need to concentrate on my schoolwork so I can graduate with good grades. It's over. I'm sorry.

Out in the hall, Bayo said, "Hi, neighbor. How's it going with you and the little lady?"

"Hit and miss," Carter replied.

The pulses leapt through my body. I quickly clicked out of his Sent Mail tab, X'd out of his email, shut the laptop, and threw myself on the bed with the Kleenex box. I even had time enough to pull out a Kleenex and start honking my nose so I could hide my face when Carter walked in.

Bayo was going to get a cookie in Wind Symphony tomorrow for no reason.

126 messages.

JHC.

So that Saturday, I escaped to my home. I was playing hymns for a baptism for one of my cousins that Sunday, and I was going to rip out this awesome Bach prelude for his benefit. And I was going to make a little side trip, too.

I didn't tell Carter where I was going. Mr. "You-Can't-Write-About-Your-Secret-Love-In-Your-Freaking-Journal-Or-I'll-Throw-A-Fit." The hell. The absolute hell.

As soon as I hit town, I stopped by Paducah's. When I walked into the hunting section, there was Wyatt, trying on a camo jacket and singing a song about ticks.

My feet took root in mid-aisle. My eyes drank him in as a parched tree drinks spring rain. Something struggled in my chest, then died.

As he zipped up the jacket, Wyatt noticed me. He did a double take and stopped singing. My heart didn't leap like it used to.

"Hey." Wyatt held out his arms in a 'ta-da' pose. "How do you like it?"

"I can't tell, you're blending in with the scenery too much," I said sadly.

"Well! I might have to get this coat after all." He stretched his arms over his head, looking at the cuffs. He twisted his head around to see how far down the coat hung. Patted all over his front to find the pockets, like a grandpa looking for his pocket watch. I smiled a teeny bit.

Wyatt ran a hand down each sleeve. "Are you okay? You look tired."

"Romance is dead and I'm not much fun either." I settled my chin onto my hands, looking at the ammo display under the counter glass.

"Is that right." He took off his coat and put it back on the hanger. "You want to talk about it?"

I sighed. A little cloud of mist spread on the glass and immediately vanished. I put my hand over the spot where my breath had been. "Nah. How are you doing?"

"My friend and I joined a fraternity," he said.

That surprised me. "You don't seem like the frat type."

"Oh, I just did it for the connections. And the guys there are good people, don't get me wrong. Problem is, I don't drink. I'll have a beer but I don't see the point of getting so drunk that you lose control."

How was it that Wyatt kept saying stuff that just made him more awesome to me? "That's a good policy."

He smiled at that. "It's just stuff I learned from Dad. But the problem is, in effect I'm paying the fraternity the big bucks so I can be their designated driver and babysitter. It wouldn't be so bad if they didn't expect me to carry out my services so damned often. So … I don't know. I met some good guys in there, made some friends, but I'm thinking about dropping out. So what's on your mind? It's not related to, I don't know, this interesting email I got a month ago, is it?"

I gawked at him until I remembered the email where I'd said too much. I looked down. "No, it's not about that. Sorry."

"That's too bad." Wyatt went back around to his side of the counter.

"My boyfriend ... I'm trying to break up with him. So ...." My thoughts rambled off like sheep. I tried to marshal them so I could continue.

Wyatt rested his arms on the counter and fixed me with his solemn gaze. "I'm listening."

"He says he'll ... he'll kill himself if I leave him. So that's why I'm staying. Yay." And here go the waterworks again. Stupid tears. I was so sick of them.

"That son of a bitch."

I huffed a laugh at the unexpected remark. "It's not nice to call people names."

"No, I'm serious. That's a terrible thing to do to you."

I shrugged, rebounding from the sympathy in his voice.

"Do you need a hug?"

I nodded like a teary-eyed four year old. Wyatt came around the counter and wrapped his arms around me.

Oh, at last. He was so warm, and smelled of cologne and that vinegar scent of his skin.

Yet ... this awful feeling climbed through my chest, using my rib cage like a ladder, like a parasite I shuddered from.

I let go. "I'm sorry. It's not right for me to be hugging you."

"You're right. And I'm on the clock." Wyatt leaned over the counter and got me a handful of Kleenex. "Look. I've been dumped a thousand times. Once I was dumped five times in three months, not that I was keeping track. Sure it hurts, but I've managed to stay alive. Your guy's awfully weak to let a little rejection kill him." Wyatt took my hand. His hands felt so large and solid around my cold fingers. I'd never realized how slim my hands were.

"You realize that I can't go out with you, right?"

"It's kind of obvious." He dropped my hand. "So what are you going to do?"

"I'll let him send me more saccharine cards and pretend I'm happy so he doesn't kill himself."

"What you need to do is call the cops."

"Um, maybe I could just tell him to stop sending cards?"

"No, I mean when he threatens to kill himself on your watch. They'll get him to the hospital. He'll get a counselor. He'll get his shit straightened out. But, and this is more important, he has trained professionals helping him."

I pushed back. "But he doesn't want professionals. He wants me."

"If he genuinely wants to commit suicide, that is not something you can fix. Let me correct that – it's not something you *should* fix. He needs to have trained professionals helping him. People who have gone to school for this shit. People who have made a living, a career, helping those who need it."

I shook my head. "I don't know."

"Is he playing you?"

"Wha – no! No, he isn't."

"Why does he want to make *you* save him, then?"

"Because he doesn't know where to go or what to do …."

Wyatt leaned forward, brown eyes full on mine. "That's bull-shit," he said. I lost my breath. "Kay. He knows exactly where he needs to go. He knows exactly what he has to do. If this were a real suicide threat, he would want to seek help. If this were real, he would not want to lay this hurt on you like this."

I couldn't breathe.

"That's what pisses me off the most. He doesn't care how you feel, as long as he gets what he wants. That's why he's laying on Powerhouse Guilt Trip #1. He's using you like a roll of toilet paper."

I got my breath back. "Toilet paper? What the hell do you know?" Oh, dear Lord, the tone of voice I was using toward the man I – the man I should have loved. I softened it. "So what? It's better than having to live with my guilt if he kills himself." I clamped my hands over my face.

Wyatt rubbed my shoulder. "Shh. I don't mean to get mad. All he wants is somebody to bleed into when he cuts himself. It should not be you."

I tried to compose myself. "I'm sorry."

"What is there to be sorry about?"

I shook my head. "For being a wreck of a person."

"I'd think that description applies more to me than to you." Wyatt reached out. We clasped hands and gazed at each other.

"It would be nice if we could be wrecks together," I said softly.

"I don't think we're wrecks, to be honest. We're just stuck in hard times. Kay. Don't let him do this to you."

"I don't know …."

"I'm telling you that if he does this again, you have got to call the police. Drive him to the hospital. If you're not sure what to do, just call the Suicide Prevention Hotline. Talk to those guys. I've called them before on behalf of one of my friends."

"You have?"

"Yes. Trust me. Even if all you want to do is talk. Kay, these are folks who have lost someone to suicide. Hell yes they want to talk. Even if you're not sure. They'll help you, and they'll help him. Okay?" He took out his phone and looked up their number. "Put this in your phone, right now. Please."

He said please. There was no way I could have resisted that. I put that number in my phone right then and there.

Wyatt leaned on the counter. "Now, just to let you know, I'm probably going to get dumped again by my current girl."

My head went up. Whaaaaa?

"She saw this, I don't know, very interesting email somebody sent to me, and she kind of went off."

I was electrified. "She didn't see the follow-up email, did she?"

"No," he said thoughtfully. "I kept that one from her. If you don't mind, I'd be happy to wait for you."

My face lit, my hands tightened on his. A great burst of joy rose in me –

Then slumped to nothing.

I cursed myself, my inability to feel. I wanted this. *He* was what I was here for. *He* was what I needed.

But I squeezed Wyatt's hands back, because respect, courtesy, deep regard – these at least I could still give him. "Don't keep yourself from happiness on my account. But if you wait for me, I'll come to you. I don't know when. But I'll do it."

"So are you going to break away?"

I sighed. "I'm so confused. Right now I think I know what I want most. But when I see Carter – even though right now I don't ever want to see him again – when I see him I want to help him. I feel like it's what I have to do."

"Couldn't he help himself on his own?"

"Yes. I mean, no." I dropped my head. "I know he's trying to do this to keep me. But at the same time, what if I leave him and he carries through?"

"Kay." I looked up. Wyatt's eyes were full on mine with such intensity that my breath caught. "Then you find a way to get through that pain. But you can *not* blame yourself. You did the best you could. Whatever he does is his shit. Not yours."

After I left Paducah's, I went to the dark church to practice the Bach prelude, and I just *nailed* that sucker.

Wyatt was going to wait for me.

Sunday morning was gray and freezing, threatening snow. I was getting ready for church in my cold upstairs room, just like old times. I'd just put on my white Victorian dress when an unfamiliar chime rang out from downstairs. The doorbell. A stranger had arrived! If it had been neighbors or family, they would have pounded on the back door and then just walked in, hollering "hello!"

"Kay!" Mom said from downstairs, sounding positively giddy. "It's Carter."

"Are you freaking serious!" I cried. What was he doing here! I came home without telling him where I was going because *I did not want to see him*!

What if I barricaded my bedroom door? I could shove the bed against it. Then I'd jump out the window and run like crazy!

I put my head in my hands. Wimp. "Just a minute."

Yep, I knew I shouldn't've gone to see Wyatt. Knew it.

Social responsibility took over. I walked downstairs, arranging my face so I didn't look like Serial Killer Prisoner #7452932.

Carter, dapper in his charcoal suit, stood on the rug by the front door, showing Mom the label of his suit jacket.

"What the hell are you doing here?" I snapped.

Whoops, wrong greeting.

Mom gawked like a snake had fallen out of my mouth. "Kay, what is the matter with you?" Carter's eyes, which had lit up when they saw me, turned hurt.

I sank into gloom and ashes.

Carter buttoned up his suit jacket. "I got up at 6 this morning so I could look nice and show up on time," he told Mom.

"You look fine. I'm just wondering about my daughter here," she said, giving me the *didn't I teach you good manners?* look.

"I'm sorry, could we just go?"

The nice thing about playing the organ that morning was that I didn't have to sit next to Carter and look ecstatic about his dropping in on me unawares. When services began, I ripped out the Prelude on the organ, which got an amazed silence from the congregation.

During the sermon, I stayed on the bench, messing around with the stops. In the past I'd always gone heavily on combinations with lots of reeds and flutes. Today, though, I was tired of such an airy, shall we even say wimpy, sound. I wanted to get all Mighty Fortress is Our God on them. What was the use of playing if I was scared to be heard?

I smiled grimly at that echo of Grandpa's.

He was right. But I honestly did not feel like I deserved a voice. Other voices had better things to say. Other voices were more important than mine.

I could imagine Grandpa sitting next to me on the organ bench – though he'd roll his eyes at all the church music.

The only sound in the church was the preacher's voice as he laced together the lessons from the Old and New Testament.

Grandpa whispered, "You wanna see those old ladies out there jump? How big of a noise can this thing make?"

I grinned. "You see my boyfriend out there?"

He made a sort of non-committal grunt. "Dolly, if he don't know 'St. Louis Blues,' you should go with someone who does."

I trailed my fingers over the tops of the keys so they wouldn't sound. "Why didn't you let Grandma go when she asked?"

He tried to start a sentence about three times before he actually spoke. "I loved her," he said, looking over the top of the organ console at her. "I never did love nobody else." Voice real quiet. He'd never talked like this when he was alive. The nice part about daydreams.

"But you knew she was … sad." The only word I could come up with.

"It ain't none of your bisness, hon." He started playing something on the organ, his ghosty fingers dipping into the keys in a slow beat, but the notes didn't sound.

"It is. But …." I started to say something else, but, too uncomfortable about the topic, I dropped it. "Now, I have a guy who refuses to give me up. See him over there? The only guy at church besides the pastor who's wearing a suit."

Grandpa looked at me, mouth open as if to talk, but then shut it and frowned over the top of the console at Carter.

"Stuff repeats through the generations," I said to him. "It's like history repeating itself."

Grandpa looked at Carter for a long moment, then looked back at me.

"I never took no for an answer," Grandpa said quietly. "I was persistent. She felt sorry for me. Made it hard for her." He kind of swallowed, then, and looked back at the keys. "Ya wanna leave him? Break his heart. Ya gotta break his goddamned heart so hard that he hates you forever. Then you never go back."

And he vanished like the daydream that he was.

Even if Grandpa was just a figment of my imagination, I was shaken.

Ya gotta break his goddamned heart so hard that he hates you forever.

After church we had dinner at our house. It was Mom, Dad, Grandma Marisa, Brandon, Carter, and me. Carter was so nice to everybody. I, on the other hand, sulked. Afterward, Carter sat in the living room and talked with Mom and Dad and Grandma. I went upstairs, lay down in my dress, and fell asleep.

It was a colorless dusk. At the edge of a lake, a wooden box, carved like an old cemetery paling, lay half out of the mud. It shone with slime from all those years underwater and smelled like rotten vegetation.

Open it, someone commanded.

But terror seized me. No. There was something inside that drowned box that waited for me, and if it came out I would die.

I ran. They grabbed me, twisted my arm until I fell to my knees. Open it! No!

A cold crowbar was in my hands. I pried and pried, and each time the nails screamed. The lid popped open a quarter-inch.

A roar of black from inside, a swarm of black bursting from the box, obliterating both box and lake.

A maelstrom of black swans filled the sky, circling so low, so close I could hear the harsh whisper of feathers as they flew, a tornado of black wings. No!

I screamed. Leave me alone, get him! The swans drew the vortex of their circling tight around me. One swan muttered in its throat. Black pinions cut my face like knives. I wrapped my hands around my head, but lost my balance and fell into the stinking water.

I startled awake. Something had trapped me in a full-body embrace. Carter had sat down on the edge of the bed, pinning my sheet around my body. My arms were locked against my sides, my legs were squished together. I tried to roll away but couldn't even squirm.

My room was dim. Outside, the wind roared, a hollow sound.

"Kay?" Carter whispered, lifting strands of my hair out of my face. "My God, you're so beautiful. You're like a sleeping Indian princess."

Don't exoticize other peoples' cultures, I thought, and shook my head, but he kept stroking my hair as if mesmerized. "Gaah, stop that." I tried to slither my arms out of the top of the sheet, but I was held so tight they didn't move. I tugged harder, panic rising. Even though I was wide awake, I still felt as if that tornado of black wings spun around me.

Carter went on stroking my hair. "Kathy. Wake up. We need to start back, a big storm's coming."

I squirmed, expecting him to maybe notice that he'd wrapped me so tight I couldn't move, but he sat there like he had no idea. "Get up, dammit! Get off my dang sheet!"

He stood abruptly. "Geez! What's your problem?"

Heart pounding, I pushed my arms free and kicked the remaining sheet off my legs. "Why'd you come down here this morning? Why?

Carter looked astonished. "I wanted to surprise you."

"I wanted to spend some time apart, but you couldn't even give me two days. That was all. Two measly days."

"You should have told me you wanted some time apart. I would have let you go."

Yeah, right, only after we experienced yet another tempestuous scene of accusations and recriminations. I should have just gotten up and left, because by this point I was a bitch on wheels. "You know what? You need to let me go. Not just *say* you will."

"What? I said I would have let you go. Didn't you hear me?"

I didn't want to touch him as I got out of bed, so I scooted ignobly over the footboard. "No. I mean from this relationship."

My words thudded like arrows into Carter's heart; his face squeezed in agony and went ashen. He breathed in, staring at me. "You saw Wyatt, didn't you?" His voice low, like the moan of a wounded lion.

Oh Lord, here we go again. "It's time we ended the relationship, if you could call it that. It's over."

"If you could call it that? What the – how can you even say that? So you're saying this was all *fake* on your part?"

"It wasn't fake." I grabbed my bag off the floor, squeezed my feet into my dress shoes. I should have changed my clothes after church, but too late now.

"Why the hell are you doing this to me?" he said. "You're going out with Wyatt now, aren't you?"

"No, but I wish that I could. Because Wyatt actually respects my wishes."

"So you're telling me that you never loved me? That you were just playacting the whole time?" His eyes hurt, astonished, angry.

"I wasn't playacting. But I can't stay with you any more. I'm tired of this."

"So everything you did over our whole relationship was fake."

"It wasn't fake! … Dammit, Carter, you are not the one for me."

"But you're the only one I want to marry."

No no no no no no no, not that. He tried to take my hands. I pulled away.

"What? Jesus, what have I done to you this time?" A despairing edge to Carter's voice. "God, Kathy, I can't do anything without totally fucking up in your eyes, can I?"

"I never said that."

Carter didn't listen. "But that's just fine with you, isn't it? It makes it so much easier for you to *despise* me."

Boy, was he was right on that score!

The ground slid away from my feet. A lucid part of me saw what was coming and cried, "Don't! Don't say it!"

Ya gotta break his goddamned heart so hard that he hates you forever.

To my shame, I grabbed that follow-up arrow, pulled the bow to full draw, and fired. "I never loved you, not the way I've loved Wyatt. And I don't love you now. What I want is for you to leave me alone. Don't ever call me, don't ever write to me again. Stop coming around my place all the damn time. Because we. Are. Through."

That just about blew Carter's hair back. But oh, the look on his face. It was like ground zero when the bomb detonates, and the world disintegrates inside the spreading fire.

Grandpa forgot one thing: The moment you break his heart, you have to start running before that explosion envelops you, too.

I grabbed my bag and stormed downstairs. Carter thudded after me saying … I didn't even know what he was saying because I was too crying too hard to hear. I dashed for the laundry room to grab my clothes, which I'd brought home to wash, but Carter blocked me in that narrow hallway. "What did I ever do to you?"

Screw laundry – get out, get out. I ducked under his arm, wriggled free from his grip, and rushed back into the kitchen. From the living room, Mom called, "Kay? Kay! What's going on?"

I couldn't let her and Dad see me cry. But Carter was coming right after me, saying, "Your daughter's gone off the deep end." His voice so calm and rational.

How he could be even sound calm and rational right now was beyond me. "We have broken up! And you should talk about going off the deep end." I yelled, heading for the back door. Just as quick, Carter blocked me.

"Kathy. Get a hold of yourself," he said – so calm. "You're overreacting."

"Get out of my damn way," I hissed, and shoved him.

"Kay!" Mom cried from the kitchen doorway. "Don't!"

"Back up *now*, young man," Dad ordered, and something rang like a bell in the kitchen at the tone of his voice. Both Mom and Dad were in the kitchen doorway, Mom shocked at me, Dad narrow-eyed at Carter.

Carter put his hands up and took two steps back as if Dad were the police. I shook myself off, sullen.

"Kay? Kay! Baby, what is going on?" Mom asked from next to Dad, and she even put her arms out to me.

I felt so stupid with my face covered with tears and snot. I scrubbed my nose on my sleeve. "We've broken up. I'm going back to school right now." As much as I wanted Mom to hug me, I did not want to be her baby.

Carter said, "Kathy, you shouldn't drive when you're like this."

"Don't tell me what to do." I headed to the front door, grabbing my coat on the way.

"Kay," Mom said, following me. "Where are you going?"

"I *said* back to school." I didn't mean to snap at her, but that's how it came out.

"You can't leave. Your laundry's in the dryer."

"Oh, just put it in a pile. I'll get it later."

"I'm not going to do your laundry again."

"I said put it in a pile, I'll get to it later!" And now I was crying again for no reason. God, was there ever going to be an end to stupid crying? I fled out the door, both Mom and Dad calling, "Kay! Get back here!"

I was such an idiot.

My phone exploded with texts and ringing until I turned the damn thing off because it's hard enough to drive when you're crying your eyes out. But I was not turning back.

I managed to get control of myself by the time I hit the highway. Which was good, because five miles after that, Carter's red car passed me like a shot, even though the snow was starting to get thick.

"Bye," I said.

Fifteen miles later, at the wide stretch at Midway, Carter's red car sat at the side of the road, hazards blinking. A dark figure stood on the other side of the car. Keep driving, I thought, but the hazards had me a little worried. I stopped and got out.

Carter was shivering at the side of the road, hands shoved deep in his pockets as he looked out over a barren snow-ridged field. No stars. Snow starting to fall thick over empty fields and blank trees. "Why do you do this to me?"

I'd really cast him down into a hole. "I'm sorry."

He looked up at the stars, his face lit by the backwash of the blinking red hazards. "You don't understand how it feels to love you this much. Look at this world. This dead place." He held out his hands to the field – they trembled – he lowered them. "It's … it's a dead world inside," he said, his voice shuddering, and shoved his hands back in his pockets. "I know it's no use asking you. But this pain. I don't know what to do. I'm scared."

Even now I cringed from touching him. Even now I felt terrible about what I had done. So many confusing emotions. "Please. You have got to find someone else. Someone who's good for you. Someone who does love you."

"God, but I love only you," he cried, and it was pain for him.

I recoiled even as that web pulled tight around me. "I'm sorry about that." I blundered through the snow to my car.

Off I went again – and a few miles later, Carter rocketed past me, skidding on the falling snow, driving like a maniac.

"Good job not setting him off, Kay." I sped up and followed him.

I drove on his tail, my headlights filling his car. Windshield wipers sweeping the snow aside. Snow piling on the windshield's edge, defrost on high. Carter kept driving onto the snow-choked shoulder. I leaned on the horn until he swerved back on the road. Then he'd accelerate 65, 70, 80, occasionally fishtailing. I accelerated with him, though my heart dipped when my car skidded. If he was going to drive off the road, I should go with him. This was my fault.

I had my phone with the number Wyatt had given me. I had the phone right there. I kept picking it up to call. But each time I lost my nerve. I was such a failure. I dropped the phone back on my seat.

There was a God, because we reached St. Francis in one piece.

Once in town, Carter pulled into McDonald's, of all places.

I clambered out of my car, leaving my coat behind in my hurry, and ran to him. "Why are you stopping here?"

"I'm going to get something to drink," he snapped. As if it was perfectly normal to pause in the middle of a cataclysmic argument for a snack.

The snow sifted from the blackness beyond the streetlights. He didn't look at me as he slammed the car door and headed in. My steps fell in with his, the freezing wind tangling my dress around my legs. I tried to suppress my unhappy grin, like a dog's grimacing smile when another dog had him on his back.

We ordered separately. He got a pop and I got a chocolate shake. When he sat at a table in the back of the room, I joined him.

Carter's eyes bored into me as took a pull on his pop. He set it down hard. "I could stop at the store and pick up some razor blades. Or maybe I could get some sleeping pills." Staring at me, gauging my reaction.

I stopped dead. I looked at my shake, forced myself to regain my poise. "You don't need those," I said quietly, toying with my straw as if this talk was perfectly normal. "They probably aren't even available. You'd only get those things, those refills with the four little blades that would just give you paper cuts."

"You don't have any right to joke about this." The hardness in Carter's voice shut me up. "And they do sell them." He stared at me for a minute. "Or maybe I should start with the sleeping pills."

"No. That's a terrible idea." I wrapped my hands around my shake. "You need to go to the hospital. I can't help you."

"Yeah. Right. That's just like you, throwing me to the curb when you're done with me."

"That's not what it's about."

"If I took the sleeping pills and then cut my wrists, then I'd be done."

The hell with him. "If you do it, so can I," I said, looking right at him. "I could kill myself too. How would you like that?"

"You said that you couldn't."

He was right, but I snorted in scorn. "Ha. You make it sound so easy. I want to die, anyway." It was the woman with the sword taunting him. I could imagine her holding a cigarette, blowing smoke at him. "It would be fun. Whee."

Carter scoffed. "Shut up. You haven't suffered the way I have. I lost my little sister, remember? You've never suffered that kind of pain, never. You sit there and talk about suicide like it's some *game*, but I have way more reason to end my life than you do. Most of all because you think it's fun to keep playing head games with me."

"I. Don't."

"Bullshit. You pretend to love me. Then you don't."

"I wasn't pretending," I said through my teeth.

"Then you act like I'm some kind of monster when all I want to do is end this pain. And the only way I can do it is to kill myself."

"Would you stop that stupid talk?"

He took another pull of his pop, eyes fixed on me. "You sit there and complain about how you have to take responsibility for me," he said in a mincing voice. "I never forced you to do that. I never forced you to do anything. But if I'm dead, I bet that would stop your complaining for good. Wouldn't it?"

I sucked in my breath as if he'd punched me in the stomach. "I said, stop it. Now."

"Wouldn't it feel nice to look down at me in my coffin and say, 'At least I don't have to put up with his shit any more.'"

"Don't. That's enough." Louder this time.

"Then you can think, 'Now I feel better that he's cold and dead.' Because what am I worth to you? Nothing."

I pushed to my feet. "I don't have to take this. I'm not going to take this. We're through."

"We'd be really through if I died," he hissed.

I grabbed my keys and stormed out the door. The steam pouring off me could have melted this hard-packed snow I strode into. So he wanted to blame his death on me. Let him! I was done with letting all this crazy eat me alive.

Carter burst out the door behind me.

"No! Leave me alone!" I yelled but before I could sprint out of reach, he grabbed me right in the middle of the drive-thru lane. I fought his grasp.

"Why are you running from me again? Why don't you listen to me?" he said, sardonic, desperate, his breath coming out in clouds in the freezing air.

"Listen to you? Why don't you listen to me?" I managed to wriggle free. He tried to grab me again.

I dodged. "Dammit, I already told you I want to leave you. I'm not taking any more of this!"

Carter shoved his hands in his pockets and glared at me, shuddering violently from the cold. His words billowed in vapor. "When you kiss me, do you see Wyatt?"

Never. I stretched back my lips and showed him my clenched teeth.

He was shaking so hard from the cold that I could see it. "You're a damned good actress," he jeered. "You can switch your emotions on and off. You can lie to me, like you are now."

I pressed my arms against my chest, shuddering as the wind reached under my dress. "Don't give me that! I told you plenty of times I wanted to leave. You're deceiving yourself because you never bothered to listen."

Carter grabbed my shoulders with a grip that hurt and pulled me close, lips puckered to kiss me. I waved wildly at this face, trying to slap him with my fists and keys (but even after this, not too hard). I wrenched myself free before his lips touched mine.

He glared at me, his whole body shaking in the cold. "I hope you go to hell." He got back in his car and peeled out across the parking lot to the road.

"I'm already there," I said.

FIFTEEN
FOR SORROW HAS ROSES AS BLACK AS NIGHT
JEAN SIBELIUS

I skipped breakfast in the cafeteria, knowing that Carter would be waiting there for me. When I went to my history class, I went by a different route so I could go into class through a different door. I needn't have gone to all that trouble, because Carter, waiting for me at his usual spot, came in as soon as I sat down, taking the chair next to mine. My heart deflated.

"You shouldn't miss class." I opened my history notebook. I skipped the pages where I'd written about our relationship, where I'd written down the talks that Wyatt and I had. I wasn't writing much in my journal these days, knowing he'd read it – but I knew he wouldn't even glance at my history notes.

Carter, his voice low, spoke only to his hands clasped on the long table. "I need to talk to you. I – I don't know what came over me last night." A broken sigh.

Yes, we do need to talk, one part of me pleaded, because I wanted so much to throw my arms around him and apologize. It would have been so easy to go back, so easy, and we'd all feel better.

But Wyatt was waiting for me.

"You'd better get to class." My voice had no air behind it. Carter got up and left without another word.

Class started. The history professor ranted on and on about waving the bloody shirt. My phone buzzed with a single text: *Please.*

I was tempted to reply NO but instead pocketed my phone. It was just about out of juice anyway. Lately I hadn't bothered to charge it. I didn't need to have the internet at my elbow 24/7 anyway. Or, for that matter, all of Carter's texts.

I was exhausted. It was over. I still had to keep an eye on him all week to be sure he'd be all right. Carter had said that he'd be going home this weekend, so once we reached Friday, he'd be safe. For a while.

I dodged him for most of the day. I had started finding hidey-holes around campus, places where Carter would never think to find me. The top of the service stairway in the Union, next to the locked door to the roof. The antechamber to the women's restroom on the third floor that no one ever used. The back staircase on the Art side of the Fine Arts Building. Random classrooms in Salmen Hall that were unoccupied until the next class came in. The staircase in the Chilcoat-Rogers Building, where I could peep through a little window and watch Carter as he walked from his dorm to the Union and wait for him to pass so he wouldn't catch me unawares.

I'd only started doing this recently. It hadn't seemed necessary before.

I hid out in the stairwell in the Fine Arts Building. They had a nice bench there and a window where I could watch the sun. When I had class, I went in a few minutes late so he'd assume I skipped it.

I grabbed my lunch while Carter was in class, and ate it in a service stairwell in the Student Union. The stairwell went clear up to a door to the roof, which was always locked. Though I occasionally heard service staff using the stairwell in the three stories below me, nobody ever came up to the roof, leaving me in peace. Earlier this fall, when Carter had been coming around to see me all the time, I'd read over half of *Life on the Mississippi* by Mark Twain while hidden up here. Nobody ever bothered me.

I finally came out of hiding to go to my bass clarinet lesson, where I was learning a Finzi composition for jury at the end of the semester. When my lesson was over, I came out, opened my case that I'd left outside the professor's door – and found a long-stemmed red rose lying there.

"Oh, come on!" I said despairingly.

On the card, Carter had written, *I need to talk to you. Call me.*

"Please no," I said. Because I knew how that talk would end.

My phone buzzed. I ignored it and set the rose on the floor so I could put up my bass. I snapped the latches shut and looked at the rose lying there all sad, and sighed. A symbol of attachment. I'm sure Carter would have said the rose was for friendship. My foot. The only friends you'd send a red rose to were the friends you wanted to make out with.

Leave the rose there! I thought, but I couldn't do that to a flower. So I brought it home, cut the stem under water, and stuck it in a vase I'd picked up when I worked at the greenhouse. The outer petals had turned black from my walk across the deep freeze that was my campus.

I lay down in bed, eyes shut, and joined my heart where it lay on a cold sidewalk in a puddle. "Bohemian Rhapsody" was playing on my iPod. I let the music settle over me the way the gray snow outside settled over everything.

My cell phone rang. I answered without getting up.

"Did you get my rose?" Carter asked hesitantly.

"Yeah. Thanks." My voice flat.

A pause. "Can we talk about this? I keep thinking about last night ...."

"That's okay. I deserved it."

"I hurt you, though. I hate myself for doing that."

Join the club, I thought, then smacked the thought down.

"Can I come over?"

I sighed into my pillow. "Please. This is kind of a bad time."

"Oh Kathy. I know you love me."

"Huh. What do you mean by that." My voice dull.

"You care enough to save my life. If that isn't love, I don't know what is."

I closed my eyes and sank and sank.

"I have another surprise for you."

My eyes popped open. "That's okay. Keep it. Please."

"Can I come over for just a little while? I really want to apologize in person."

"Yeah. I guess so."

He sighed. "Thank you. I'll see you in a minute."

I hauled my sorry butt out of bed, my body heavy and aching, grabbed my bookbag, and fled through the snow to the Union.

One of these days, he's going to figure out that he shouldn't call before he comes over.

So I sat in the women's restroom antechamber, which had a nice chair and a bitty window in the wall above it, and worked on my homework, which needed to be done. After about three texts (*K, where are you?* and, *U there?* and, *K please!*) I shut my phone off.

When I'd finished my homework, I suddenly took a crazy (for me) step and texted Yvonne from Wind Symphony. *What are you doing? Are you at home?*

After a little while (and two more texts from Carter) she replied, *Yeah wazzup?*

Can I come over?

Sure!! P.S. U don't have 2 spell words out u no.

Antidisestablishmentarianism, I texted back, and picked up my book bag.

Yvonne's side of her dorm room was plastered with posters of classical music playbills and ska artists. Elizabeth of the regal braids was her roomie, with Pentatonix picures and a big poster of Octavia Butler, and gorgeous Harry Potter fan art that Elizabeth had drawn herself. The stereo was playing country music. Elizabeth's side was tidy while Yvonne's side was like a train wreck that a tornado had passed through.

"Best. Room. Ever!" I cried, which they liked.

We went to the coffeehouse for supper, a cozy little place that smelled of coffee and spice, with big shelves of used books, and we talked about music and books and goofy stuff. I told them about reading Jane Eyre for class, and they were all down with that book. Then we trooped back to the Fine Arts Building and played upside-down etudes on the grand piano in the bandroom. I made sure to keep out of sight from the windows in the bandroom doors, just in case.

I played blues standards while Yvonne and Elizabeth leaned on the grand piano, then I leaned on it while Elizabeth played upside-down etudes, which were basically classical pieces that she messed up with a few wrong notes in the exact right places, and then she'd do stuff like turn the etude into a mashup of Chopin vs. Lady Gaga.

I leaned on the piano case, watching the damper jump and the felt hammers striking and making the notes ring through my body, and Elizabeth's shoulders moving as she chased down notes across the keyboard and Yvonne leaning in, trying to play additional notes as Elizabeth's fingers roared by – I watched all this, and I sighed.

"I miss this life so much," I said under the cascade of notes.

Then Elizabeth hit a chord that just crunched the etude into a little pile of screeching metal, and Yvonne and I yowled and laughed.

It was very late when I walked home, keeping a wary eye out for every dark shape that came up the sidewalk that might possibly be Carter, but to my relief he never materialized. My phone was stone dead, so no more texts.

The next day I ate breakfast in my dorm, took a roundabout

route to class, and managed to dodge Carter by ducking into the women's bathroom as he came up the hall. I stayed there until I was five minutes late for class – but he was gone when I came out.

Later that morning, I was hiding out in the periodical section in the library when Carter came through the door past the microfilm. I sank into my chair.

Carter kind of hesitated when he saw me – his face was pale and drawn – but he opened his notebook and pulled out yet another card. "I'm sorry, but I had to find you," he said, handing the card to me.

"Thanks." I read it. It was so saccharine, my teeth ached.

Carter sank into a squat next to my chair, one long hand on the armrest. I moved my arm off, heart thudding, and looked only at my magazine.

"I feel terrible about what happened. I've wanted to talk to you for the past two days, but you keep running from me like a scared mouse. Why can't you stay for just a moment and talk to me?" His voice broke.

That break in his voice brought my head up, and all my compassion. But when I opened my mouth, when I met his worn eyes, all that came out was an exasperated sigh. I lowered my head again quickly, praying he'd misunderstood.

It was like I was two people inhabiting the same body at the same time. One person wanted to love and help him, and the other one wanted to head-butt him so hard that his eyes would be purple for weeks.

"Carter," I said dully. "Just stop it. It's over."

Carter sagged. His eyes went exhausted past all help.

"We're finished," I said.

He slumped, turning his eyes from me. Took a shaky breath.

I thought about hugging him and begging his pardon, but instead I shook my head. "Hey," I said, trying to make my voice gentle. "Sometimes I get tired too."

"Tired of life?"

The irritation flashed back. Tired of you, I thought.

I huffed and turned back to the magazine, but forced myself to keep my voice gentle, not wanting to send him over the edge. "This isn't a good time."

Thunk went that arrow. He fought to his feet. "Yeah. Maybe you're right." He walked away. The glass door thumped shut behind him.

Thank God.

Two hours later, I went to my dorm to grab my books for Comp and check my e-mail on my computer, since my phone was dead.

Another Carter message, sent a couple of minutes ago. Yadda yadda – wait, WHAT THE HELL IS THIS.

Kathy –

I hope this act will release you of your obligation to me. It's too hard for me to go on in this way. I think about all the pain I've caused you and I think you will be glad to be able to move on.

This is not your fault. I know you will be happier without me so this is the best thing to do.

Good bye. I love you.

Carter

"What? What?" I cried.

I hope this act will release you of your obligation to me.

I called his room and his cell, jittering next to my desk. No answer.

Oh, great, so this was going to be a "Where's Carter" game.

I asked the computer, "So what do you expect of me? Am I supposed to find you? This is ridiculous!" My mind was whirling, so, logically, I let out an exasperated groan, grabbed my books and started walking to class, doing my best to ignore that part of me that was pinwheeling its arms and hollering WHAT ARE YOU GOING TO DO WHEN HE FOLLOWS THROUGH?

Ugh, what indeed? I thought as I headed out into the sea of students coming to and from class, walking on my tiptoes so I could scan the crowds.

I was 95 percent sure that Carter was playing me by raising the emotional ante beyond anything he'd done before. But *only* 95 percent. That other 5 percent was scaring the hell out of me.

Miracle of miracles, I spotted Carter walking across the commons toward the cafeteria. I gasped with relief, my legs going shaky. Well, this was his usual lunchtime, wasn't it? But then anger settled in, and I followed at a short distance, fuming. Mr. Manipulator. Put death aside for a little snack. Another part of me felt differently. I followed him inside.

I should be going to class! I raged, until I met his eyes in the lunch line. His set face shocked me – that flat, exhausted stare with an edge of contempt in the quirked corner of his mouth. I was grinning again, trying not to. I embraced him and started to cry. He held me, emotionless.

All the people in the lunch line were staring. Embarrassed, I tugged at his hand. "Come on." I led him upstairs, where all the empty conference rooms were, and found an armchair in the hallway. "What on earth is going on?"

Carter sank into the armchair and pulled out a bottle of sleeping pills. "I was going to take them at lunch," he said, his voice flat. "They wouldn't have noticed. They never notice."

I gawked until I got my head around what he was saying. "Why don't you see a counselor?"

"I'm sick of them." His hand holding the bottle sagged over the chair's armrest.

"But everything is on me! Just like --" Just like Wyatt said.

"Nobody else cares."

I pulled out my phone. I had the Suicide Prevention Lifeline on my phone from the night that Wyatt had given me their number. This seemed like a super-good time to do it.

I hit the on button. Again. The screen stayed black: My phone was dead as a rock.

Oh, great job, Kay! Way to think ahead.

"You really think some stranger is going to help?" he said, eyeing my phone, too tired to even sneer.

I had to pull him out of the abyss again. Why not. I was already down there in it with him.

I pocketed the phone and crawled into his lap. "You can't do this. I need you, your parents need you."

"You don't need me." His eyes refused to even acknowledge mine. "You're through with me, remember?"

"Your parents."

"Dad can go to hell."

"Your mom."

"Stop it. It's not going to work. I'm done."

We stopped talking. I cleaned out his shirt pocket so I could put my head down on his chest and found a playlist. What, were these songs for his funeral? I went cold. But then I actually read the song titles. "Vertigo," "Every Rose Has Its Thorn," "Shoots and Ladders," "For Those About to Rock." Hell of a funeral.

"What's this?"

He looked away. "Some songs I want to get for my music library."

After you die? But, as I'd been trained, I said nothing. I tucked it back into his pocket and put my head on his chest. His arms didn't move, refused to encircle me. His face was stone, as if a monolith sat in his place.

"I'm sorry you're angry at me."

"I'm not angry."

I sighed, raising my head. "Why don't you go to the Counseling Center with me? Please."

"I'm not going. I'm sick of psychologists."

"I can't do this. I can't save you."

"Then don't. Go off with Wyatt and let me kill myself."

I had to let it go. Yet I snapped, "I'm not with Wyatt."

He said nothing. Refused to look at me. Freezing me out.

I climbed out of his lap. "Please. Don't do this to yourself."

Still wouldn't look at me. The only way he'd come back was if I started crying and telling him that he was right and I was wrong, please don't kill yourself, please.

My heart started pounding with a strange, sideways motion, like it was squeezed in a vise. Carter stared at the ceiling, the pill bottle loose in his hand.

I lunged to my knees and snatched the bottle out of his hand.

"Hey!" He struggled out of his chair. "Dammit, give those back!"

I fought to my feet, those damn pills tight in my hand and my heart about to leap out of my chest at the look on his face. He wasn't emotionally distant anymore. "Um, these are bad for you? So, no?"

He grabbed for me. I half-screamed and lunged out of his reach, and then kept running because he was coming for me like a linebacker, and oh Jesus he was fast. I put my head down and flew down that hall, his heavy steps and breathing right behind me, close enough to where he could almost step on my heels. I rounded a corner and plowed into the wall, just barely leapt out of his way in time. His fingers brushed the back of my neck and my shirt yanked back, in his grip, nearly choking me. I made some kind of rattle in my throat and yanked away so hard that something the back of my shirt ripped, but I was free. With a weird despairing laugh I pulled away. He fell down with a thud I felt through the floor and an "oof!"

The women's restroom was ahead. I burst through the door so fast I was in a stall before the door slammed against the tile. I stood over the toilet, trying to open the pill bottle. My panting echoed off the walls. You damn child-proof cap! Stop clicking at me and just open!

Kay, for God's sake lock the door! I whirled but Carter filled the doorway, heaving for breath, face florid.

I shrieked and grabbed the stall door to shut it, but he was already there. The door bounced off his arm. He swore. I couldn't get back any farther. I started laughing, this weird laugh that had never come out of my mouth before.

"Do you think this is funny?" He grabbed my hand and squeezed. I hissed. With his other hand he tried to pull the bottle out of my hand.

I fought to hold on. "Ow, stop!"

"Let go!" he yelled, his voice at a roar in that echoing room.

I cowered, certain I'd feel his hand across my face. The hiss of the ocean filled my ears.

He opened the bottle, click click, no problem.

"No, don't!" I grabbed his arm but he shoved me aside. He shook pills into his hand, tossed them in his mouth, and stuck his face under the faucet, sucking down water.

Birds winged around my face, pinions striking me. I ran at him and slammed against his back. He pushed me back and dumped more in his mouth with a hateful glare and put his head under the faucet for another drink. Gave me that look, mouth and chin dripping water, as if he put a good one over on me. But something else was entering his face, an uncertainty. All around my head wheeled the birds, a great flock of them, not letting me think straight.

I burst out of the bathroom, hyperventilating, looking left and right. Where's the nearest phone? That's right, there's an office down the hall.

Before I could make my dash, Carter came out, looking worried. "Kathy?" he said in this scared little-boy voice.

"Where's your cell phone?"

"I ... I left it at home."

I sprinted faster than I'd ever run in my life. The birds flew straight as an arrow.

I dashed down the hall, around the corner. There, through the door of the office, I saw, on the corner of a desk, a telephone lit up by a stray sunbeam, all glittery and lovely. Oh wonderful phone, sent by God! Or Radio Shack. I burst into the office, startling the heck out of the student secretary. "Emergency, sorry." I grabbed the receiver.

And even now, when the dispatcher said, "911, what's your emergency?" I still hesitated, because even now, I was going to ruin his life by making this call. I had no right. But I pulled my head together and started talking.

Once the cops were on their way, I ran back to Carter, who was sitting on the floor by the bathroom, chest heaving, tears leaking from his eyes. The pill bottle lay at his feet. I kicked it. Nothing clattered out.

My insides were shaking like they were on spin cycle. How do you stop somebody from dying? Did I need to stick a finger down his throat? I shoved away the panic, shoved away the tears, and shook his shoulders. "Carter! Talk to me."

Carter's teary eyes opened right to mine. Looking relieved. "I'm sorry," he slurred, laying his head back against the wall. "It's for the best."

I knelt, held his face in my two hands, rested my forehead on his. "Please don't. Please."

He brought his hand up over mine, and now peace flooded his face. "It's okay. It's okay. Hannah's just up ahead. I'm gonna see her now. I miss her so much ...."

"No!" I shrieked. "No! Hannah wants you to stay here!"

His eyes closed. I pulled back, breathing hard. A wild idea flashed into my mind to smack him hard – *make him stay here!* – but instead I shook him. "Don't. You. Dare. Leave. Me."

Carter's eyes flitted open. Met mine with such love, which I did not deserve.

Except a sudden wave passed over his face, and he burped. A second wave passed up his body, and with a long "urrggh" he thrust his head forward … and threw up. I shrieked but couldn't jump back fast enough. The hot vomit splashed down my jeans, over my shoes, and the stink made me gag and cough.

Carter fell sideways, passing out into the pool of vomit he was still choking up. Hands shaking, I grabbed his shoulders and struggled unsuccessfully to pull his face out of it, just as boots came thundering up the stairs.

SIXTEEN
SOMEONE SAVED MY LIFE TONIGHT
ELTON JOHN

I'd been alone in the waiting room at the little hospital for about two hours. I had changed my clothes and washed up but I could still smell the vomit on myself. At this point, I wasn't really caring. I paced, a hand on the back of my neck. I smacked a rolled-up magazine against the furniture. I shut my eyes and tried to rest but the pictures behind my eyelids pushed me to my feet again.

How long did it take to pump out a stomach? Was he dying? Was he already dead?

SHUT UP. SHUT UP. SHUT UP.

I got to my feet. Rubbed my hands over my face.

I stared at my reflection in the black window. I had my coat on; I hadn't taken it off since I'd been at the hospital. My hair floated around my head, a victim of static. My reflection was wavery and faint like a ghost, superimposed on the night.

A movement reflected from behind me. I turned. Carter's mom Stella stood in the doorway. Not the friendly mom I'd met in Omaha. Eyes like she was firing up the photon torpedoes.

Oh, no. No no.

"Save it. He's fine," she said.

I sagged back against the windowsill. "Can I see him?"

She jerked her head to the side – come on – and I followed.

When we reached a room on the third floor, a guy wearing a nice black overcoat, snow still on his shoulders, turned to see us, shiny black shoes squeaking slightly from the wet on them. Carter's dad, I knew instantly, though I'd never met him in person. When he saw me, his eyes were like headlights. "Are you the little girl who did this to my son?"

"Um ... um ...."

"Nice to see you too, Bill," Stella said curtly, her hand now on my shoulder. I didn't dare breathe or blink.

"God, what's that smell?" he asked, wrinkling his nose.

But I was looking only at Carter, pale in the hospital bed. Eyes half-open, staring straight ahead. A chill shot through me. For a second I thought he was dead.

Stella went to Carter's bedside. "How dare you come here. After all you put him through." She jerked an open hand at Carter. "So you stood by and watched him do this?"

I gasped. "No, no, no! Look, I took the bottle from him. But he wrestled it out of my hands." I thrust out my hands, which still hurt from Carter's rough attention, but realized to my consternation that no tell-tale bruises showed. "I tried to flush the pills down the toilet. He was trying to ..." *manipulate me,* but I couldn't say that to his mom.

"Well, maybe he wouldn't have done anything if you hadn't been toying with him!" Stella's hands were tight on the bed's rail. She leaned over Carter, her glare like a punch to my gut. "For four months you've been treating him like this. And then you ask him if he's all right. Seems like you bear a lot of the blame."

Yes I do!

No I don't!

"There's a lot of things that he's not telling you," I croaked. The world hissed around me.

Bill, who had been staring at me the whole time, broke in. "Stop crying. You're not hurt."

I snapped my head up, aghast.

"Don't listen to her," Bill told Stella. "She's just some hysterical little girl trying to get attention for herself. This bid for attention isn't going to work, you know," he told me.

What the! How was this my fault!

Even though part of me was sure he was right.

Stella ignored him, her voice going rattlesnake-deadly. "Carter told me how he wanted to marry you someday. He trusted you ...."

She stopped because her face was struggling. She turned her cheek toward me, pressed a fist against her mouth, eyes clenched shut, chest heaving. Her mouth opened. Air burst into her lungs with a yelp. She started sobbing against her fist, awful cries that tore at my heart.

Carter didn't respond. His dad stepped back, hands in front: keep your distance.

Stella looked at me, her face like a horrible Greek mask. I'm sure my face looked the same. She turned toward me.

I ran to her. We threw our arms around each other. For one awful moment we cried together.

Then Stella jerked away and said in this awful cracked voice, "Get out." So I did.

The rest of Thursday, as well as Friday, Saturday, and Sunday was a train wreck with the tracks all torn up and twisted metal everywhere. Carter didn't call. No e-mails, nothing. At the hospital his room was empty and the nurse said she wasn't allowed to disclose his status.

As I studied, or tried to, I kept glancing at the phone. It was Self-Castigation Night at my dorm. So much guilt that my eyes kept sliding down the text without registering. Rage so strong at Carter that it would drive me into the winter night, walking fast, hands deep in my coat pockets. Which faded as quickly as it came into grief at the suffering he was going through. Then right back to the guilt.

I didn't know what to do. I just didn't know what to do anymore – if there was anything that I could do.

On Sunday night I heard a knock on the doorframe behind me. I turned. Carter stood there, eyes filled with love.

Oh my goodness. He was okay. I ran to him, nearly knocking my chair over. We squeezed each other tight.

Carter shut the door and gave me a long kiss. "You love me. You wouldn't have saved my life if you didn't love me."

And all the crappy feelings crawled back into my heart and went around sliming everything. "Where were you?"

"Dad pulled a few strings and got me out of the hospital. It was a mistake. I shouldn't have been in there in the first place."

"What?" My voice wheezed like an accordion that had been stepped on.

"Then I went to Mom's house. We went shopping at the mall. I helped her make supper, and we sat around watching TV. Went out for breakfast. We had a pretty good time."

"A good time? How'd you manage that?"

Carter, studying my face, turned serious. "Oh, you mean my little hospital visit. No, I was fine. Mom was real glad to have me over."

I heard again his mom's awful yelp as she started to cry. I pushed out of the embrace. "You act as though it didn't bother you to try and kill yourself in front of me. Whereas I am deeply disturbed."

Carter started to say something, but changed his mind. "I told you. Nobody cared," he said, his voice hard. "I was in a lot of pain and I couldn't take it anymore. Get it through your head, Kathy. You think I'm a monster. You think I'm doing this to hurt you. I'm not. *I'm* the one who's hurting, Kathy. *I'm* the one who's in pain. And if I get rid of myself, you don't have to deal with me anymore."

"I don't know, Carter," I said dully. "That's a heck of a way to do it."

"You'll be happier."

"Not if you killed yourself. Besides, you sure wouldn't be happy."

He sighed, a defeated sound. "Sure I would. I'd be dead. Better than dealing with this. Sometimes I see you and it helps me get through the day, you know? But sometimes, like when you're cruel to me, I can't deal with it."

"But what about me?" I burst out. "I have to deal with you doing this to me – how do you think that feels? When I work so hard to try and save you, and then you just throw this into my face – do you really think I'm that heartless?"

"Oh, God, Kathy, I don't. You matter so much to me." He wrapped me in his arms. "Don't you know how much it tears me up to see you like this?"

"Then why don't ....?" I began, but a huge breaker of confusion swamped my brain, and all I could do was sputter. But I held him tight.

"You're right. I feel so rotten, doing this to you. But I can't help it. You're all I have to hold on to. My mom, my family, my friends, are so far away. You're all I have. Haven't you ever felt this way?"

My sight cleared. Because hell yeah. I was feeling this way right now. But I'd never, never, *never* demanded that Wyatt save me from my despair.

"So are you going to try again?" I asked him.

Carter looked spent, as if he'd been in a long race and lost. "I don't know. But if I'm in a lot of pain, then yes, I might."

I pressed my fists together. "Wait a minute. I gotta go to the bathroom."

Alone in the bathroom, I leaned over the sink and glared at myself in the mirror.

"This is what I really want to tell you," I hissed. "Even if you were in a lot of pain, what you did was wrong. I'm sick at myself for letting you get away with it. And I'm sick at you for manipulating me like this. You're in pain and I'm sorry about that. But that doesn't give you the right to transfer your pain into me."

I wanted to slam my fist into the mirror, a sledgehammer blow that would send shards flying.

But I held my fist in my hand, tight, working my palm against the knuckles.

"I have to stop being afraid. I have to leave you. I know you're going to hit me with another suicide attempt when I do. And this attempt is going to be a heck of a lot worse. Because now you know what you have to take to succeed."

I thought of how I felt about Wyatt, as if a gap were missing from my soul that made me frantic. That's how Carter felt about me.

I rubbed my hands over my face, shaking off the voice. Met my eyes in the mirror.

"Look, I never ran after Wyatt. I never forced him to love me. I never asked Wyatt to sacrifice himself for me. I would think you could do me the courtesy of behaving the same way."

My rage was still there, but now it was tempered with determination.

"So I'm going to leave you. It scares me. But I can't live the way Grandma did. There are alternatives. They just ain't very pretty."

I got right up against the mirror, so close I could see my pores and the laugh lines around my eyes, so close that my nose smudged the glass. Me and I looked at each other.

She was kind of ungainly-looking this close. Nose a little big, face a little plain. But I kind of liked her. I wanted her to be all right.

I wrinkled my nose in a secret smile, as if at a conspirator, and returned to my room.

After Carter went home, I felt like a wrung-out dishcloth, but I sat down at my laptop.

· · ·

Hey Yvonne.

I need some help. My boyfriend tried to commit suicide. I think he did it to make me stay with him. I have to leave him. But I don't know how.

I don't want to freak you out. But I don't know what to do.

I hit send and lay my head on my desk.

My computer quacked.

k!

good to hear from u!!!!!!!

*im SO SORRY. hes emotionally blackmailing you, using whats most precious to u to get his way. its a kind of abuse. it shouldn't b tolerated! *hugs**

the goddess is booked 2night (music theory class) or else she'd come rt over.

but she wants u 2 google "my boyfriend wants to kill himself."

DO IT DO IT DO IT.

she has some personal experience with this.

y

p.s. if i was freaked out you'd know it

"Okay," I said. It hadn't occurred to me that I could Google it. But emotional blackmail? That was a new one.

But a trembling started up when I Googled "my boyfriend will kill himself if I break up with him." (Auto-add suggested the second part.)

129 million results. I began scrolling through them.

I can't leave him. Do you know how selfish it would be to leave him now, when he's suffering so much?

. . .

I spent night after night trying to make him feel better and begging him not to kill himself.

He tells me over and over again that I'm the only one who can save him.

I can't live with the burden if he kills himself.

So many people saying that they felt like it would be selfish to leave. So many people saying that they can't help but feel responsible for their significant other's well-being.

And so many more people trying to help them.

He's manipulating you and it's working. He's turned your relationship into a hostage situation.

Whoa. I leaned forward, staring at the screen. Was that true?

Please call the authorities. My ex ended up shooting himself in front of me. This is not something you should handle alone, whatever he tells you.

He doesn't want you to be happy. He wants to keep you guilt ridden, hanging on his every word, trying to talk him down. It's working, too. He is abusing your kind heart and gentle nature.

. . .

*You expect people to respect your boundaries. These guys? They don't **want** you to have boundaries. They steamroll right across them. As far as they're concerned, you are only a part of them.*

Even if he is bluffing, the fact that he's toying with your wellbeing is inexcusable and not something a well-balanced person should do.

By staying, you're not helping him. He will not get better as long as he can use you as a crutch.

Please get the police involved.

This is pretty much a straightforward attempt at gaslighting. He minimizes abuse, downplays whatever circumstances led to your restraining order, minimizes his transparent attempts at manipulation, and polishes everything off with a plea for sympathy.

Gaslighting. That was a new one on me. I'd look it up in a little bit – right now I was too fascinated, too amazed at how my whole mind was being turned upside down by all this new information. I kept reading.

Healthy relationships include breaking things and threats of suicide, right?

I never called 911 because I didn't want to ruin his life. I wish I'd done it sooner, before he ruined mine.

.   .   .

So let's say you stay with him. You spend the rest of your life chained to someone you don't want to be with. In time you will start to hate him. Nobody wins.

RUN! Before he sucks you into his vortex of evil.

If my partner broke up with me, I'd be devastated. I'd cry, drink a lot, and maybe leave him a sorrowful rambly message on his phone. But would I threaten to kill myself over this? Oh hell no.

To repeat – suicide is NEVER committed out of love.

My God. I wasn't crazy at all.

All this time I thought I was wrong. That I was the bad guy. That I brought this all on myself.

Yvonne texted back: *i want to talk to u abt this but i'm stuck here til 9 ... sorry!*

That was okay. I needed some time to read all this and let this new view of my world sink in. It was a LOT for me to handle. Even though I understood it – part of me still rebelled. Those charges against him were too severe! Unjust!

And – this doesn't mean I have to abandon Carter, does it?

I sat back in my chair, still staring at the screen. Ah, there lies the rub. Because I couldn't just turn my back on Carter like that, after all I'd sacrificed so much of myself to save him.

You don't just turn your back on a friend. Ever. Especially one who's in so much pain.

. . .

It's wrong for you to give your man false hope by trying to let him down easy. If you are going to end it, end it. Don't keep leading him on.

I read that one over and over. Had I been leading him on? No! Not … not intentionally.

So, he's learned that he can control others by upping the ante emotionally.

"I did nothing wrong!" my boyfriend said every time he did something wrong.

A suicide threat during an argument is ALWAYS a bid for control.

"But is it?" I asked the screen. "What if he's hurting so much he can't help it?"

When my boyfriend broke up with me, I cried for weeks and weeks and sunk into depression. Funny thing, it didn't occur to me to threaten him with my suicide. I guess that means I never really loved him. Which, actually, is a relief, because he was a dick.

From my experience, I have threatened suicide many times when he threatened to leave, but I'm still alive! Most abusers do this as a way to continue to control you! Your husband sees you're not going to put up with it anymore and feels weak! The only way he can regain control is by threatening suicide! Do NOT fall for it! Tell a professional or a family member of your husband's what is happening.

• • •

These guys are experts in not taking responsibility for their own actions, in downplaying the harm they do, and in projecting blame onto others. The stories they tell are heavily edited, revisionist histories.

Bzzt! Yvonne texted me again.

i went out with this guy in HS. he <3 me so much. i wasn't crazy about him. hadn't come out of the closet yet. he was driving me home. i said i had 2 break up w/him. he got so mad he drove the car off the road. both of us in it.

What!! I texted back.

one of those live & learn moments.

It's strange, I texted. *I thought that I was the only one in this situation.*

not at all my dear. we r the wronged women & we r legion.

My phone was quiet for a while. I went on scrolling through posts. Once in a while you'd see a troll, but overall people were concerned, wanted to help. I could not believe how many of them had been through the same problems that I was neck-deep in right now.

A relationship with a borderline is ALWAYS fraught with drama, manipulative sob stories, general crazy making. I should know. Ugh.

That man broke something in my empathy file.

The problem was not with his girlfriend. The problem was with HIM not taking the hint: Dude, this relationship is soooooo over.

Are you sure that you, the girlfriend, are not concerned that maybe if you leave, he'll get along just fine without you. Do you stay because you like the feeling of being needed?

. . .

I made myself read that last one a couple of times.

You believe you deserve this treatment. You're a good girl that doesn't want others to think badly of you — you want love and validation from others because you can't get it from yourself.

I read that one over and over as well. Take your medicine, Kay.

He's very good at persuading people he's the victim — and did a good job of convincing me of it, too.

They do everything they can to control your self-image — they make you feel inferior, like you can't solve your own problems, and make you feel like you screw up all the time.

He'd call me begging for help, crying, and I'm listening in my bed and I wouldn't know what to do. I felt like I had to go comfort him because there was no one else to help him get through the pain.

The Centers for Disease Control and Prevention say that occurrences of intimate-partner violence, rape, or stalking takes place mainly before age 25. This happens to both men and women alike.

My father frequently told my mother he intended to kill himself. After she died, however, he admitted that he never considered it. He said that he threat-

*ened suicide only because he wanted her, and us, under his thumb. The manip-
ulation took its toll, and we no longer have a relationship.*

*It's easy to mistake this kind of abuse for the exact opposite emotion —
undying devotion. He loves you so much that he can't spend a minute away
from you. A whirlwind "romance" is also a hallmark of these relationships.*

*A lot of people make lightweight remarks about how the victims should have
known better. But abuse is otherworldly and deeply frightening. If you've never
had your whole world on tilt, you don't truly understand what it's like to be
there.*

Some fears mark your soul for life.

Bzzt! A text from Carter.

    missing you. come over?

    Later, I texted back grimly. *I have business to conduct.*

SEVENTEEN
SOMETIMES YOU CAN'T MAKE IT ON YOUR OWN
U2

The next morning at breakfast, I read an article about emotional blackmail on my phone as I ate my cereal.

Threatening suicide is a powerful form of emotional blackmail. In threatening suicide, the abuser takes a simple argument and turns it into a life-or-death situation – and they do this only to get their way.

Emotional blackmailers know what is most important to you, and they use this knowledge to control you. *Don't leave me or I'll kill myself.* Or they might say, *If you leave me, I'll take the kids and you will never see them again.* If you give in, they reward you with loving intimacy. If you tell them no, they dump a world of guilt on your head.

Remember: emotional blackmail is ALWAYS a type of emotional abuse.

Emotional abuse.

I looked over at Carter. He stood in the serving line, hand on his tray, chatting with the gray-haired serving lady over the reconstituted eggs. She said something and they both laughed and she served him a dollop of eggs.

How could you imagine him as an emotional abuser? One part of me railed. That's stupid. He's never hit you. He never screamed at your or called you names. And he's never made rude comments about you in front of others.

But yet, but yet ….

Carter, carrying his tray, sat down next to me. He took an extra glass of chocolate milk off his tray and set it down next to my cereal. "There you go."

That was nice of him. "Thanks," I said, X-ing out of my window on my phone so he wouldn't see the article.

Carter talked about this TV show that he'd watched last night, "but I really wish you'd been there to watch it with me." I let that slide as I pretended to listen.

I'd read so much last night. Emotional blackmail, the term Yvonne had used, really hit the target. Threatening suicide in order to control me. Jesus.

There were some other terms that kind of fit. People kept talking about borderlines, or Borderline Personality Disorder, in a lot of those stories. I read about gaslighting, which was where a person would start making you doubt your own mind by subtly changing their story. And that seemed way over the top when applied to Carter.

But then again, when I'd read some of his old emails in this new light, I noticed that he would often change the narrative on me. There was one email where I told him we'd broken up once every month since September – and I knew this because I'd written about each event in my journal. He wrote back and said that those weren't breakups at all. Then he went on this long spiel about what a breakup actually was and how those times where I said "I am breaking up with you" were not actually breakups.

So was that gaslighting? But that was such a minor quibble, wasn't it?

I sighed and drank my chocolate milk. Well, it's not like reading a bunch of Wikipedia entries makes me a mental health expert.

"Haven't we broken up?" I asked as I jabbed my fork into my eggs. "I mean, we're still acting the same as we did when we were together."

He didn't seem perturbed. "We're friends. Friends eat breakfast together, don't they?"

And it was interesting how he would redefine the word "friend" in whatever way suited him.

Escaping sounded awesome, but a huge exhaustion settled over me at the amount of energy I was going to have to spend on the subsequent drama.

After lunch I went to Wind Symphony. As I was walking down the sidewalk to class, the snow blowing around me, my phone rang. Carter.

"Can you skip class?" he asked, his voice dull.

A leaden winter sky hung low over the snowy town. I steeled myself. "No. I'm sorry."

"I need you. I know I shouldn't think about how bad I feel, but all I can think about is how you want to leave me. I'm scared, Kathy."

This was the first time I'd realized this: That everything he did, and I mean *everything*, was done to keep me from leaving him. So how much leverage was he willing to use if I followed through?

I hoped he mistook my sigh as a gust of cold winter wind blowing over the phone. I pushed the glass doors open and was met by the delicious sound of the Wind Symphony warming up. "I am too. But I can't keep skipping classes. Dr. Byrd would kill me." Actually she wouldn't, but it was so important to be a part of her class – any of them, actually, I grumped.

Carter sighed. "I don't want to bother you. I'm sorry."

That sigh oozed through the phone, into my ear, down over my brain as I went into the instrument room.

And hello, there was Yvonne, waving at me. "Hey! … whoa, you talking to your boyfriend?"

I didn't even want to think about what was on my face. "Sorry, Carter. I gotta go." I hung up just as he started to say something else. Crap, I was going to hear about that later. "Yeah." I switched the phone to silent, pocketed it, and opened the bass case.

She shut her trumpet case with a smart click. "I'm sorry I couldn't come over last night. Dr. Moser teaches my music theory class. If you skip, she'll write a song about you and sing it to the class."

"Seriously?"

"Yeah. Once I missed class because I was out with a cold, and when I came back she sang this ditty about how I'd been kidnapped by aliens because they needed a supply of snot."

"That sounds … interesting …."

"Do you want to talk after Symphony?" she asked as we went into the bandroom. "Go to the coffeeshop again? I haven't seen you much lately."

"I don't know." I felt like I was cheating on Carter, even though going to a coffeeshop with a friend was something that normal people did. I didn't want to go back to Carter's room and spend the whole afternoon there, crying my head off. But I was, for no reason, a little bit mad at Yvonne, though I wasn't sure why. "Nah. Maybe later."

"Let me know if you change your mind," Yvonne said.

I put the reed on my tongue with its sharp wooden taste, and headed for my seat. Dr. Byrd was standing on the podium joking with one of the French horns as everybody warmed up. She always started promptly at 1, "because if you think this promptness is unnecessary, wait until you join the musician's union."

As I passed the concert grand that had been pushed off to the side, I ran my fingers over the keys as I always did.

You and Arden, always hanging around a piano, Grandma had said. *Sometimes I would see you two at the piano, and I'd worry.*

You'd worry ... that I'd turn out like Grandpa?

Nooooo. Of course not.

I stopped dead.

My eyes got wide.

I pressed my hand into the keys, gently, so they wouldn't sound. I couldn't move, swamped by a realization that hit my brain and flipped everything I'd known upside down.

Grandma had not been worried about me turning out like Grandpa. No.

She'd been worried that I would turn out like *her*.

Dr. Byrd raised her eyebrows at me. Whoops. I hurried back to my seat, slipped the reed under the ligature, and ran a few quick scales into the lovely cacophony just as Bayo, the oboist, stood up and played concert A.

Even though we were working on Holst's *Second Suite*, which was one of my favorite pieces in the world, I couldn't keep my mind on the music.

I'd turned into my own grandma. I was scuttling from place to place like a fugitive, hiding from someone whose love I no longer could accept, just the way she did, years and years ago. All those alternate routes I used to get to class, all those hidey-holes I had around campus when I didn't want Carter to find me. And yet I'd write him all these emails, pretending nothing was wrong, writing to him like everything was sunshine and roses, because I was so afraid of setting him off. I wanted so much to make this work – but not for myself. I was doing this because I had to keep Carter alive, and if I didn't play by his rules, he'd punish me by killing himself.

How on earth did anybody ever manage to get free? Carter and I were going to be on this campus together for the next four years. How on earth was I going to deal with Carter for the next four years?

Grandma never really did get free of Grandpa, did she? Not until he died.

After Symphony, I met Yvonne in the instrument room. "I

changed my mind," I said as I carried my bass in. "I do want to go to the coffeeshop. I just … realized something." Shamefaced, I looked at my phone and found 10 texts from Carter. Here we go again.

"Yay!" she said, sliding her trumpet case onto its shelf. "I'm happy to … Kay? Kay?"

I was staring at Carter's texts, mouth agape.

Ive been thinking about Hannah
  when I found her in the pool

Oh God. I very gently set down my bass and picked up my phone in both shaking hands.

I went outside to the pool b/c it was time to eat
  I said come on its time to eat. Get in here.
  It was really quiet in the pool. I opened the gate and went in
  And saw her in the water I thought she was playing a trick pretending
  I said you aint fooling me and jumped into the water and grabbed her
ankles.
  She hated when I grabbed her ankls
  I knew right away what happened as soon as I touched her.
  Kathy, I need you so bad. I cant wait. Im coming to meet you aft. class.

Oh God.

Yvonne said, "Kay? Is something the matter?"

I grabbed my blue scarf, ready to rocket away without an explanation. But I drew a breath and forced myself to stop. "I have to cancel, sorry. I need to go help Carter." I might have said that with a tiny bit of exasperation, though I didn't mean to. I handed her the phone. "Hannah's his sister." I rubbed my face and leaned against the wall, because the image of the little girl in the pool was making me lightheaded.

"Wow," Yvonne said softly, scrolling through. "I'm sorry. He's really applying the screws to you, isn't he?"

Harsh, are we? I lifted the phone out of her hands, turned my back to her with a motion that belled out my overcoat, and strode toward the door.

But I'd only taken three steps when I made myself stop and turn back to her, shamefaced. "Sorry. I know perfectly well why he sent those texts. But ... he's never talked about Hannah before. I still need to go to him."

Yvonne lowered her face as she reached into her hair and readjusted a silver clip. "Yeah. I knew I shouldn't've said that. It just popped out. God! I wish I could disguise myself as you and go in your place. You know? I mean, my ex-boyfriend did the exact same thing to me after he ran the car off the road."

I looked down the hall through the milling crowd of musicians, thespians, and art students. "Carter's not a bad guy, is he?" I said plaintively.

Yvonne relented. "He's a super-nice guy. Personally, if I had no idea what you were going through, I would like him a lot. He just happens to have this huge character flaw, and I'm sorry, but because of what he's doing to you, he really pisses me off." She wrapped her scarf around her neck and zipped up her fleece. "Those men! Just thinking about the way they treat you – and me – gaah! I gotta get out of here or I'm going to break something. I would still like it if you went to the coffeehouse with me."

I was surprised Carter wasn't here yet. Maybe I'd have enough time to drag Yvonne out of one of my alternate routes before he showed up. I'd taken to going clear to the back entrance in the art side so I could get out without Carter catching me.

Except just then he came in through the front door. He didn't even stop to stomp the snow off his shoes the way he normally did, but came right up the hall toward us, face grim. He wore a black overcoat, Dockers, nice shirt. Among all the art students he looked like a CEO lost in Greenwich Village.

I gripped Yvonne's arm as if she were the one who wanted to bolt. "I could use a cup of good tea."

Carter spotted me and his face melted into relief. "Oh my God, Kathy, I'm so glad to see you." He sprang to me, scooped me up, and spun me around. I held on to his neck, whee! surprised out of my fear, and laughed with him. I was flattered that he did this in front of my friend. But sad. I gave him a squeeze when he set me down.

Yvonne piped, "So, Kay, is this your boyfriend?"

What snark! I just about fainted.

"Of course I am." Carter's hurt eyes flashed to mine.

Even worse!

Yvonne smiled. "I thought you two had broken up."

Carter pulled away. "Kathy and I have a very special relationship." A hint of *this is none of your business* crept into his voice.

"I see," Yvonne said, her black eyes crinkled with mirth. She shot a quick look at me.

My hands fluttered. I folded them. "Yvonne and I were going to head out for a little bit and talk."

Carter wrapped his hand around my shoulder. "Okay. Let's go." Yvonne frowned; Carter's smile brightened.

Oh, shoot. "I mean – oh, I'm sorry. I mean – I know you walked all this way, but I was just going to go out with Yvonne for a while. By ourselves. I'll catch up with you later. If that's all right."

Hm, my ability to make a straightforward statement has apparently gone all to hell.

Not that it mattered, because as the meaning gradually came out, Carter's grin faded and faded and faded and vanished.

"Kathy, didn't you get my texts? Didn't you read them?" He searched my face and saw my answer there. He started to speak, noticed Yvonne standing a little too close, and lowered his voice.

"That's why I need you to come over. I can't go through this alone."

Aaaaaand this is the part where he applies the pressure.

Except Yvonne cut through all that back and forth like a shark. "To be honest, Carter, I don't see where it's going to hurt you to let her do her own thing for once."

Yikes! The only times I'd seen the color drain that fast from Carter's face were the times I'd end up staying with him for hours afterwards, crying and explaining that I really didn't mean it and I was sorry.

Yvonne just rolled her eyes. "Come on, Kay, let's go."

When Yvonne walked away, I joined her, plunging my shaking hands deep in my coat pockets. As soon as we got out the front door, I asked, "Was that necessary?" under my breath as we went out the front door and down the sidewalk.

She just about spoke, but paused when the sound of crunching snow rose behind me. "You should ask, 'Was it enough?' because the answer would be 'no.'"

And then Carter's hands rested on my shoulders from behind. He tried to get between us as we walked but Yvonne, apparently, was determined not to cede him any sidewalk space. "Kathy. Please. I can't help this," he murmured in my ear. "I need you and I'm scared to be alone. I'm afraid I might do something to myself."

I stopped on the sidewalk and turned to face Carter. Yvonne came back and stood just behind my right side, vibrating with impatience – the way my mom used to stand behind me when Grandpa and I were playing piano. I sensed the woman with the sword in the back of my mind, waiting. I hated them both.

Carter, visibly relieved, gathered both my hands in his. "I'll make it worth your while."

And Grandpa would play "Paper Doll" and wink at me.

My heart sped up. I cut my eyes away. "Later."

Carter shot a glance at Yvonne, who had her arms crossed. His face looked worn, the way it had when he was in the hospital. "You're busy. Don't let me get in your way."

I nearly said, *I'm sorry,* but caught the words before they could squeak out. "I'll call you. Okay?"

"Yeah. Right." Carter squeezed my hand so tight it hurt, his eyes moving over my face as if caressing something he might never see again. He dropped it and walked away.

The jangly feeling started up in my chest. The worst part wasn't when he tried to kill himself. It was the suspense. Wondering when it was going to happen. Wondering if I would be the one to find him.

I wondered if Grandma had ever watched Grandpa walk away like that. If she'd thought those same thoughts. *He put the bottle to his head and pulled the trigger.*

Yvonne brisk-walked away. "He's hard to shake, isn't he?"

I followed, my heart too full to talk, wriggling my fingers to get the hurt out.

"You're aware that he considers you his property."

"Really? I couldn't tell." And now it was Yvonne's turn to look like a chastened child.

"Have you ever called the police on him?"

"Yeah. The last time I did, his dad sprung him out of psychiatric care after only 24 hours."

Yvonne was aghast. "OMG. Are you serious?"

"If I called again, he'd just get sprung. And then, what if his dad got tired of me calling the police on his little boy and put a cease and desist thingy out against me? or some kind of lawsuit? Because he's rich, he can do that. Me, I'm not exactly rolling in the dough here."

We walked under the crabapples that surrounded Salmen Hall. Snow sifted down from their branches, dusting us.

I remembered Wyatt squeezing my arm in the library the day I fell in love with him. How vulnerable his face became when he looked down at the page of his almanac. How upset he'd been when

I turned him down at Paducah's. How he'd listened to me when I crawled back asking for help. Yet the memories no longer called up any feeling up inside my heart. My heart was dead.

Each branch and twig of the crabapples wore a cap of snow that followed their contours exactly, drawing white lines against the sky. The sap that made the trees blossom was frozen inside those barren limbs. The satin blossoms were packed inside tiny buds that had forgotten the touch of the sun.

♬

"So are you done with your snarky Asian friend?" Carter said when I walked into his dorm after supper.

He was still okay. Thank God. I put my coat over the back of his desk chair and unwound my blue scarf. "I'm sorry about that. I wasn't happy about the way she talked to you, either. But her race doesn't have anything to do with that."

Carter was lying on the bed, watching TV in his nice plaid lounge pants and a University of St. Francis T-shirt that featured the saint wearing sunglasses and giving a peace sign. "What was up her ass? You saw her. Acting like I was some kind of criminal."

"Hey. Don't talk about my friends like that. And turn off that dang TV. That thing is the bane of my existence."

He did, tossing the remote onto the side table, where it knocked over … a bottle of sleeping pills.

I went still, my blue scarf in my hands. "What's that doing there?"

"That's where I keep my remote, derp."

"No. Those pills."

He tossed them a glance as if they didn't even register. "They're supposed to help me sleep, because this floor is so noisy. But when I wake up the next morning I don't feel like I've slept at all."

"Give those things to me."

Genuine irritation flashed into his face. "Why do you want them?"

He knew full well why. "You don't remember that little incident where you took a bunch of them right in front of me? You know, just last week."

He swung his legs over the side of the bed. "Are you still on that?"

"Only because you seem to be intent on repeating it."

"What's wrong with you? You think I'm some kind of psycho freak? If I'd really intended anything, then they would have made me stay in the hospital for a week."

There were so many things wrong with this statement that I swear my brain melted. I pulled out his desk chair and slowly wrapped my scarf around my hands so I wouldn't have to look at him.

He went on. "Do you really think that some idiots in a hospital will get me the help I need? I've already had to go through that hell once. I am not going to do it again. If you turn me in, you're going to ruin my life."

"Fine, fine," I snapped. "Just leave off."

I glared at Carter, who shook his head. I looked away. He got up, sighed, and closed the blinds. "I know you're worried about me. I'm sorry. But I don't need outside help. Okay?"

A feeling of doom settled over me. "Do you really see us getting married?" I asked.

That had been a rhetorical question, but Carter's face lit up before I could say more. He came over to me and knelt down before me, his face glowing. "It's what I want more than anything."

Yeah. Like my face when I looked upon Wyatt.

I wasn't reflecting that joy back, and he saw it, and the joy in his eyes started to fade. Thinking of the sleeping pills right on his dresser, of the depth charge that his suicide attempt sent through me, I pulled him to me and kissed him before he could start talking. He was fine with that, from the force of his return liplock. He liked

198 MELINDA R. CORDELL

making out. I am sure that he didn't like that I insisted we keep our clothes on during our makeout sessions. Oh well! I wasn't doing this for his benefit.

Give him just enough to make him happy.

Later, I walked home alone, my blue scarf wrapped around my head and neck. The stars shivered in the cold wind. Orion stood in the southern sky with the Seven Sisters and Taurus and the Dog Star. Venus had already set. I took a roundabout route to avoid the streetlamps so I could enjoy the stars. Even though it was too cold for attackers, I kept my ears open and my keys laced between my fingers, deep in my overcoat pocket.

So how much longer are you going to stay with Carter? I asked myself. Do you really plan to marry him?

My sigh came out as a billow of vapor, briefly obscuring the stars. I was trying to get serious about leaving Carter, though okay, if I ended up in a makeout session in his room, I wasn't being serious enough. Now he thought I was his again. My heart sank.

"Wyatt said he'd wait for me," I said aloud.

So why do you keep putting Wyatt aside for someone you don't really love? How long is it going to take for you to live your own life and maybe get your heart back?

The winter stars shone cold and sharp. There was an edge to the cold that smelled like snow, and the lightest of breezes touched my upturned face.

"What's the one thing you can do to let Carter know it's over for good?" I asked aloud.

Oh, I knew the answer to that one.

I thought the past few weeks had been filled with drama. Guess what, now it's going to be the Soap Opera Wrestlemania of drama.

Because Wyatt would be in play.

I took out my phone.

The wind had stopped whispering the snow around, and the world was still in the grainy half-dark, with all the streetlights creating their white-orange glow in the air and the clouded night above. Quiet flakes drifted down, touching my eyelashes and nose with their friendly cold taps, settling their silence over the land.

Both of them I loved, but both loves were so different. It was hard for me to be alone – how much more difficult it would be for Carter. He would say I'd betrayed him. So be it.

I hurried up to my room where I shut the door behind me, and, not bothering to turn on the light, my hand shaking, I dialed Wyatt's number, which I had memorized ages ago.

Dialing this number was not as easy as it sounded. My mind was filled with all the things that could go wrong. Maybe he'd see my name come up and not answer. Or maybe Wyatt would get annoyed that I was bothering him. Or we'd go out, and I'd do something that would screw up our relationship forever.

Or I'd find Carter's body ....

Before I finished dialing, my phone lit up. Carter.

I was going to have to take this new relationship way underground if I was going to be in it at all.

I waited forever for him to go to voicemail. Then, with my final gasp of courage, I punched the last number.

It rang. And rang. And ....

"Hello?" Wyatt's warm chocolate voice.

I gripped the phone so hard that it beeped. My knees took a vacation. I thumped into my chair, hugging myself, my insides buzzing like a beehive. "Hello?" I squeaked.

"Hello?"

"Hello."

"Are you going to talk or are we going to greet each other the rest of the evening?"

"Do you know who this is?" I squinched my eyes shut.

"Of course I do. It's Kay, isn't it? My favorite customer in sporting goods." A note of genuine pleasure in his voice. Went straight to my heart.

I swallowed. "Yes. Yes. It's me. I'm not calling at a bad time, am I?"

"Not at all. I was just thinking about you and hoping you were all right."

"Oh, man." How amazing it was that he was thinking about me. "I'm fine. Well, actually, no, I'm not fine. There's a reason I called you." I had to take a breath. "My boyfriend tried to commit suicide last weekend."

A stunned silence from Wyatt. "That bastard."

"I keep trying to break up with him but each time he goes off the deep end." I sighed, suddenly realizing how stupid this sounded. "Can you help me? I need some moral support. I don't think I can get away from him on my own."

"Oh, hell yes I can help you. I'd do anything for you."

Tears started running down my face.

"Do you want to meet in person, so we can talk face-to-face?"

A spasm of joy hit my heart, fading almost immediately into anxiety. Everything I knew about love, I associated with Carter. Part of me cringed away from starting a new relationship, while part of me was over the moon that FINALLY I'd meet Wyatt outside of Paducah's! "Could we meet tomorrow night? Is that too soon?"

"Let me look at my schedule." A little rustle of papers on Wyatt's end. "Yeah, that'll work. We could meet at Polly-Eye's Pizza in St. Francis if you're cool with that." What tenderness. "By the way … you realize this would qualify as a date, don't you?"

"Don't call it that." Panic rose in my chest. "This whole love thing scares the bejesus out of me. Love has treated me like an old shoe."

"Well, then, call it an e-tad."

"E-tad? What the heck is that?"

"It's just "date" spelled backwards."

I put my head in my hand with a short laugh. "You have a heck of a way of instilling confidence in a girl. But it's working."

As we talked, and talked, I paced my room, sat on the floor, lay on my bed. His voice was warm and tender, and only for me. I felt as if a current moved between us, and it made my heart look up in surprise. As if we were saying, in roundabout ways, "I love you." And though it was too soon, I found my voice expressing that love, felt his voice returning it. So strange, this connection, as if a thread ran from his heart to mine.

It was after eleven when I let him go, though I wanted to keep talking to him and I felt like he hated to go, too, which thrilled me. He really does like me! I shut off the light and threw myself on the bed, hugging my pillow.

Is there such a thing as being made for each other? Can two souls meet and find the things they need in the other? I wanted to know. I needed to find out.

My cell phone starting singing *What is love? Baby don't hurt me, don't hurt me, no more.* Carter's ringtone. I shut the phone off. Though I hadn't answered, Carter kept talking. Telling me what he'd do when he found out. Eyes glaring, water dripping off his chin, as he shook more pills into his hand.

EIGHTEEN
HERE I STAND BEFORE YOU WITH MY HEART IN MY HAND
JAY MCSHANN

Carter caught up to me at lunch the next day. He tapped me on the shoulder and I startled and knocked my salad everywhere. He was smiling, which surprised me.

He sat down and took a bite of one of my cookies while eating me up with his eyes. "How's your day been?"

I didn't have air enough in my lungs to demand my cookie back. Oh, I'm going out with Wyatt tonight. How's *your* day been? Getting over that suicide attempt yet? I started putting my salad back so I wouldn't have to look at him.

"I was thinking about our trip to Omaha a few months ago," Carter said. "Didn't we have a great time?"

I softened. "Yes, we did." But things are different now.

"I showed you so much of my life. You were so sad when we left. I know how you like that jade turtle bracelet."

I shrugged. I really did like it, but I had stopped wearing it because Carter seemed to consider it a symbol of attachment.

"You deserve something pricier. I should take you out to Borsheim's and buy a real ring for you. Lots of carats."

I recoiled. "No thanks."

His flame-blue eyes met mine, sexy, alluring. "Only the best for you."

I started gathering up my food. "Um. I have class. Gotta go."

"I'll walk you there." He leaned on the table, all elbows, to push to his feet. "I have a surprise for you later. I can't wait."

I walked with my head down. I was pretty sure he didn't want to hear about the surprise I had for him.

For the rest of the day, I couldn't think about anything besides my e-tad with Wyatt, and my poor dead heart had even revived, so I was a bundle of nerves all afternoon. I had a hard time dressing because my hands were shaking.

Finally, vibrating with excitement, I was ready to go. I took one last look at my French twist and my nice black dress with the fine, wide skirt that belled out when I twirled. I tried to imagine what Wyatt would see, looking at me. A mature girl, a straightforward gaze through brown eyes, a gentle smile.

Or would he think, Well, she looks nice but I bet she's psychotic!

"That's enough," I told my reflection. "This is not the time to freak out."

I threw on my overcoat and raced out the door like a rocket sled on rails.

And slammed hard against somebody standing right outside my door, hitting my skull against his sternum and hurting my nose and ear.

We ricocheted apart. I managed to keep my feet. Carter fell against the wall and slid part way down before he stopped. I'd busted the bouquet he was carrying. At least I'd crashed it over my own head before he had a chance to crash it over mine.

Carter's hand was splayed on the wall. He pushed to his feet, staring, not noticing the flowers broken in his hand.

"You're beautiful," he said like the air had been knocked from his lungs. He reached toward me. "Come here."

My heart threw itself against my rib cage like a frantic bird.

Because Carter had his charcoal suit on, slim and tailored, and his favorite blue shirt, crisp as a new dollar bill. Make that a hundred-dollar bill. "I was going to invite you to dinner. Surprise you." He gave this short laugh. "I didn't realize you'd be ready to go."

I looked at my black dress. I'd spent all day fussing over accessories and my hair. Something I never did for Carter.

Carter laid the flowers in my hands. Broken sky-blue delphiniums and those little yellow thingies and blood-red roses with some of the petals knocked off. Like the flowers I put on Hannah's grave.

"Um. They're beautiful." The words stuck in my throat like chicken bones.

"Come on. I have reservations at the really nice restaurant. They're having crème brulee." I was a fiend for those little bitty custards.

A shaking spread from my gut into my arms and legs. "I wish you'd told me earlier," I croaked. "I ... I already have plans."

"Cancel them." Something strained crept into his voice. "There's something I want to tell you tonight. Something important," he said, taking my hand. His was cold and clammy.

I had a deep, almost painful urge to yank free and do a wind sprint up the hall. "I, I can't."

Carter's grip tightened as he brought his face close to mine. I smelled mint on his breath ... and something that reminded me of Grandpa Arden. "It's because of that Asian girl, isn't it? And then after she was all bitchy at me, you went trailing off down the sidewalk after her like she was right and I was wrong. And when you were with her, you lost all interest in me. What's the deal with that?"

"I need to go," I blurted. And cringed.

"So where are you going?"

I'm going to go see the man you hate more than anyone else in the world and initiate a relationship! Instead I said, "I'm going to meet some friends tonight, and I don't want to be late." I stared down at the flowers, chewing on my lip. My heart fluttered up and down against the bars of my ribs, calling Wyatt! Wyatt! Wyatt!

Carter put one hand on his hip. "Look, I've already made the reservations. I can't cancel them."

"You should have asked before you made them."

"How could I? You wouldn't answer the phone!"

That echoed up and down the hall.

"I'm sorry, Carter."

"Sorry. Sorry, hell. You never were sorry. Never."

Stunned, I backed away.

"Just leave. Go be with your snarky friend." He put a hand over his eyes.

I bolted to my car, trailing bits of broken flowers.

I drove all over town, up and down back roads, obsessively watching my rear-view mirror to be sure Carter wasn't following me. Finally satisfied, I parked out of sight of the road behind Polly-Eye's, which was actually Pagliai's. Our local awesome radio station was playing "Take Me for a Little While" by Coverdale and Page. I opened and closed my sweaty hands on the wheel. Oh man, I should have been frantic about leaving Carter with broken flowers around his feet. Instead, my heart was like a little kid grabbing my hand and going into tractor pull mode: Come on, come on! Let's go see Wyatt! And I was digging in my heels, going, Wait! Slow down! Don't pull my arm off.

The pizza shop was bustling. Over the door was a small plaque that said "Sempre Famiglia." Behind the counter, high school and college students stretched dough, slid pizza in and out of ovens, rung the cash register. Customers, from kids to college students to farmers, swarmed the buffet. The air was busy with conversations, plastic plates clattering, and people in the back throwing around pizza pans with great crashes. I stood there, breathing that smell of baking bread and melting mozzarella, vibrating from nervousness. Okay, make that outright fear.

Then Wyatt rose from a booth by the buffet, wearing a red

flannel shirt and work jeans. The same brown eyes, the straight brows, the rumpled jet hair, and that amazing, radiant smile that had welcomed me a million times before. I wondered if he would mind terribly if I sat on the floor because my knees were giving out. I looked down, embarrassed at my gigantic, scared grin.

"Hey. Haven't seen you for a while." Wyatt opened his arms, head tipped to the side. I hesitated ... then walked to him. He wrapped me up and rocked me. He felt so solid and so needed, and I felt like a shipwrecked mariner washed ashore, crawling to where the sand was dry, clinging to the lovely warmth, the still, the solid, the safe.

True to form, I started bawling.

"Oh, now, I don't want you to be traumatized," he said.

"You're fine, you're fine!"

The pizza production crew said, "Awww!" We released each other and laughed.

Wyatt turned. "Do we get a free pizza for bringing you that heart-touching moment?"

"How about a senior citizen's discount?" the manager called, and we all laughed again.

"We'll take it," Wyatt said.

Right off, bam, pizza at a discount. Sly, very sly.

As soon as we sat down, my cell started singing its song. Carter.

"You going to answer that?"

Shakily I said, "Well, if I do, I'll be on the phone for the next hour."

"I can wait." Wyatt stretched his legs on the seat, sending me such a cool, friendly look that I got flustered answering the phone.

"Are you having fun with your new *boyfriend*?" Carter asked.

I sputtered as if a big cooler of ice water had been dumped on my head. "What are you talking –"

"This Pag-lee-ay's Pizza, that's what, and you're –"

I hung up. "Holy crap! How did he find me!"

"Well, this'll be fun," Wyatt said as the door burst open.

Carter steamed right to our booth and crashed his hands on our table.

I jumped. "Don't!"

Wyatt steadied his pop, eyes dark and calm. "May I help you?"

"What are you doing with my girlfriend?" Carter demanded of Wyatt.

"Waiting for our pizza. Do you want some? You're welcome to sit down and join us."

"I wouldn't joke about it, lowlife," Carter snarled.

"Carter!"

Wyatt's eyes never left Carter's, but his voice stayed casual, as if talking to a friend. "I'm not joking. If you want to sit down and stay, go ahead."

Carter leaned across the table at me. "All that stuff you said about being loyal. Then you cheat on me while I'm going through the toughest time of my life. I was going to take you to dinner, I bought you flowers. Ten minutes later you're off with some other guy. You really don't care if I die, don't you?"

"Don't do this," I gasped.

He slammed his fist into the table in front of Wyatt.

Wyatt cast a look past Carter, then back to him. "You might want to idle down. You've got a lot of people staring at you right now."

"I don't give a damn." Carter stole a look around. Several people were at the buffet line behind him, sort of sidling past. The pizza production people were staring outright, and little kids had their mouths open.

Carter turned his face, pale with fury, on me. This time his voice was so low I could hardly hear it. "You think you've won, haven't you? I'm not finished yet." He put his hands on the table, showing his bleeding knuckles, the scars he'd opened up. "You can't beat me that easy."

Wyatt glanced my way. I know he saw how my face was crumpling. "Whoa, stallion. I don't know anything about your plans, and

I'm sorry about that. Now, you're welcome to stay and salvage some of your evening. But not if you keep trash-talking Kay."

"You need to keep your fucking mouth shut."

I froze, hands over my mouth.

They locked eyes for a moment, Carter poised like he was going to take Wyatt out, Wyatt sitting back but frowning, his gaze intense. I could not believe that Wyatt wasn't just yelling at Carter for that.

Wyatt's face was turning red. But he merely stated, "You'd be surprised, but a little civility works wonders."

"Don't lecture me."

"You might apologize to Kay for busting in here and disturbing the peace. She wanted to have a nice evening…"

Carter snapped, "She was going to have a nice evening, but not with you."

Wyatt held Carter's gaze for a moment. Then he turned to me. "You're able to make these decisions for yourself, aren't you?"

I caught myself before I could nod and looked at my drink. "I'm sorry."

A shocked silence. Carter drew back, stunned. "You know what you can do to yourself." He stormed out.

I could feel my face dissolving under Wyatt's concerned stare. I covered it so he wouldn't see my stupid tears.

His fingers warmed my arm. "It's okay."

I managed to pull myself together. "No, it's not." I wiped my face on my napkin, threw it down, and followed Carter into the parking lot, where he was of course waiting on me.

Carter turned on me like a lion, breath billowing in the cold night. "How nice that you and that *shit* of a boyfriend can cut me down behind my back."

"We're not cutting you down."

Carter snorted. "Bullshit. Didn't you hear that bastard, scolding me, giving me that superior act?"

I forced myself to quell my exasperation. "I'd rather you come in and hang out with us. Please?" Trying to borrow a page from Wyatt's book.

"You really don't care whether I live or die, do you?"

Oh God. My heart wanted to lie down on the cold, wet parking lot and die in a puddle as the snow fell on it. But Wyatt was inside, waiting for me. Wyatt, who I'd been wanting since that day in the library so long ago.

"Don't do this to me," I said, a new note in my quavering voice. "Don't do this. You keep saying that if I want to end the relationship, I can. Well, what I want is in that pizza shop, and I am tired of waiting for him. He's the one I want to spend my life with. And if you truly loved me, you'd give me my damn freedom!"

That was what I wanted to say. But the last thing I wanted was to come home from my first e-tad with Wyatt and find Carter dead in his dorm.

"I can't leave. At least give me this. Just this one evening with …." I started to cry. "That's all I want."

That took off some of Carter's speed. "He's a dick." But his sneer was half-hearted.

"I'm not your girlfriend any more. I thought we'd already agreed on that."

I was sincere, and Carter saw it. But he shook his head with a small, knowing smile. "Whatever."

A long silence as I looked into the sky. Not many stars tonight.

Carter unclenched his hands and stretched them. His face went gentle as he gazed at me, a fatherly look, an expression I hadn't seen since he helped me in the library so long ago. Then his face clouded. "What am I standing here for, anyway? Waiting for you to hurt me?"

I scrubbed the tears from my eyes with my overcoat sleeve. "No. It's time to move on."

"Yeah, well." He hesitated, then walked to his car, jacket hanging over his shoulder.

I went back to Wyatt, drained. The pizza had arrived, but Wyatt hadn't touched it yet. Waiting for me.

As I sat, he took my plate and loaded two pieces on it. "Aw, Kay, don't be sad."

"I'm sorry you had to see all that." The steaming pizza slid under my downcast face, and all that mozzarella smelled great, but my throat was too tight to eat.

"It's okay."

"Well, at least you have an idea of what I'm dealing with."

"That bastard should have apologized to you."

I shrugged. "How did you keep your cool through all that? I couldn't believe you could just sit there and not start yelling back."

"That's what he wanted me to do, but I wasn't going to play his game. I wasn't about to lose control just because some dumbass wants to lose his shit over you choosing to have a nice evening with whoever she pleases." Wyatt shook his head, putting down his pop. "That's what really pissed me off, because you do have a choice. You can do anything you want. But he doesn't want that. It threatens everything he knows, because he knows that once you choose, you're going to leave. Once you're gone, you're never coming back."

Wyatt's eyes met mine. "Kay, you can make your own decisions. Your life is yours to live; your choices are yours to make. Not his."

I drew a shaky breath.

I had forgotten how refreshing truth could be. How it cleared away all the confusion that had clouded my brain since September.

I wanted truth. Not confusion.

Wyatt's voice softened. "I don't want to drag your evening through the gutter all over again. Come on, let's start over."

He stretched his hand across the table, palm up. I put my hand in it. His fingers massaged mine, and his touch was so soothing that my tense shoulders relaxed. I could hear "When I Said I Do" by Clint Black playing on the jukebox as Wyatt started talking. "First, there's some business I'd like to deal with. I'm going to ask you a question but I don't want you to take it the wrong way." He gave me a particularly penetrating look that scared the heck out of me. "So exactly how long have you been, let us say, interested in me?"

A tingling burn started under my skin as I hit that rare five-alarm red. I forced myself to look at him. "Since March 31. During second lunch. At the reference table in the library, when you were supposed to be doing a make-up test, but you were actually studying for Brain Bowl."

He sat back. I felt a small surge of pride that I'd floored him. "Huh. I didn't know it was that long. But I still got you beat. As far as an interest in you goes, of course." Wyatt frowned at his hands, clenching and unclenching them. "Just so you know."

For that one instant, all his verve was wiped out by the rawness of his voice.

I gripped his hand and jumped in to rescue him. "I guess I can say that I'm in love with you." Staggered with the enormity of what I'd said – and by the sudden glow in his face – I began to stammer. "I've, I've been in love with you that whole time, even when I didn't want to be, even when I was a complete nutso idiot toward you. I always thought I'd end up driving you away every time I did something stupid. Which I managed to do anyway. So I was afraid to talk to you at all."

"I always thought I did something wrong."

"Not at all, never. I'm really sorry about that. I just felt like, you know, you were too good for me. I don't mean arrogant or snooty," I added. "I just mean that ... I was scared. Scared of being hurt if it didn't work out."

"Well. Let's just say I was hesitant about approaching you, too. For similar reasons."

I gripped his hand. "You? Scared of me? But it's just me, Kay, a no-account gal who's scared of her own shadow."

"Well, there's a little more to you than that or else I wouldn't have been interested."

We sat there for a long, lovely moment, hands clasped. He was smiling at me and I was grinning at him.

"You're like the gal in the Clint Black song," he said. "You don't want the love you can live with – you want the love you can't live without."

"You nailed it," I said, and my mind was full of what that meant. Then I became so abashed I couldn't even look at him. "I can't even believe this is happening," I said to his hands. "I don't feel like it's possible to have happiness this close, where I can reach out and just take it. I always feel like it's going to vanish by morning."

"Well, it's possible, and you're doing it," Wyatt said with a chuckle. "But maybe we'd better reach out and take some of this pizza, too, before it gets cold."

Wyatt and I talked as our pizza diminished, as our pop grew flat. As I talked about my troubles with Carter, I kept sneaking looks at Wyatt, trying to study his olive skin, the curve of his jaw when he looked down, that little cleft in his chin. I couldn't get enough of looking at him. He caught me staring and gave me a mock-puzzled look, and I busted out laughing in embarrassment. When our server came by, Wyatt joked with him. He had an easy way of bantering with people as if he knew them, and they bantered right back. Was that how you talked to people? I had no idea.

When the pizza place closed, Wyatt put on his dad's bomber jacket and we went outside. We climbed into Wyatt's truck, turned on the radio, and kicked the heater to high. I should not have been feeling this bubbly, but Wyatt smelled spicy, like manly cologne, and I wanted to put my lips to my face like he was a hot-fudge sundae and he'd melt if I didn't, um … well, let us not continue the simile. Instead I cuddled up against his side, and I fit nicely under his arm.

Chuckling, he leaned down and kissed me where my hair meets the forehead. My heart combusted in a nuclear fireball. The ice that encased me steamed away. I gasped. There was something deeply resistant and scared, but my heart's combustion felt so *good* that my fear stayed way off in the corner.

Wyatt gave me a little squeeze and went on talking as if he didn't notice me rocketing to the moon. "Look. I'm tired of messing around. I'm twenty years old, and what am I doing with my life? Spending money on stupid crap, going out with girls who, in the end, dump you for something better. My God, I'm tired of this. I want to settle down with someone I can trust. You seemed like the right one, but I wanted to be sure. So I went back and read your emails. I did a little googlestalking on your social media, nothing major. I asked some of my friends about you. They all had good things to say. But it comes down to this: every time I talk to you, your face brightens, and I feel mine doing the same."

I shoved away the cold of the black fleck in my heart. "I'm glad I passed the test."

He took a drink from his sweating glass, then brushed the hair back from my face. Water from his hand clung to my forehead. We were quiet. In the silence our gazes locked and held, as they had done once before, as if we had fallen into a moment together and didn't really want to leave it.

I felt time open like a flower, the world on pause. Our breaths meeting, combining.

I blinked, looked away with a soft laugh, and time started again. I said almost to myself, "Maybe it was fate."

"What'd you say?" Wyatt tipped his head, his eyes sparkling. But I knew he'd heard.

"So can I count on you to be on my side with this Carter thing?"

"Hell, yes. What do you think? Wonder Twin powers, activate!" Wyatt shook my hand in his. Neither of us seemed ready to let go quite yet.

"There's something else," he said.

He reached into his wallet and pulled out a worn newspaper clipping and gave it to me. A wedding announcement for Ghenna Richards.

I stared at it for a moment, because the name wasn't familiar to me. Then I gasped. "Oh, no! Was this your girlfriend? The one you told me about?"

I tried to hand it back to him, but Wyatt folded his arms. "Keep it. I thought she was the one. But she's chosen her road now. It's time for me to choose mine."

I threw my arms around him. His arms tightened around me.

He chose me.

Well, technically, we chose each other.

NINETEEN
OBSESSION
ANIMATRONICS

The next afternoon I sat at my desk, writing in my journal and drinking chai tea, my replacement brain for when I had none. I'd stayed up late last night with Wyatt. In some ways, we were two old friends who thought the world of each other and had so much to catch up on. But we were so much more than friends, so much more, and his every kiss made my heart combust. Even now, sitting at my desk, I pressed my hand over my heart, like it was going to bust out of my chest from all that joy.

A little part of me felt sorry for Carter, but I also wanted to shake my fists at him and dance around and yell "I'm free now I'm free I'm free and there's nothing you can do that will hold me down ever again! Cage me, would you? Lock me up, eh? Hah!" But then I imagined him looking sad and felt bad about it.

Carter knocked on the doorframe. I jumped. I was so relieved to see that he was okay, and yet my heart plummeted. Seeing him coming in and taking off his coat just brought home the huge gulf between him and Wyatt, The way I felt toward Carter was nothing, nothing, *nothing* compared to the lightning that Wyatt inflicted on my heart. I put my head down on my desk and almost groaned aloud.

"Hi." Carter sat down, got a wad of Kleenex, and wiped rainwater off his shoes.

"You're obsessed with me," I said into my desktop.

"I'm not obsessed with you." His voice was hurt, defensive. "It's a very deep, very pure love I feel for you. It's not obsession at all."

His knuckles were still raw and bleeding. I winced. "By the way, how'd you find me last night?"

He shrugged, throwing away the Kleenex. "I was just driving around and saw your car."

How on earth did Carter see my car? I had parked it behind the building, out of sight from the road and side streets. And I know he couldn't have followed me. I was pretty much staring at my rearview mirror the *whole time* I was driving. So how –

"Kathy, what are you doing this weekend?"

I kind of imitated a fish for a moment before I blurted, "Well, Wyatt's at work until Sunday night, so I was going to see him then …."

"I have a really great idea. Why don't we get away the way we used to?"

"We? As in you and me? But – ?"

Carter leaned back in his chair, hands behind his head, smiling. "I was thinking that tomorrow we could go to Omaha. You could visit that bookstore you like so much, take in the botanical gardens and the zoo. We can wander around the Old Market and look at the shops. I'll take you for a carriage ride."

Truth be told, the very thought of Jackson Street Books made me drool. But to go up there? With him? Did someone spike his pop with an illegal substance?

"Um, Carter, don't you remember that little debacle last night at the pizza shop?"

Carter rubbed my shoulder with his scarred hand. "Don't be

argumentative. I thought about it a lot. I want you to be happy. And if that means being with Wyatt, then do it."

"Thank you," I said, feeling like I'd fallen into the Twilight Zone. "So if I'm going out with Wyatt, then I can't go to Omaha with you. I already have plans …."

"Not until Sunday."

"But I was going to do other stuff this weekend." Like obsessively visit Wyatt at work.

"But you kind of canceled the plans I'd made for you last night," Carter growled.

"I …." And I let my breath out with a hiss. Even though I knew the kind of hell I'd get for talking back, I said, "I'm old enough to make my own plans."

Carter shrugged, turning amiable again. Geez, he was good at doing the opposite of what I expected. "Sure, you are. But I am too. It's okay if we go to Omaha. We're still friends, aren't we? We can still have fun together."

"But … but no. Friends don't go on carriage rides together."

He didn't even hear me. "In fact, look." Carter pulled a rolled-up catalog out of his inside jacket pocket and put it in my hands. "Look at what I'm going to get you."

A dress catalog. Filled with models wearing sumptuous dresses, low-cut numbers, and elegant styles. High style and … good Lord, look at the prices!

"Yikes! If I had this kind of money I could fund my college education." I handed it back. "No, it's fine. I'd rather skip."

Carter smiled and caressed my cheek with the back of his hand. His fingers trembled. "Guess what? You're not going to skip. You'll go to Omaha in style. You'll be the most beautiful girl to walk through the Old Market."

The blood drained from my face. "I'm sorry, but this is too …."
Bizarre.

"Don't be silly. There's nothing that says that you and I can't go on a little weekend trip together." He pulled his wallet out of his pocket. "How much do you need for your dress? A hundred dollars? Two hundred?"

I sort of laughed. "No, really, Carter."

He dangled five twenties in front of me, grinning. "Tell you what. Let's go shopping. You don't have any classes until tomorrow."

I was really sweating by now, because how do you respond to something like this? "But you have a 2 o'clock class. And I don't need a dress. I'm not going," I croaked.

"No, no, I insist." Under the velvet of his voice, an edge. "Do you know why? Ever since I've known you, Kathy, you've been running from me. But not anymore." He lifted my hand and closed it gently in his fist, fixing me with his intense, flame blue eyes. "I know where you live. I know the names of your relatives and where they live. I know where Wyatt and Yvonne live. It doesn't matter where you run. I can always find you. Like I did last night."

He said all this with a smile.

I started chewing on my lip. My insides felt jangly, like when you're walking through the percussion section and it's a mess and you trip on some drum thing and fall into the chimes.

And I thought: Give in, say yes. He won't take no for an answer.

And some other part of me stated NO NO NO NO NO.

And some other part of me wondered how badly I would suffer if I threw myself out the damn window right now, and how much of a running start I'd need to bust through those aluminum panes holding it together. Which was a dumb idea.

Carter led me into the fancy-name department store where the artificial salesladies glittered and the lighting was subdued and the mannequins were faceless. I was reeling, like the Tilt-a-Whirl was going way too fast.

And I was walking through the store, looking at these dresses like I was going to go through with the whole Omaha ordeal – *No!* He knows I'm going with Wyatt!

And, how did Carter find me last night?

Carter, sorting through a rack of dresses, said, "Ooooh, look at this one." A slinky number that barely reached my knees. White with a hint of lace. "Let's go try it on."

Inside the dressing room, I put the dress in a heap and sat, head in hands.

Bzzt! A text from Wyatt. *How's it going, hot stuff?*

I quickly tapped back, *Could C. track me thru my phone?*

Jesus. No doubt yr serious. I'm Googling ....

"Kathy?" Carter asked just outside my door. "Put it on for me. I want to see it."

My hands squeezed into fists, and I started to strip. When I picked up the dress, I felt the *No!* all through my being. "Carter, I can't."

Silence.

"It's a shame you parked your car in the parking lot next to my dorm. If you try to run, I'll know it."

I dropped the dress. "So what? What's it going to matter to you?"

He pressed his face against the slatted door so it creaked. A whisper: "I have something that'll make you stay."

His words went through me like a shock of cold.

"You can't win my love by making me your prisoner," I whispered, borrowing Raoul's line from *Phantom of the Opera*.

"What did you say?"

"Nothing."

Bzzt!

Turn off "Find my iPhone" in Settings and that might do the trick. Now if he's installed spyware on yr phone, that might be a problem. Googling ....

I scrolled over to Settings and shut that thing off. Spyware ... so was it possible that Carter could see my texts? My email? Listen in on my calls?

Carter tapped on the door. "Hurry up. I need to get back to classes before 2."

Well gosh, maybe you shouldn't have taken me out dress shopping. "Hold on," I said.

I hauled the dress over my head, tucked everything in, and modeled it for Carter. Ms. Zombie, the lovely creature without a soul.

When I went to change into my regular duds, Wyatt had texted again: *Shut yr phone OFF until you can fix it. I'm sending links to yr email that show how to get rid of spyware. Just in case. CHANGE YR PASS-WORD ON EVERYTHING.*

P.S. Don't let the bastards grind you down.

OK, I texted. I shut off my phone. Now I was really paranoid. I couldn't wait to look at those links.

After he bought the dress, Carter was happy again. "Now you're all set. Meet me at my dorm tomorrow at 4 o'clock and bring your bags. Okay? I'll drive."

I put my brain back in gear. "Um. Carter, this is a terrible idea."

"Why are you saying that?" Genuinely surprised. How could he be surprised?

"Because we've broken up, remember? You don't go running around with your ex when you're going out with someone else. That's like the rule Number 1 of dating."

His voice had an edge to it. "Look. I am trying to be your friend. Don't friends hang out after the end of the relationship? And it's not like I'm going to do any romantic crap. I just want to spend time with you. Nothing else."

"I want to spend time with Wyatt now."

Fear flashed into Carter's face as if an undertow had him. Then he went cold. "Do you really think I give a damn about what he thinks?"

"Maybe you should give a damn about what *I* think."

"If you're as smart as you say you are, maybe you'd better go along with me, and stop arguing," he said, crossing his arms.

The heat in his voice made my pulses jump. Mute, I walked at his side as we left the store.

We walked past the bedding department. Maybe I could hide out in the store and sleep on the mattresses at night.

We walked past domestics. Maybe I could get a cast-iron skillet to defend myself with. And then a horse called Maximus would show up with a sword in his mouth, and I'd hop on his back and we'd gallop away, and I'd use my magical brown hair to whack Carter if he tried to chase us.

I'm not grasping at straws because I'm panicked, no, not at all.

We walked past the sporting goods. Fishing rods, guns, camping equipment. I stared at the tents as we passed. Thinking of sleeping bags rated for 40 degrees down to zero. Propane heaters. Lanterns. Hand warmers. Space blankets. Wool socks.

My heart caught, thinking of all those times I stood in the hunting and camping section at Paducah's with Wyatt.

… and I still had that tent I bought when I turned him down.

And a sleeping bag that I had found on clearance.

I stood as if dumbstruck, staring at the space blankets. These were pretty cheap. Wyatt had talked about using them when he'd gone winter camping.

"Come on," Carter snapped.

Hello, Kay, would you please answer the clue phone? It's December! There's snow in the forecast!

Back in my dorm, I surfed the internet, read Wyatt's links, and cleared my phone. I changed my password on my email account, then had a long email exchange with Wyatt. I packed my overnight bag and set out some stuff for my trip, despite this fear that made my insides feel like they were liquidating.

I didn't take any calls, ignored all texts. Naturally, Carter came a-knocking on my door, so I showed him my bags all packed for tomorrow's trip. He liked that. Then we had a long makeout session because oh well. He finally went back to his dorm at 11, and I crawled into bed and tried to sleep.

At 2 a.m. my clock radio went off.

Who knew that a quiet radio could make me sit up like it was a fire bell.

I got dressed and headed to my car in the late-night blackness. Carter's window, which overlooked the parking lot, was dark. Good.

I drove to the Paducah's there in St. Francis, the moon shining through my windshield. The place was dead. I headed to the sporting goods section at the back of the store. Camp stoves, unbreakable dishes, tents with multiple rooms, instant dinner in a bag, compasses.

I already had my tent and sleeping bag, thanks to Wyatt. I got a space blanket (Wyatt had strongly recommended this), a flashlight, batteries, wool socks, and a packet of chemical hand warmers that lasted up to 18 hours. Then I went to the grocery side and got chocolate milk, almonds, dried cranberries, peanut butter, and bread.

What on earth was I was doing? I thought at the checkout. Of course that was the exact same question Wyatt had asked during our email exchange a few hours ago.

You're at work all weekend, I'd written back. *I can't hide out at your house, not to mention that Carter would be all over your folks looking for me. I can't go home. I can't stay in my dorm. I'm just going to run to a place where he is not going to find me, and the freaking woods is the only place I can think of. Not to mention that I have all these useful items, thanks to you.*

The temperature's going to be in the 20s, Wyatt had replied. *If you have the sleeping bag that's rated to 20 degrees, and if you wore a warm stocking hat to bed, you should be okay with that alone. I used to go out camping with my buddies with only Spider-Man sleeping bags, the cheapo kind, with snow out. You should be fine.*

I should be fine. Except for that little issue of how Carter was going to react to my disappearance, that was going to be fun. I blanched and grabbed my bags.

But screw him. If Carter refused to respect my wishes, then I would *make* him respect them. If he wanted to run a steamroller right through my boundaries, then I'd go someplace where he couldn't steamroll me at all. What he did as a result was *not* my fault ... though, even now, I was having a hard time believing that last part.

I parked in front of my dorm. Carried out my two quilts, my sleeping bag, a fully-packed overnight bag, my pillow, and my tent, and fit everything into the trunk with my purchases.

I drove back to the parking lot. My spot was still open. Not like anybody was going to take this spot at this hour. Except for me.

Tottered back to my dorm. Crashed on my pillowless bed at 3:30 a.m.

I even slept.

TWENTY
RUN LIKE HELL
PINK FLOYD

The next morning, I was dazed and groggy, and I had a crick in my neck from sleeping without a pillow. Worse, Carter showed up at my door at 7:30 a.m. to walk me to breakfast. Then to my 8 o'clock class.

His hands kept touching my arms, my face. I could see in his eyes that he'd won over Wyatt. I couldn't bear to look at him.

What Carter didn't know – what he didn't know now, since I killed whatever spyware he'd put on my phone – was that during class, I was texting with Wyatt.

This is a good day, Wyatt texted. *Woke up feeling really good, then had to go to school, so much for a good feeling. But now I'm very able to deal with day to day life now that you are with me.*

I just about fainted from joy when I read that, except it would have been terrible form to pass out in history.

When class let out Carter was leaning on the wall, waiting for me. He walked me to the next one. When I stopped by the bathroom, he leaned against the wall just outside the door until I reappeared. At least he didn't follow me into the stall.

This unsubtle shadowing went on all day. I didn't tell Carter how much I hated this. Instead Wyatt and I texted constantly whenever I was out of Carter's sight and whenever Wyatt wasn't in class. My God! My time needed to be given to Wyatt, not to Carter!

At 1:50, as the slow tide of students traveling to and from classes churned around us, Carter stopped dead in the middle of the commons. "I don't think I'll go to my 2:00 class."

"No! I mean, why not? There's only two weeks until finals. And haven't you skipped more classes than you're allowed?"

Carter's blue eyes snapped to mine. "Let's go to Omaha early."

"No."

"Oh, yes."

We regarded each other as students pushed past. I had expected him to pull something like this. I looked at the Union. "Fine. If that's what you want, let's get some snacks and drinks to take on the road."

I got him a 32-ounce pop, no ice, and a big bag of vinegar and salt potato chips, his favorite. I waved the bag at him teasingly. He grinned and grabbed it out of my hand.

When we stood in line at the checkout, I opened the bag.

"Hey, those are for the ride," Carter said.

I fished a chip out and popped it in his mouth. He seemed to like that, the way he smiled, and he shrugged and picked out another.

I encouraged him to eat every one of those ultra-salty chips. Because of the chips, he drank a lot of his pop. I know because I watched him. In the meantime, I dragged him to Salmen Hall to talk to my favorite English professor about all those classes I'd skipped at Carter's insistence. On the way back to Carter's dorm, we stopped by the library, and I wandered around for ages, looking for a book to read in the car. Try as he might, Carter's bladder was no match for all that pop. When he finally vanished into the bathroom, I sprinted for my life.

I jumped into my car and spun out of the parking lot faster than you could say "impending disaster!" Except my cell phone started singing "What is Love?" and my heart thudded.

"Kathy, where are you?"

"That's classified," I said, dead serious.

There was a long silence, as if Carter were trying to keep from crying or yelling. Then he said, his voice shaking, "I'm going to find you."

"No, you're not."

"I am. I'll call the police."

I imagined Carter talking to the police:

Police: *How long's she been gone?*

Carter: *Oh, about five minutes.*

"Okay, you do that," I told him. "And while you're at it, tell them about your suicidal tendencies."

"What suicidal tendencies!" he exploded into the phone. "You seem to have a problem with understanding that I'm not like that!"

I had to pull over because it was like all the air had been sucked out of the car. "Are you freaking serious?" I cried into the phone. "What the hell, Carter! After you took all those sleeping pills on me?"

No answer. "Hello. Hello? Hello!" I looked at my phone. He'd hung up!

Furious, almost out of my head, I called Carter back. He picked up. "Where are you at?" I demanded.

"Heading to my dorm. Meet me there."

"No, I won't. But the police will."

Silence. "What for?"

"To make sure you aren't going to take the pills again."

"Why the hell would I do that?"

"To get back at me in the most hurtful way you possibly can. To make me the bad guy. To make me come and save you."

"That's bullshit! That's --" It sounded like he was crying. "Why the hell do you have to hurt me like this? Do you get some kind of enjoyment out of it? Do you like to see me suffer?"

I put my head on the steering wheel, and took a deep breath. "Go on up to Omaha without me. See your mom. Make her happy. She feels bad enough for what you did last week."

"What the! Why the hell would she think it's her fault!"

"I don't know, maybe you should ask her why she was crying over you."

"She was crying because she was upset with the way you treated me. Playing your games. Telling me one thing, then running away. Telling me it's my fault that you make promises to me that you refuse to keep. Promises, Kathy. You know what those are?"

Another deep breath. "So do I need to call the police, or what?"

"Fuck you, Kathy." The line went dead.

On a scale of 1 to 10, the chaos in my head was at about 9.5.

I dialed Bayo's number. He was the musical genius from Wind Symphony who played 500 instruments, though not at the same time.

Bayo answered, and some kind of awesome symphony was playing in the background. It sounded like something American from out of the 1940s. He had good taste. I explained that Carter and I had broken up and he was having a really hard time; could he go and check up on him?

"Sure, girl," Bayo said. "How much are you gonna pay me?"

"I'm out of money," I said, thinking of all my new camping equipment in the back. "It's a long story …."

"I'm kidding. But hey, I had a girl break up with me a little while ago, so I know what he's thinking. I gotta give you some credit. My girl, she never called anybody or gave me a hand. More like gave me the finger."

"I'm sorry to hear that. Listen, I care about Carter, but … well, that's a long story, too. But he's upset and I don't want to make things worse."

"Sure, I'll see him. I'll go over there soon as I get off the phone."

"Thank you so much. Oh, thank you. You are an angel."

"Whoa, now! You want to ruin my bad reputation?"

"What bad reputation? You are a total music nut. You don't have time for a bad reputation."

He sighed. "A man can dream."

As soon as I'd hung up, I shut off the phone, took a deep breath, and roared off campus.

About 15 minutes later, I pulled up by a campsite overlooking Lake Sundry. Lots of cedars to block the wind, and eastern exposure for morning sun. The temperature was almost 50, really decent for December, and a dim sun shone.

You're crazy! You're going to die!

Well, it won't be the first time.

I looked over the dark, half-frozen lake with its cedars and winter-bare trees climbing the hills around it, thinking of Wyatt thinking of me. The sun on the back of my coat soothed me. I couldn't be scared.

But I was. Whatever I told myself, whatever I knew, logically, to be true – it still could not touch that guilt, anxiety, fear, of what I would find when I returned. This logic did nothing, and I mean nothing, to quell the panic. By asserting myself, I was bringing this catastrophe down on Carter's head. And on my own.

To distract myself from the circles that my mind was running in, I got out my tent and pitched it. I slid the bendy poles into place and grinned when the tent stood up, all ready to go. But when I tried to push the aluminum pegs into the ground to keep it from blowing away, they bent. The ground was frozen.

I placed the space blanket on the ground inside the tent to keep the cold out, as Wyatt had recommended. I put a folded blanket on that, then the sleeping bag, and my two quilts on top.

My cell phone rang. Carter. I shut it off. At least he was still alive.

The sun was low in the hazy west. Two sun dogs, those half-rainbows that tell you that a storm is on the way, lit up the haze. Just my luck. I hopped in place to warm up, watching the sunset.

I was wholly alone and, let's face it, scared. I was sure some weirdo would go driving around the barren place, find me, and do violence to me. Looming large over that fear, as a castle looms: I'd go back and find Carter dead. I was sure of it.

The fear curled across my shoulders like a devil cat, pricked its claws in my heart, hissed in my ear. It stayed with me as I walked around the lake, kept hitting that one note of fear, made my heart run fast. At one point I stood by my car, keys in hand, half of me ready to speed back to the campus, the other half ready to throw them in the lake just so I'd stop this foolishness.

After two hours of this, the fear congealed in my chest, sickening me. I sat down with my notebook and started writing. I wrote about Grandma and why she didn't leave sooner. About how Grandpa had hit Mom when she was just a girl. About being brave in the face of danger, like when Dad was in Iraq and got hit, point-blank, with machine-gun fire. The only reason he was still alive was that he happened to be wearing the bulletproof vest that day. He said it was like having a huge wooden plank swung full-force into his chest.

I wrote a lot of things. And when my hand tired, I got out my copy of *Jane Eyre* and read again the scene where Jane leaves Rochester, whom she loved passionately, though she was his only chance of happiness in the world. She was indomitable; she knew what was right; she stood by her principles though Rochester's pleas rent her heart.

Reading it, I was shaken, not only by the story itself, the heights of Rochester's fury toward the woman he loved most, but also what the story demonstrated: It was quite *correct* to be courageous for one's own sake. To give in for the sake of someone else, when their desires for you were wrong, was a sin. The difficulty of leaving was what lent power to Jane's courage. And so it must be with me.

I was able to breathe at last.

When I returned to the campsite, the temperature had started falling. I slid into my sleeping bag like a turtle ducking into its shell. It was cold for a second but then I warmed right up. I snuggled in. I

230 MELINDA R. CORDELL

read *Jane Eyre* for a little longer until it got dark and I got tired of holding the flashlight. So I shut it off, turned on my phone, and lay in the dark.

My thoughts spun in the mind-blunting tedium. It was still hours before my bedtime, but it was too cold to walk, too dark to read, and music wasn't doing a thing for me.

Here, alone in the tent, the only tiny speck of warmth for miles and miles, I was facing The End of the Line.

Where was I going to hide next time? On a Greyhound bus to nowhere? On an extended camping trip into the mountains 300 miles away? This had to stop.

Just then my phone started singing the Queen of the Night's aria from the *Magic Flute*. Mom.

"Kay, what is going on?" she cried. "Carter came to our house looking for you. He said you ran away. Where are you?"

"I didn't run away. Well, not technically. I'm at a friend's house." Seeing as God was my friend, and this is my Father's world. "Carter says I'm his girlfriend, and I say I'm not, and things got … a little hairy. Is he still there? Don't let him know you're talking to me!"

"He's not here. Tell me where you are so I can come get you."

"Um! No, I can't."

"Don't talk to me like that. Where are you?"

Geez! "No. This is my problem, and I'm going to solve it."

"Huh? How are you solving this problem?"

"By not giving in to his insane demands." I sighed. Everything seemed like so much trouble to explain, especially when I was about to get the third degree.

"There's no need to get huffy at me. I'm worried. When I came home, Carter was up in your room."

"He was WHAT?"

"Your dad let him in and let him get a sandwich, then went to watch TV, thinking Carter would join him in a minute. When I came home from work, Carter was coming down the stairs, saying he couldn't find you. Then he went next door to Grandmother Bachmann's and then over to your uncle's house."

At least he was still alive. For the moment. "Did he take anything?"

"Your room looked like the usual mess, so I don't know. Kay, what is going on? Did you break up with Carter?"

"Yes, but he won't believe it." Quailing from the heart-to-heart that I knew was coming.

"Honey, I got into law because I wanted to make a difference. I see a lot of domestic cases, and yes, they are painful, but I know I'm helping those who are afraid to speak for themselves. I never dreamed I'd have a domestic case-in-progress right under my nose. Why didn't you tell me about Carter before?"

I nearly snapped, *It was a question of trust,* but didn't. I was having one of those moments where I wanted to say a number of emotionally intense things that my harried brain was saying no to.

Because I was ashamed to be weak in this way.

Because I was ashamed of myself.

Because I didn't want to burden you.

Because I didn't want to depend on you because you think I'm nothing but a little kid.

Because we have a code of silence, things we must never talk about because they hurt too much or make us uncomfortable and scared.

The electric fence went up. There was enough power in that strand of wire to throw me to the ground, muscles twitching, drowning the world in static.

But who was on the other side? My mom, who I hardly ever hugged, who'd been so hard to live with. But it was possible that I was hard to live with, too. It was so hard to fight for my independence. I wanted to be free, my own person. If gave in, I'd be back to being a baby again.

But it didn't mean I had to keep her at arm's length forever.

"I didn't want to tell you," I said. "I didn't want you to know. I was scared. I'm sorry."

"I don't understand why you're scared of me."

I nearly took it as an attack. I didn't say I was scared of her; I was simply scared to *tell* her. Then I realized that it could have been a plea from the heart. "I'm not sure how to reply to that. Because I don't know."

"I've raised you ever since you were a baby. Don't you think I care?"

"I love you too, Mom."

She stopped, surprised. Who knew that I could say the right thing for once.

"Well, I love you, Kay. I want to help."

"But I wasn't sure what you could do except give me cookies and advice. I mean, if you came up to campus and kickboxed Carter into submission, that might have legal ramifications."

"I'm getting ready to pass the bar, and you think I can't deal with a few legal ramifications?" She laughed. "I'd be more worried about wrecking my high heels."

"You want to do it? I'll give you his dorm number."

"Honey, it would be better if you dealt with your own problems."

I tried not to take it wrong, but I did. "I have been. That's why I didn't want to tell you about this in the first place."

"Don't get short with me."

"I'm not!"

"Yes, you are."

"How can we change the ways we talk to each other?" I asked.

A pause as if she'd been caught off-guard again. "I don't know, honey. I'm trying to."

Again we were quiet.

"Mom, I know I'm no ray of sunshine, but at the same time, I don't like being cut down over things I like."

"I don't cut you down."

"Mom. You do."

"Don't put the whole blame on me. Every time I see you, or talk to you, you snap at me. It doesn't matter what I say, but you have to turn it around."

"No! That's not true! Stop it, I'm trying to do this right!" I really meant to have that come out in a loving, gentle voice, but that did not happen. "But I can't even get that much."

"Me neither," she said. "Even after I've worked so hard to raise you, when you've left all the chores and laundry and dishes to me … I'm trying to go after my dream, but you have no idea that when I come home from a long day fighting to free people from their abusive spouses, I still come home to my life as an indentured servant. I keep thinking, if I weren't a mom, I could have gone farther; I would have finished my classes years ago. I'm jealous of you, Kay. Part of that's my own fault. I wanted to protect you and give you the childhood I never had. Yet …."

Another tense moment, but now I felt sorry.

"Did it work?"

"I don't know. The jury's still out on that one."

A cold front moved in. The wind started blowing.

"Where are you? Are you outside?"

"I'm in the sunroom or porch or whatever."

"I mean, where are you? Which friend's house?"

"Mom, I'm sorry, but I'm not coming home. I don't want to be protected. I want to go out and make stupid mistakes that I can learn from. I promise I'm not going to do anything life-threatening."

"I didn't say you were. I just wanted to pick you up."

"I know. And I said I didn't want to be."

"You don't need to repeat yourself … and here we go again," she sighed.

"Huh?"

"Talking to each other the same old way."

"Oh." It was very strange to hear her say that.

"And I'm sorry I talked to you that way."

I was stunned. I don't know if she had ever apologized to me before. But then again, I'd never told her that I loved her during an argument before, either. Maybe we could both change.

After I hung up, I listened to the wind shake the tent.

I realized that I needed to climb out of the bag to go outside and pee. It took me nearly an hour before I had to go bad enough to crawl out of that lovely warmth into that evil cruel cold. That was the worst moment of the night. Snow was flying where snow was never supposed to go. I crawled back into my bag and fell into a coma.

Hooo hoo hoo hooo! Hoo hoo hoo hooaalllll....

I woke up.

Hooo hoo hoo hooo! Hoo hoo hoo hooaalllll....

A barred owl called from right next to the campsite, loud, like it was calling into a megaphone. There was a faint light from all around that allowed me to see the tent, though I didn't know where on earth the light could be coming from. Was the moon out? I put my hand on the ice cube that was my nose. From far away, a different owl called back.

Still in my sleeping bag, I squirmed to the tent flap and opened it. And gasped.

Stars. I'd never seen so many stars, never seen them so bright. Like God had turned the switch up high, and each star was a glory of white light. I had no idea you could see by starlight. And by the starlight I could see the oncoming front of clouds coming out of the east, bringing the wind and Lord knows what else. The tent shuddered in a gust of wind, then subsided.

The owl called again, so close, like the voice of God.

"Hannah, if you can hear me now, please help your brother," I whispered.

Under the beauty of that night I thought about Carter. I did care for him. Not the passionate, bone-deep terror/need I felt for Wyatt. Not like my brother, who could be a pain in the kazoo but he was still my brother, and family is worth fighting for. But a friend. Not that friendship is less powerful than other loves. It's as strong, can be stronger.

But what Carter had was not friendship. What he was doing was saying that we were friends, but acting like we were lovers. That wasn't friendship. That was deception. He was actively trying to deceive me, but he also was willfully deceiving himself. Acting with his eyes closed, telling himself it was all right to be this way.

Whatever this relationship was, it was not going to have a happy ending. Not for me, not for him.

The wind began to pick up, and I ducked back into my sleeping bag.

When I woke up, I thought for a moment that I was still dreaming. Except now it was morning, all sullen and gray. There was frost on my sleeping bag and on my pillow where I'd been breathing. The wind was bellowing outside, flapping my tent. Lord. And I had to pee like nobody's business.

I sat up, my nice warm air billowing out of my sleeping bag (I grabbed the bag opening to shut it) and unzipped the window to peep outside. A light dusting of snow. Trees leaning in the wind, branches dancing. I would have to go to the truck stop and use the bathroom there. And I could get a nice breakfast, too.

A mean gust of wind lifted the sides of my tent, since I hadn't been able to peg it down last night. If I was going to the truck stop, I would have to break camp – impossible. At that point I was all for letting that little tent blow away like a scrap in the wind.

I pulled the bag under my armpits and crawled out of the tent, getting snagged on the zipper twice. I was shivering like a druggie coming off his fix. When I got out, the wind caught the tent and tipped it on its side. I grabbed it. The sleeping bag fell around my ankles and the wind stripped away all my warmth. I might as well have been naked. My teeth were chattering like something out of a cartoon. I had no idea they could make that kind of noise.

I wrestled with the tent, trying to collapse it as if in some nightmare. My numb hands couldn't take hold of anything as the terrible wind snapped parts of the tent against my face or yanked them out of my icy fingers. My fingers hurt from the cold, an ache that cut through bone and flesh. When I got the last fiberglass pole out of its little peg, my fingers were too stiff – I couldn't unloop the pegs from the tent. I gave up. I broke down the poles only enough to cram the whole tent, with all my stuff still inside, into the back seat of my car.

My carton of chocolate milk, half-full, fell over but nothing came out – frozen solid. I laughed a sad little laugh, more like a moan. I climbed into the front seat, found the keys in the ignition, and started the car. Freezing air roared out of the registers. I was shivering so hard I thought I'd die. I gunned it for the truck stop.

Ten minutes seemed like forever when I was freezing to death in my car and I was shivering so hard that I was probably going to pee my pants, not that I would have noticed at this point.

But walking into the truck stop – well, technically, busting straight through the front door – and feeling that delicious warmth wash over my body as I flew past the convenience store section, and smelling that cigarette smoke and the smell of bacon and eggs cooking in the back – that was the best feeling I'd had for a long time.

I was very happy to get that bathroom break taken care of. I thawed my hands in hot water and put my face under the hot-air machine, and that was so nice. When I walked back out, much more slowly this time, I found a booth and sat down.

I got hot chocolate so piping hot that I didn't dare drink it. I leaned my face over it. I heated my hands on that deliciously warm mug, put my hot hands on my cold ears, my face, my neck, my nose. The nice waitress brought two pancakes, all light and fluffy, with butter melting everywhere. I poured on the syrup and the pancakes soaked it right up and they tasted like marshmallows almost.

I ate the whole stack. About halfway through, I started dozing. I snapped awake to find the fork drooping in front of my face, pancake sliding off the tines.

Time to head back to my dorm and get some sleep. Then I'd face the music.

I drove back to campus and parked behind the science building, where Carter would never look. I tottered for what seemed like a half-mile through the blowing snow until I reached my room. Snow was pasted to my hair, my coat, my jeans. I opened my door ... and groaned. My bed was bare, with nothing but a flat sheet on it. My pillow, blanket, and all my quilts were in the back of my car inside my old tent.

At this point I didn't give a damn. I kicked the thermostat up, shed my coat and shoes and wet jeans, put on snuggly-warm clothes and fresh socks, rolled a sweatshirt into a pillow, and threw myself onto the bed.

Let's go camping when it's warmer, I thought, and my brain shut off the lights.

TWENTY-ONE

I WILL MAKE YOU HURT
JOHNNY CASH

W hen I woke up, it was noon, and I was groggy. I rolled out of bed, knowing that now I had to see if Carter ... oh Lord.

But then I stopped. Something wasn't right.

I kept looking at my desk trying to figure out what it was.

My little turtle that I'd given Grandpa had been knocked over, and several pieces had broken off. But I hadn't knocked it over.

My computer was on, even though I always shut it off when I'd finished with it. I jiggled the mouse to bring the screen up. My email account was open, though it had logged me off last night due to inactivity.

I logged back in. There was a new message from Carter from an hour ago.

Guess what? I didn't get any sleep last night. Can you figure out why. Besides that knife in my back. And all those emails from your socalled friends saying what an asshat I was. What were you telling these people? Were you telling them that I abused you? That I manipulated you? You sure weren't saying anything good about me because my god, they all wanted to save you from this demon that I am. I can't believe the things you said about me.

I cant believe you told them that I was abusing you!!!! I don't even know where to begin with that one. I never hit you. I never yelled at you. WTF? How do I abuse you?

I deleted your emails. And the emails from your loser boyfriend.

As for me, don't worry. I'm in a better place now, thanks to you.

sayonara

I ran through the falling snow, dialing him on my cell phone. No answer. I took the stairs up to his dorm, not wanting to wait for the elevator. He was all right an hour ago, I kept telling myself. It's only been an hour. For all I know, he could be sitting there, waiting to yell at me.

Or worse.

I was an idiot. How could I have gone off on that damn camping trip and expect everything to be okay? Didn't I know? That wasn't my call to make.

His door was open. I saw the shine of packaging tape over the lock. I pushed it open. The stink hit me a millisecond before the door swung back far enough to reveal Carter lying on the floor, his head wreathed by a pool of vomit and small decaying pills.

My breath had been ripped out of my body. Which was good, because I was unable to inflict a nightmare-inducing scream on the tenants of the fifth floor.

I shook and shook him, making a teakettle noise. It took a damned long time for me to realize that he was still warm. I cupped my hand over his vomit-spattered nose. The air moved cool against my palm.

They took him to the hospital. Instead of riding with him in the ambulance, I walked to my dorm. The trees were webs of black, barren limbs, cold as the snow that fell through them.

I stood at the sink, running water over my hands for what seemed like an hour to wash the vomit smell off. Too stunned to do more. I mechanically added soap and rubbed and rubbed. Yet, when I lay down on my bare bed, curled up, I still smelled it.

I dozed off. All these people were being shoved into a wood chipper, and everything was hot blood and shredded meat and screaming, like a torture porn movie. I grabbed people and begged and pleaded with them to stop, pulling them away from the machinery, but they shoved me aside with bloodied hands. I couldn't make them stop.

The phone rang, jolting me out of my sleep. It was the hospital.

A policeman sat outside of Carter's hospital room, a coalrock fellow reading about Thai cooking on his tablet. His eyes flashed as he looked me over, and he gave me a nod. "Go on in," he said in the bassest of bass voices.

Even though I was a trembling mess, his voice impressed me. "Are you in a choir by any chance?" My own voice just a shadow.

He laughed, an amazing rumble. "I wish. I can't even sing Happy Birthday in tune." He waved me in. "If you need anything, I'll be right here."

Well, one good thing. Chewing on my lip, I went in. I wanted to draw myself up and look tall and strong, but I couldn't even muster the will to do that. I was done. I had nothing left.

Carter lay in his bed like a discarded husk, yellow-brown bruises around his mouth. He didn't look at me. The window he looked at showed only overcast white-gray skies.

My eyes ached.

"Proud of yourself, now?" Carter's voice barely a whisper.

"No."

He continued staring out the window. I just stood there. Neither of us spoke.

"So I'm an abuser now."

"No."

"So that's what you really think of me. After all this time, after you told me lie after lie, you've really outdone yourself."

"No," I whispered, my face crumpling. I needed to reply, to fight back, but for some reason his judgment just froze me in my tracks.

"So did you tell everybody I hit you? Did you tell them how I dragged you around by your hair? How I smacked you around? Burned you?" Carter tried to push himself up in bed, failed, lay back on his pillow, staring at the ceiling.

"I didn't say any of that."

"Oh my God, Kathy. What did you tell those people about me? When I treated you better than any woman I'd ever met before in my life."

Like Rebecca? I thought.

I hugged my arms tightly to myself. "Except for that part where I wanted to leave and you never let me."

Carter snorted. "How the hell is that abuse? If you can't tell the difference between abuse and love, then you have some real issues."

Are you kidding me? I sputtered, "You can't force me to love you by making me your prisoner. The only thing I wanted was the one thing you couldn't give – my freedom."

His eyes got big. "You never wanted freedom!" His voice, already weakened by the vomiting and the tubes, broke from the strain. "Every time you came running back to me," he said in a thin, angry voice. "Every time. And you have the balls to blame that on me?"

I laughed incredulously. "Of course I came running back to you, because I had no choice. What about all those suicide attempts? All those sad emails and texts and all those times you made me stay and talked at me until I had no choice but come back to you? Stopping me was like the freaking biggest part of your life! It gave you purpose! Because what I wanted – what I want right now – doesn't include you! and that's the biggest, worst thing you can possibly think of!"

Carter leveled a hard-eyed look at me. "No. The worst thing is to be lied to, to be deceived, by somebody who says she's so proud of being loyal. Somebody who says she'll stand by every promise she's made."

Now I was seething. "You knew I wanted to save you, and you took advantage of that. All I wanted to do was help."

"Uh-huh," he spat. "And now here I am, in the fucking hospital, because all you wanted to do was save me, and all you wanted to do was help."

"I did not force you to take those pills."

"Yeah, of course not. You just lied and deceived me and made me think you loved me when in reality, you were plunging that knife in my back. Stabbing me when you know I was hanging off my last rope. No, of course you didn't make me take those pills, somebody else must have done that."

I wanted so bad to just scream at him, but the policeman shifted in his chair outside the door, and I remembered myself. I made myself breathe. "Carter. I'm sorry. You want me to be honest? It's time we ended this relationship. For good."

He forced himself to sit up, a helpless expression in his eyes. "You can't do this to me now. Look at me. My God, Kathy, what kind of heartless ... person are you?"

I could imagine Carter telling everybody he knew, "Hey, you know what Kathy did? She broke up with me while I was lying in my hospital bed."

What the hell was wrong with me? I pressed my hand into my forehead, tried to stay on topic. "If I stay, what good is it going to do? I'd have to break up with you down the road anyway."

"Then do it later. I need you now, don't you see that? Don't you see that you're killing me?"

Carter's voice hit me like a hurricane west wind. Waves and wind thundered over me. The ocean pulled my legs with a grip like a giant's, a blind force that sought to pull me down.

I'd heard him say these words so many times. But I understood their true message: *I'm so afraid of this pain inside me that I'd do anything for relief. I honestly don't know what the pain will make me do to myself. Or to others.*

Those words I'd spoken of myself many times, when I was longing for Wyatt with a pain that could hardly be endured. When my heart constantly struggled in my chest like a blackbird gripped in two strong hands, and all she wanted to do was to burst free and fly.

Carter's words died out into tears.

I wanted to crumple to my knees right there. Anger. Pain. Love. Part of me begged myself to show mercy to Carter. Instead I had to take my sword into my hand and hold onto it for all I was worth.

"I've been cruel," I said. "I let you believe something that was not the truth, because the truth hurt too much. Carter. There's no good way to say this. But I do not love you."

Carter held one hand out to me like a drowning man. His voice wobbled up and down. "What … are you trying … to do to me?"

"I'm making a clean break, the way I should have done a long time ago."

Carter put his face in his hands. "What did I do? What did I do wrong?"

I went to him then, and took both his hands off his face. Now that I was so close, the yellow and purple bruises around his mouth made my stomach drop. "You have not done anything. You're a good and loving man. But I cannot make any kind of long-term commitment to you."

He took a long, shaky breath and pulled his hands away. "Wow. You are cold. Telling me this right after I tried to kill myself, right after you screwed with me and generally fucked me over. Yeah, you're the considerate one."

A great wave swamped me, dashed into my eyes, nose, and mouth. I sputtered. "There was no really good time …."

"Oh, yeah, right. You think this piece of bullshit news would make me feel better? Like everything's going to be all right now?"

"I didn't mean it like that."

"Yeah. Like you didn't *mean* to put me in the hospital, and you didn't *mean* to come to the hospital and dump me right after they pumped out my stomach."

"No! No! No!" I screamed, and stamped my foot. "Stop it! How can you think this relationship offers anything good if it makes you take sleeping pills! If you hate this relationship so badly, then let me go! Unless you are enjoying this unmitigated misery or something!"

"The sleeping pills were an accident," he snapped. "It didn't have anything to do with this relationship."

"Oh really? Then if it's not me, I'm better off out of your way so you can cope better and heal."

He immediately took another tack. "I can't live without you. Don't you understand what you're doing to me?"

"It's clear that you can't live *with* me, if you have to take sleeping pills."

"What does that have to do with anything?" And from the frustrated rise in his voice, I saw that he really didn't get it. He really didn't. It was his blind spot.

But then, Lord be praised, a bird flew past the window, distracting me. I threw myself into a chair and covered my face with both hands, folding myself in half. Carter was beyond logic. There was no way I was ever going to talk him out of it, any more than he was going to talk me into loving him.

I concentrated on breathing.

Carter rustled in the bed. His hand stroked my back, the gentle caress I loved.

I burst into tears. How could I be so wrong? Wyatt didn't need me. I could survive without him. Here was a man who needed me more than life.

That voice, speaking up for Carter again.

You know what? Carter wasn't the bad guy here.

I was.

I have this amazing capacity for working against myself, I'd told Wyatt once.

It wasn't enough for me to want something. I also had to understand, in both my mind and heart, that I could claim what I wanted. That my choice wasn't up to Carter, or Mom, or Grandpa, or even Wyatt. It was up to me.

All these years I'd believed that I had no power to make choices. That others' wishes were more important. I had to act. The power was mine to claim, if I dared.

This was my choice to make. Not his. Not anybody's. My choice.

So I had to break off the relationship. I had to choose my own life over Carter's. And I had to pray that I wasn't going to second-guess this decision for the rest of my life. Well, okay, that's not going to turn out so well. There's just no good way to do this. There just isn't.

But. I had to do it. It was my choice. Not his.

I pulled away from Carter's hand. With a shaky breath I sat up. "I need to return your stuff to you. I'm hurting both of us more by staying."

The words hit Carter. Shaken, his eyes searched my face. "Don't do this. Please."

"These people are qualified to help you. I'm not."

"But you've saved my life over and over again."

I closed my eyes, took a breath. "Stop. It's over, Carter."

He turned away from me and began to shake with sobs.

Oh Jesus, help me. I was the lowest dog on earth for walking away from someone that I'd wounded to the heart. I cleared my throat so I could talk. "I'll bring the stuff you got me back to your dorm later on."

A long moment passed, and he didn't move. I started to get to my feet.

Carter turned over. "Don't."

"I gotta," I whispered.

"I mean, don't give it back."

I stopped.

"They were gifts. All of them. To you." He turned over all the way now, his eyes burning and sad. "Keep them."

I'd gotten to my feet, my hands clasped over my heart. "Are you sure?"

"Well, yes. It's not my money. Take it and have a little fun."

I couldn't speak. Finally I stuttered, "Thank you."

We were quiet.

"Kathy, I'm going to go home at the end of the semester. And what you said put the final nail in my coffin." I went pale. "No!" Carter said, putting his hands out. "I don't mean like that. No pills, I hope. I mean that ... I don't think I'll be coming back to school. I'm flunking anyway. And if you don't want me ...." He raised a hand helplessly.

I let him hug me. "It's for the best that you go home," I said. "Spend some time with your mom. Talk with her about what happened. About Hannah. Her death broke you, and you never got it fixed. Start seeing a therapist. I bet you could get better help up there than you could down here in Podunkville."

"Yeah ...." Now Carter wavered. Hurt filled his eyes as he gazed at me.

"Please," I said into his shoulder. "You have a hole in your heart that needs to be filled. So fill it. And once you're better, go find the right woman. I am not the one."

"Don't say that. Don't. I want only you." He held me so tight, I could hardly breathe.

I pulled away and took a step back, just enough to be out of reach. Guilt ate at me. But there was no alternative. "For what it's worth, there will be somebody better."

"You can't do this. Why can't you and I be friends?"

And there was no way on earth I could make him see that we could not be friends. He honestly could not see that. "It's better if we never see each other again."

His breath caught in his throat. "You must really hate me, to turn your back on me like this. Especially right after you put me in the hospital."

Though I knew that was only his hurt speaking, I said the only words that were left. "Goodbye, Carter."

TWENTY-TWO

THE RESOLUTION OF ALL MY FRUITLESS SEARCHES

PETER GABRIEL

On a hot day in July, Wyatt and I roared up to the little country church in his truck. I held on to the "Oh sht!" handle over the door as we whipped into the gravel parking lot and braked. The limestone dust from the tires rushed past us. The instant Wyatt shut off the ignition, I opened my door. "I can't believe you're late to this!" I cried, unceremoniously dumping myself into the parking lot.

"We're not late. Idle down, darling," Wyatt said, climbing out, then reaching back in for his digital camera. He looked very natty in his good suit, though I was just about vibrating from nerves, as usual.

We walked into the church, hand in hand. A bunch of folks stood up at the front of the church, and a sprinkling of people sat in the pews, and the whole place was festive with flowers: altar arrangements, bows on the pews, bouquets in hands and corsages on tuxes. All heads swiveled right around to look at us as we came in. I ducked slightly, grinning.

"There you are," called Wyatt's uncle. "Let's get started."

Wyatt took his place, and I stood beside him. He was the official photographer for his uncle's wedding, and I had come along for the fun.

So I followed him around as he squinted into the viewfinder of his digital camera, looking very attractive even with his face all screwed up, holding the camera ready, then taking a little burst of pictures at the right moment.

During the wedding ceremony, I sat in the front pew as Wyatt lurked around the wedding party, snapping shots. I watched the service, watched him, with great attention.

It had been over a year since I'd finally broken up with Carter, who was back in Omaha with his mom. He still sent me emails, asking why we couldn't see each other, asking why I never wrote him, telling me that I must have hated him to be treating him like this.

He'd even tried to visit me a couple of times, but each time I fled before he managed to see me. His most recent visit was in March. District music contest was being held on campus that very day, so I hid out in the mixed wind ensembles room way back in the Union, working as door monitor for the judge. I stayed there all day, leaving the room only to hit the bathroom, grab a sandwich, or go to class. Carter never saw me.

Wyatt and I had gotten off to a rocky start. Unfortunately, I was something of a basket case after having gotten away from Carter, because EVERYTHING I'd learned about being in a relationship, I'd learned from him. I responded to a lot of things with hysterics. I was needy. Though Wyatt and I were crazy about each other, I had a lot of learning to do, but he was patient. It wasn't until Wyatt lent me his copy of *Seven Habits of Highly Effective People* that I saw the light. Now I was trying to do better for him, and he was trying to do better for me.

The unity candle part of the service was over. As the bride and groom moved back to their places to wrap up the service, Wyatt looked at me from behind his camera and winked. I was warmed through.

Later, after the reception in the church basement, and after the bride and groom drove away in their balloon-covered, toilet-paper-wrapped, shoe-polish-messaged car, Wyatt and I walked up the aisle through the empty sanctuary and stood before the altar.

"Can you see us standing up here someday?" Wyatt asked, his words rumbling in his chest.

"Maybe not here, but at my church. If that's okay with you." I rested my forehead against his face, the tiny prickles of his chin. "That's where all my people are. That's where I want to go."

"Oh, that would be fine."

He kissed the top of my head.

"Do you know that my heart always combusts when you do that?"

"How about this?" He gently raised my face to his and we kissed ... well, for a while. Nothing over the top, of course, since we were standing in front of the altar in God's house, good heavens.

I slumped against Wyatt. "Help help! My knees are all rubbery."

"I'm already holding you up."

"You always have held me up," I said, now serious again. "I'd like it very much if we could do this for the long term."

"I'd be fine with that." Wyatt smiled at me. Oh, man, that smile. It always gets me, every time.

"Me too."

"How do you think we'll do?" Wyatt asked, gazing down into my face.

It was a strangely thrilling moment, our faces so close together – it seemed as if, without ceremony, without even saying so, we were dedicating our lives to each other.

We held each other tight.

"I think we'll do just fine."

THIS IS JUST IN CASE YOU
LOOKED BACK HERE.

I'm just really taken with you
and I hope you will have me as I
am. I always think of you, my dear
and what more can I say...
I love you and only you
Katherine Marisa Bachmann
if you can live with that —

then well, I'll go out on a limb and
say will probably live happily from
now on.
Love,
Wyatt

08953

TWENTY-THREE
ONE FINAL NOTE

Remember: Somebody's life is never your responsibility alone. Never.

If you are in a situation like Kay's, please ask for help. There are resources available. People who have been where you are, who understand what you are going through, and they want you to get out and be safe.

Hell, I'm one of those people. And you are doing a noble thing. But if it's killing you, it's not noble.

You deserve, more than anything, to live a life with freedom, with people who love you. You deserve joy.

Read *Emotional Blackmail: When the People in Your Life Use Fear, Obligation, and Guilt to Manipulate You* by Susan Forward. I wish to God I'd read it when I was 18. Read *Why Does He Do That?* by Lundy Bancroft.

Emotional abuse is not your fault, no matter how your partner spins it.

College students, go to your campus counseling services and talk to someone about what you're going through. If that doesn't work, go to student health services. Contact WomensLaw.org for more information. Call the National Domestic Violence Hotline at 1-800-799-SAFE (7233) or TTY 1-800-787-3224. Or just Google "escape an abusive relationship" and start reading. Knowledge is power.

If your loved one is threatening suicide, please call 988 in the United States. This is the number for all mental health, substance abuse, and suicide crises, replacing the National Suicide Prevention Lifeline (1-800-273-8255).

Please take care of yourself. Reach out for help.

ABOUT THE AUTHOR

Melinda R. Cordell started out with a degree in horticulture, then earned her MFA for writing for children from Hamline University in 2012, where she worked with a ton of great writers, including Gary Schmidt, Mary Logue, Laura Ruby, Anne Ursu, Swati Avasthi, and Gene Luen Yang. It was the best time ever.
Her book, *Courageous Women of the Civil War: Soldiers, Spies, Medics, and More* was published by Chicago Review Press in August 2016. This was a series of profiles of women who fought or cared for the wounded during the Civil War. She was able to discover stories about these women that had not been seen for decades.
As soon as *Courageous Women* came out, she immediately self-published a short stack of gardening books, a short-story collection called *Angel in the Whirlwind*, then a fantasy novel called *Butterfly Chaos*, which she worked on with Gary and Mary at Hamline. She'll be publishing a fantasy trilogy about raccoons in the Missouri forest. It's like *Watership Down* only with raccoons that fight evil spirits with music. She lives in northwest Missouri with the best family on earth, as well as two red hens and two baby chicks.

If you like this book, please take five minutes to leave a review. Also, look me up on melindacordell.com and sign up for my newsletter.

ALSO BY MELINDA R. CORDELL

If you enjoyed *Those Black Wings*, take a look at *Butterfly Chaos*. It's a contemporary YA novel set in the same part of Missouri as *Black Wings* -- only with ghosts and a deadly tornado.

The building shook from ceiling to floor as the tornado tried to yank it off its foundation. From outside came a series of huge, electric-blue bursts that sent shadows all over the building from a million different angles as transformers blew. Everything went black. The world began to pull apart around us.

Butterfly Chaos
by Melinda R. Cordell

Here's the first chapter. Enjoy!

TWENTY-FOUR
FROM BUTTERFLY CHAOS
GHOSTS

The second-worst day of my life (so far) began on Wednesday, when I pushed through the swinging door into the junior high bathroom. It was a pretty September afternoon outside, with a warm happy sun perfect for basking in, but in this old crumbling school you'd never know it. The bitty window let in only the teeniest teardrop of sunshine.

As I moved through the girls crowded in front of the mirrors, their voices quieted. At least it wasn't the circle of silence it had been a month ago, when I started school and Toni's death was on everybody's lips. But still.

Fluorescent lights flickered overhead, and even those tiny flicker s buzzes echoed in this high-ceilinged, stone-floored bathroom. Everything you did could be heard two miles away , so I came in here only when my bladder was set to declare a national emergency. Otherwise I held it until I got home. A girl washed her hands, the water hissing like Niagara Falls. A roar of a flush from a stall. I cringed.

Seventh grade at Schopfer Junior High, where kids from every elementary school around the county had been dumped, was like having a bit part in a zombie movie, only the zombies looked like kids who were better than you, and instead of brains they ate your heart. I missed Amazonia Elementary with its small classes and comfy reading nooks and big windows letting in tons of sunlight and air, and all the kids were so nice there, not like they were at this stupid place. I sat alone at lunch, my curly black hair was a wreck, and the level of mean from some of these girls was beyond anything I'd ever experienced.

Here was a stall that looked empty. I pushed the door open.

But when I opened the stall door, a wave of deathly cold rolled out from the door and washed over my feet, my body, like I'd stepped into a full-sized freezer. I could almost feel the ice crystals.

At the same moment, I lifted my eyes and was immediately was thrown into confusion. A girl was in the stall, standing on the toilet seat. What? No! The girl was *floating* in mid-air at the back of the toilet stall. And what was wrong with her –?

A shock shot through my body into my feet. *The floating girl was Toni.* Toni, my dead cousin, suspended in mid-air only a few feet from where I stood. Her toes dangled above the ground, and she clawed at the air. She wore the same black Adidas t-shirt and jean shorts she'd worn the night she'd died, but one of her flip-flops was missing. She might have been climbing an invisible ladder, except her reddish hair drifted around her face like she was still underwater, and her head was thrown back as if she watched salvation floating up, and up, and up, out of her reach.

My screech propelled me backward out of the stall, reverberating off the stone walls and the ceiling and floor. I flung the stall door closed. But it rebounded right back open, shuddering, and Toni was still there, but now – worse – her eyes moved – clicked on mine. *She saw me.* Her glazed, glassy eyes were the same as those I'd met when she sank under the surface. And the whole time, my body was awash in the cold that drifted off her, cold so deep that it would sink into flesh and bone and silence it forever.

With a sob I ran, shoving past the amazed girls who'd turned from their mirrors, and I burst out the bathroom door, crashing into the mill of students going to class and knocking some books out of a girl's hands. "Hey, loser!" somebody yelled, but I didn't even look. My entire laser focus was on running, and running, and running, and never returning.

Except at that moment, Toni's cold hand locked around my bicep.

I went completely out of my head, fighting to pull free. I probably could have pulled down a house, but I could not break from that steel grip. "No! No!" I shrieked, and spun to face Toni's ghost, ready to punch, kick, bite.

But it wasn't Toni. It was Jake from English class who held my arm, his black hair curling down over his eyes, his usual sarcastic grin vanishing when he saw my face.

"Whoa, Cassie. Calm down, calm down," he said. "What is going on?"

My heart staggered as if it had tripped. Jake's face was so close to mine that I could smell peppermint on his breath. I made a strangled gasping sound. Jake had been there the night Toni had drowned. I'd never had the nerve to thank him for helping us. I could barely manage to talk to him at all.

But even now, even now when I was going out of my head, I had enough brain to notice the girl snarling at me as she gathered up her books, the glowers from the passers-by, and the bathroom door springing open as a flock of prettified girls, hair half-straightened, burst out to watch the insane misfit – i.e., me – die in flames of eternal humiliation.

"Th-there's a rat in the bathroom!" I shouted at Jake.

Best. Save. Ever.

In that split second, when the word *rat* hit the air, the shock waves moved out around me. Jake jerked upright. "Oh, really?" he cried, and whirled toward the girl's bathroom – and recoiled. The next second, the plastic girls realized what I'd said, and the shock washed over their faces, followed by screaming and hairbrush-clutching. One girl pulled open the bathroom door and shouted, "There's a rat in the bathroom, get out!" New shrieks, amplified by the stone walls and floors, rang out of the bathroom, and a bunch of girls pushed out. Some of the kids in the hall surged toward us to see, while others just as quickly surged back, squealing. The word *Rat!* spread in a ripple of voices.

I was amazed. I had started all this excitement, me!

For the merest instant, I wondered if this was how Toni felt when she watched her pranks turn out successfully.

I tore away from Jake and hurried down the hall, dodging through the crowds of students. I pushed through the big double doors to the outside, but instead of going to gym – my next class – I ducked around the corner of the building, out of sight, and pressed my back against the rough brick wall as if I could melt into it.

Around the corner, crowds of shouting kids hurried to and from the outbuildings where they had band and art and gym. Alone, I shuddered, hugging myself tight.

It's Toni's ghost.

I laughed the awfullest laugh I ever felt, just to keep myself from crying.

Review: "This book was a delightful departure from many of typical stories I read. The author did a wonderful job of building the conflicts throughout the book. She chose the real things that a 7th grader deals with AND this was the genius of it that reminds me of some of my favorite TV shows, she didn't hyperbolize to do it. She was a real girl dealing with real things like having her first crush and fighting with her relatives."

· · ·

Review: "Things I enjoyed about this book: good writing, good dialogue, Cassie's snark and no b.s. attitude, the tension-filled storm scenes, Cassie's big family with a ton of cousins and aunts and uncles. I wanted her family."

Butterfly Chaos is available on your favorite online booksellers, in ebook and paperback. Grab a copy today.